# S. O. D.

# SWORDS OF DAVID

—— A NOVEL BY ——

# L. J. FEINSTEIN

*Swords of David*
Copyright © 2015 Graphic Sales Ind. LLC

Cover design by Scott Weinberg

*Swords of David*
L. J. Feinstein

1. Title 2. Author 3. Fiction

Library of Congress Control Number: 2014922099
ISBN: 978-0-692-33593-2

*To every man and woman hoping and praying for World Peace:*
*May it be a reality sooner than later.*

# ACKNOWLEDGMENTS

I wish to thank Evelyn, my first wife of 40 years who passed away far too prematurely. I am grateful for all the faith you had in me during both the good as well as hard times.

Special words of thanks I extend to Sandy, my second wife who has kept me laughing and happy for almost 20 years.

Thanks to my children and grandchildren who have made me proud in so many different ways.

I express gratitude to the wonderful Italian family who helped me during a very bleak time in my life.

Last but not least I especially wish to thank Nancy Genovese. I am not sure I could have completed *Swords of David* without your help. Thank you for believing in my dream, for sharing my passion for the literary word, and for your amazing expertise.

# PREFACE

The tall dark-skinned man lay prone in the pitch blackness of night. Hidden behind a sand dune, he was as invisible as the twirling specks of sand blowing across his face and body. A pair of steely-blue eyes remained protected by special night goggles. The tan body suit he had slipped into earlier not only provided cover, but concealed him even from the steady stream of helicopters flying overhead.

Fourteen hundred meters in the distance, a retinue of stone-faced guards paced around a massive gray building: rather intrusive in the Clay and Saltmarsh Iranian desert. Air vents encouraged workers deep inside the bowels of the utilitarian structure to inhale fresh air into their lungs.

Avi Levine smiled. One of the few people in the world who knew the events about to unfold, he stood at attention, while caressing his custom-made snipers rifle as if his hands entwined the body of an enticing woman. Only, this beauty would bring no pleasure to the madmen below who were working to destroy Israel, Avi's beloved homeland.

In the drab building well beneath the amorphous surface of the desert, people were convening not solely to plot the destruction of Israel, but to exhume and bring to the light of day decades later, Adolph Hitler's vow to resolve the "Jewish Problem."

Darkness blanketed the area. In Avi's mind it was a Temple of Doom for Israel, and for the entire free world. The only available light came from either the headlamps of a few motor vehicles entering and leaving the compound, or the tiny slivers of illumination escaping through the air vents. When they appeared, they glowed like the beacons guiding planes to safe landings.

From his vantage point, Ari had a clear view. Elevating his rifle he positioned his eye directly in front of the magnifying scope mounted on the weapon. Undoubtedly he was ready for action. Reviewing the discussed strategies in his mind, he smiled. A quick distraction, a turn of the head—even a glance at his watch could be fatal. Taking a deep breath, Avi realized every ticking second brought him closer to the completion of his mission. He had to stay alert. Yet the absence of movement lured his attention back to how and when it all started.

This is his story.

# I

My name is Antonio Bastone. Many however, remember me as Avi Levine. I was born on June 22, 1975 to Demetri Bastone and Shanna Levine in a small hospital located approximately 30 miles outside of Haifa in Israel. For the first 10 years of my life, I enjoyed a privileged childhood many children could only covet, though at the time I was unaware of my good fortune. Children and youth take much for granted.

My family name, Bastone is scribbled across the label of one of the most lucrative and well known olive oil companies in Italy. Founded by my grandfather in 1947, the business was built and expanded from a small olive tree field to thousands of acres cultivated to produce one of the best ranking, and sought-after olive oils in the world. Therefore, it was no surprise that my father would be groomed early on to take over upon my grandfather's passing or retirement.

Demetri's life was a smooth run until a destiny changing day when on a business trip in Israel he spotted Shanna Levine walking among the ripe colorful fruits and vegetables displayed at a local market place. As their eyes locked, the tall handsome man from a far off country, and the fair skinned beauty with hair the color of the setting sun knew something exciting had occurred: each had met their soul-mate. It was inexplicable but electrifying!

Regrettably their parents were not in agreement. Yet in spite of all the pleas, protestations and threats of disinheritance by both families, the couple was married on July 25th 1974.

Holding firm to their religious origins and their wishes not to offend Demetri's father and Shanna's mother, Mom and Father said their *I dos* and promised to love and honor each other until death parts them, in the presences of a priest and rabbi.

An eye catching twosome despite their pronounced physical differences, the olive skinned heir to an oil fortune and his light complexioned school teacher bride with a dazzling almost angelic smile, were undeniably *hors d'oeuvre* for cocktail party banter.

I'm happy to say that in time their respective families grew to love the spouses their children had chosen. On the rare occasions in which they argued, Demetri's passionate nature led him to wave his muscular arms while shouting in Italian. Meanwhile, Shanna's rebuttals torpedoed in English, German, Arabic and Hebrew with a tinting of Yiddish. As a young boy, eager to defend my position amid the verbal bombasts, I busied myself, learning all six languages.

My father was quite a tennis player as a youth in Italy, consequently at the age of five I was signed up for tennis lessons. To make my tennis game more conducive to improvement, a court was built right in our back yard. This left me with little if any valid excuses to justify not getting out on the clay and practicing my serve and returns. Many mornings and afternoons especially when the weather was not exactly in tune with my comfort level, I'd slam the ball across the net in spoiled brat protest. Little did I know what a useful skill this would become in the years ahead.

# II

It was Father's wishes that the family be transferred to my grandfather's palatial estate in Italy. His concerns were safety as well as a reluctance to compromise all the comforts unlimited money could afford. However, he failed to take into consideration Shanna's thoughts on the matter. Although petite in stature, Mom was unbending in her refusal to leave the country she, as well as her mother, and grandmother affectionately called Bubby Fanny, now called home.

Both Anna and Bubby had lost their beloved mates. Grandma's father, my great Grandpa Saul died a hero. He was killed fighting to create this beautiful land for displaced Jews from all nations; men and women who not only wanted, but deserved a land to call their own. Sadly Grandpa Max was fated to end his days, the victim of a suicide bombing attack that took place in one of the many coffee shops scattered across the landscape of Israel.

Firm in her resolve, Mom would not yield to my father's many requests. So strong were her refusals that he finally gave in and sacrificed his time to travel back and forth to work with Grandpa Antonio after whom I was named. However, it didn't end with a name. I was expected to walk in his footsteps, which meant taking over the business.

Meeting with distributors and learning all aspects of the olive oil industry was part of the job description. Nevertheless, what I failed to realize was the bi-polar nature of the business—its Jekyll and Hyde aura.

Grandpa Antonio, a self-made man, had friends on both sides of the law. In fact he was often called upon to arbitrate disputes between the various *Cosa Nostra* families, in addition to government issues.

Everyone knew his word was his bond, and those who counted respected his one request to never be summoned to where physical harm was a threat. Moreover, he had been asked to run for political office many times, yet refused, unwilling to forfeit the things he loved most in life—family and business.

Grandpa's wife had died during child birth, and although there were other women in his life, he found himself a single parent raising my father. Irreplaceable in his heart, Grandmother Sofia's passing was difficult to digest. But circumstances change. Eventually he opted in favor of preserving the relationships he shared with his many contacts on the flip side of the law.

Friends had bestowed upon Grandpa Antonio, the title *Il Fidato*, which means the Trusted One in Italian. One day, assuming my father proved worthy, he too would earn the title.

On May 6, 1985 my world crumbled. At home with his Israeli family, Father received word that Grandpa Antonio had suffered a massive stroke. No longer able to rule his empire, it was necessary for Demetri to return to Italy to execute his father's wishes, step into the lead role, and accept the responsibility to oversee the family business on a permanent basis. Although he pleaded way into the wee hours of the morning, until their eyelids drooped from exhaustion, Mom was unfaltering in her decision to remain near her family.

Shanna's mother and grandmother had endured far too much pain and hardship in their lives and were unwavering. They wished to be near their loved ones buried beneath the hallowed ground in the Holy Land. Eventually, Father relented proposing two conditions. He insisted I spend each summer in Italy with the family. The second clause of the condition stated that he and my mother would enjoy a couple of weeks in the spring and fall away from everything and everyone, honeymooning like newlyweds, on a deserted island.

Declaring their love for each other, Mom and Father swore never to stray from their marriage vows, but live their lives as one. It was beyond romantic especially for a young naive mind.

The next seven years literally flew by, and I always looked forward to the summer months with Grandpa Antonio and my parents. It was in beautiful Italy that I learned to ride, hunt and best of all play tennis with Father, who despite his advancing age managed to beat me until I reached the age of 15.

I had beautiful memories. During my trips to Italy I met some of the most fascinating people in the world; people with easily recognizable faces; people whose names alone brought fear and awe to both kings and leaders of both free and captive nations.

The trip itself was an adventure. To insure my safety, I flew with an Israeli passport into J.F.K. International Airport. Driven by limo to a private airstrip on Long Island, I used a passport with the name Antonio Bastone to board the waiting Lear Jet, owned by the Bastone Olive Oil Company. My destination was Naples. Once air bound I breathed a sigh of relief. It was time to enjoy the ride: after all, the complicated family bureaucratic protocol had been completed.

Over the years as my grandfather's physical frailties became more pronounced, Demetri Bastone took over the role of mediator to appease the disputes between crime families. In fact he had even been solicited to resolve several government problems. Finally, during the year of my 16th birthday, Father, having achieved the same level of trust as Grandfather, had earned the right to be called, *Il Fidato*.

# III

Tennis had become my passion. It was impossible to keep abreast of my wining streaks at various tournaments in Israel. Just fifteen years ago my instructor (who could no longer keep up with me) had been ranked fifth in the world. From time to time, he would play on the senior circuit where he challenged some of the best players from my youth to highly competitive matches.

Notwithstanding my skills and reputation, Mom was reluctant to let me play outside the country; thus on the International circuit, I was an unknown, revered exclusively in my native land.

To celebrate my 17th birthday, my father gave me a gift I will always remember. He invited Stefan Bjornberg at the time the *numero uno* pro tennis player from Sweden, along with his entourage to join us during an upcoming event. *Herr* Bjornberg liked the idea of staying in quiet surroundings. The serene environment was beneficial and enabled him to prepare for the Italian Open, held in Rome. Much to my delight Father had asked Stefan to play a few sets with me.

It was not easy to refuse my father's requests. Besides, going a few matches with me would help him unwind before his workout with the coach.

Turning pale in spite of his sun tanned complexion, I noticed the smile quickly faded from Bjornberg's face the moment I fired a 130 mile an hour serve down the left side of the court. It landed three inches from the end line, and darted left like a mongoose chasing after a cobra.

We battled back and forth, for the next four hours, until Bjornberg's experience and energized ego brought him victory in five sets. I thanked him for treating me gently on the court, but later was thrilled to hear he had mumbled under his breath; "Who the hell was that kid, and where the hell did he come from?" It was a phenomenal gift though not the only one I received that summer.

The 23 year old daughter of the cook, Rosa Maria had come to work with her mother. In addition to culinary skills with the power to tantalize any palate, she possessed all the prerequisites to spin a male into delirium—long smooth shapely legs, silky black hair, a pair of radiant eyes that outshone the moon in mid-July, and a set of well rounded full breasts, which stood at attention even braless.

Initially her attention was focused on my father until she realized he regarded her solely as the cook's nice young daughter. Father was a hopeless romantic with dreams of his beautiful Shanna. Every year they religiously honored their vow to fly off to renew the passion they felt for each other, and simply join hands, lock glances and be in each others company smiling and laughing. They were truly a fairy tale couple.

I was amazed at the rapid passage of time. One day I was a child and then suddenly I stood 6 ft. 2 inches tall and weighed 175 pounds. At this point it was not necessary to run DNA testing to prove I was the son of Demetri Bastone. I had his long black hair, dark olive complexion, a pronounced square jaw, high cheek bones, and my mother's deepest blue eyes. I was repeatedly told I would break the hearts of many women when I reached manhood.

It was a scorching July morning. I was swimming laps in the family pool as I did frequently, weather permitting. Lifting my head for air, I noticed Rosa Maria approach carrying a cool drink, white towel, and long robe with the initials A.B. embroidered in gold letters on the breast pocket.

When she flashed a coquettish smile, I jumped out of the water. Instantaneously my body betrayed me. The cooling effects of the water evaporated into beads of sweat.

"If this doesn't help, perhaps a massage in the guesthouse by the pool would do the job," Rosa Maria said, handing me the drink. Embarrassed, I realized she noticed my discomfort.

"Sounds good," I said, not daring to make eye contact.

I took the towel from her extended arm, dried myself off, slipped into the soft robe she held open between her hands, and proceeded to the guesthouse. Since girls in Israel were rather uninhibited, I had enjoyed several amorous encounters. However, the art of love making remained an unsolvable mystery for my young mind, a mystery I wanted to explore in greater depth.

"I will meet you in the guest house," Rosa Maria shouted as I walked away sipping the cool drink.

Peering over my shoulder I noticed she smiled, turned on her heels, and headed in my direction, cutting the distance between us. Settling in the lounge chair, I paused, emptied the glass and prepared myself for a pleasant experience, watching her stroll toward the guest house.

Like a loyal puppy I followed. When I entered through the main door eyes darted towards Rosa Maria, clad in a shear black cover-up. I chuckled at the term cover-up as she was stark naked beneath the transparent robe.

There were no surprises—her body was an exact replica of the alluring form running through my thoughts on many sleepless nights.

"Come join me," she beckoned, patting the mattress with her dainty hand.

I was so ready! I walked over to the bed elaborately made in the finest silks only great wealth could buy. My father spared no expense when it came to entertaining both famous and infamous guests.

I dropped my robe, climbed in beside Rosa Maria and lifted the transparent garment which served exclusively as a teaser for what was to come. She parted her lips before moistening them with the tip of her tongue. I accepted the invitation, covering her waiting mouth with mine. Gradually I worked my way down to her breasts. How ready she was! They had peaked and hardened, as I stroked her with the tips of my fingers.

With outstretched arms, she searched for my head, pushing it lower and lower, until I was positioned where she intended. Instinctively I knew my mouth was being enticed to give her pleasure. Within moments the volcano between her legs erupted echoing sounds I had never heard before. Reaching for my throbbing manhood, Rosa Maria pushed it into the cave of heat and moisture I had helped create.

"Deeper deeper! Faster faster!" she shouted breathlessly. I felt her long nails burrow into my back.

"*Vengo vengo*—I'm coming…I'm coming" she gasped again and again in Italian. Delirious, I moved in and out as if I were gliding across the tennis court. I kept pace until I could no longer restrain myself. I surrendered. She surrendered. What an extravaganza of sheer pleasure shot through our pulsating bodies.

Her moans and groans joined mine. Exploring with ecstasy we fell powerless on the royal blue silk sheets marred by the evidence of our lovemaking.

"*Dormi bene, amore mio bello,*" "Sleep well my handsome love" she crooned as I drifted off; when you awaken, I will show you even greater pleasure than you have felt before."

Amid all the rapture I had no idea this was destined to be my last summer with Father and Grandfather for a very long time.

# IV

In Israel military service was not an option, and I was now approaching the age at which all young men and women were required to complete a year's service. Though I tried to slip into denial not to ruin my vacation, I knew I had to face this obligation when I returned home

I dreaded saying goodbye to Rosa Maria and was not surprised to note it was far more difficult than I initially thought. During the summer, I had grown more than just fond of her. Undoubtedly our time together created memories that would stay with me for more years than I anticipated.

Our final meeting prior to my departure was filled with endless lovemaking. On the last morning, at the first sign of dawn she reached over and softly kissed me on the cheek.

"*Amore mio bello, tu sei il migliore amante che una donna possa avere—*" My handsome love, you are the best lover a woman could have," she murmured.

There was sadness in her eyes. It was as if she knew many years would pass before we would meet again. Furthermore, things would never be the same. I kissed Rosa Maria gently and departed her company to prepare for the return trip.

"Be careful my son. You and your mother are the two most precious things in the world to me," Father said, encircling his arm around my shoulders. I said my goodbyes and headed for the jet which would fly me back to Israel where a year in the service would plot the course of my destiny.

As soon as I celebrated my 18th Birthday, I began gun and physical training in the Israeli Armed Forces. Holding the much coveted title of number one tennis player was totally insignificant. The few "good job" originating from the mouths of I.D.F. (Israeli Defense Force) instructors had to be earned through determination, perseverance, coping with stress and fatigue, and the acquisition of fine tuned skills. Nothing was easy, and no one was privileged because of family or fortune.

The aptitude test I was administered revealed to the top brass in command that my scores were off the chart. Tennis had developed my eye-hand coordination, but my fluency in six languages allowed me to by pass the infantryman stage. Consequently, it was decided that I would spend the following 11 months involved in intense training with Special Forces, an elite branch of the *Zroa HaAvir VeHahalal*, Israeli Air Force, (I.A.F).

It was discovered that I excelled in Total Recall, a skill I had developed in my youth. This made attaining and absorbing knowledge an uncomplicated task throughout my schooling years. Learning the intricacies of bomb or crude weapon construction using things most people would cast off as useless was child's play. Actually I had been told that my skill with the long range snipers rifle was the pulp of legends. Some actually swore I could take out the eye of a fly at 2000 meters.

It was no secret I enjoyed hand to hand combat. With forearms that rippled like steel cables, and a speed and dexterity refined on the courts, I was a very different 19 year old. The experience went quickly. I did as I was ordered and satisfied my military obligation.

My tour of duty was just about up when fate stepped in to revolutionize the story of my life. While on guard duty just days prior to my return to civilian status, and my previous life, complete with Father's dream of grand slam fame for me, my unit was attacked by Hamas, the Palestinian Islamist Organization terrorist group operating inside the West Bank borders.

Shots echoed in the darkness outside the campsite my unit had set up for the night. Like a gazelle tormented by a cheetah, I sprang into action, setting my sight on the flashes of light coming from the weapons spewing their deadly message. Firing round after round in response to the unforeseen attack, I was rewarded upon hearing agonizing cries resonating in the darkness. The lack of light served as a convenient camouflage, concealing people whose only goal was the total destruction of Israel.

Suddenly I felt a piercing pain in my right shoulder just as an Israeli tank rumbled up. Intruders scrambled back across the border to their hideouts among the innocent people, people who had grown tired of war. Although my wound was not serious, I immediately knew my tennis dream was dead. I would never be able to compete at the level needed to rank among the world's greats. The bullet had burrowed into my rotor cuff disabling most of the power in my 135 mile an hour serve. Additionally, my slashing cross court forehand would certainly be affected.

Upon learning of my injury, Father flew to Israel joining my mother, grandmother, and Bubby Fanny. Of course he had to inspect my wound first hand to be certain it was nothing more than a small scar—a souvenir of my military service. Perhaps it was denial; perhaps it would all disappear in a cloud of smoke; perhaps my father knew it was time to face the truth. Denial was not my forte. Looking truth in the eye, I faced my new reality.

Demetri and Shanna's dream to witness their son crowned number one on the court, the first Jewish/Italian player to ever reach the top in the tennis world had been shattered by a bullet. Face to face with my shoulder they had to accept the web fate had spun, like it or not, willing or otherwise. Seeking respite from the disquieting reality, Father once again asked Mom to take up residence with him among the fertile olive trees on the family estate. Somehow the fecund farmland provided respite from the sting of life's nasty curve balls.

Upon completion of my military obligation I was no longer under the jurisdiction of my parents' decisions. Even though I had not yet turned 21, in Israel I was considered an adult with full faculties and responsibilities. Moreover, Mother was concerned about Grandmother who although too old to up-route her life, had just become involved in a relationship with a new suitor.

"Who is Grandma's new lover boy?" I asked playfully.

"The local butcher," she replied. "I think he was recently widowed. Apparently she went to the shop to buy some meat and he was taken by her," Mom continued smiling; "after all she is still a very attractive woman. You know your grandmother—she always does the meat shopping. Claims she is the most qualified in the family to select the best cuts."

"Really?" I chuckled. "What is the basis of her assessment?"

"Oh Antonio who knows—she says experience."

"Well I guess it makes sense. The meat is always wonderful."

Shanna found it strange when her mother began returning from the butcher shop with far more provisions than she had requested, but never seized the opportunity to confront her. There were always other more pressing issues to tackle.

Much to the dismay of my parents, I felt a certain kinship with the military even though it forced me to forgo a college education to remain in service. Needless to say the army took full advantage of my decision. Immediately I was sent to Israel's Special Forces unit for additional espionage training as well as a higher level of close quarters-weapons and unarmed combat. This was defined as military hand to hand combat.

Within a few short weeks, my leadership qualities became evident to all my instructors. Unanimously they suggested I enroll in Officers' Training School. What I didn't know was that one person of elevated rank in the ruling cabinet had her eye on me, fully aware of my relationship to Demetri Bastone. In her mind I was already starring in the plan for the future of her beloved nation. I was destined to become the first of the chosen ones. *Les jeux sont faits* as the French say: The die is cast!

# V

Ziva Mizrahi swam lap after lap in the dimly-lit pool inside Haifa University's training facility. Mile after mile of water passed under her long slender arms, legs and body. At 17 she already showed signs of the beautiful woman she would eventually mature into.

Finally growing tired, she climbed up the pool ladder and grabbed a towel to dry her model-like figure. The shine of her wet brunette hair and flawless cocoa complexion left little room for doubt about her Sephardic Jewish heritage. History records how many Spaniards and Turks, as in Ziva's case migrated from their birth countries to pursue new beginnings in Israel.

Arriving just nine months ago with her parents, the young teen's mind was filled with thoughts of her exciting adventure. There would be new friends, a safe life, and the joy of growing up in a bright sunny paradise with her parents, Aunt, Uncle, and the cousins who had preceded them.

However, a Palestinian worker hired by the farmer living about three miles down the road brought her optimistic expectations to a crashing halt. Distracted, he had plowed into their car killing her parents and two cousins; a tragic turn of events that would re-write the course of Ziva's life.

A university freshman, she sought solace from the agony, submerging herself in the professors lectures and studies. Of course her alluring physical attributes did not go unnoticed on campus. The flirtatious looks and invitations of her male peers were met with a gracious smile and a polite no. She was not yet ready to cross that path.

But ready or not, she faced a patriotic call. Upon celebrating her 18th birthday, Ziva was summoned to serve her adopted country.

The discipline of years of swimming gifted her with a great physical condition rendering the rigors of training rather uneventful. The acquired upper body strength provided an advantage in hand-to-hand combat. In fact more than one instructor commented—"Ziva is the female equivalent of Avi Levine." I wondered if she realized what a compliment that was.

At this point I had attained officer rank in Israel's elite Special Forces. But I was not the headliner. News travels fast and reports of Ziva's beauty and skills soon reached the Prime Minister's attention.

"I want to learn more about this young woman," she told her subordinates smiling. "Bring me the latest up-dates." The pieces of the puzzle were falling into place. The Prime Minister's plan required the participation of a male and female, who were compatible in looks and skills. They would have to work together as a team. Consequently, Ziva was deemed my perfect match: code name S.O.D. (Swords of David) was born.

# VI

During my sixth year in Israel's Special Forces my different experiences resulted in worlds of personal changes. News of my great grandmother's death quickly followed by Grandfather Antonio's second stroke and eventual demise two months thereafter, left both sides of the family grief-stricken. Granted a leave for the funeral and mourning process, I spoke to my mother about joining Father in Italy to enjoy life in a serene and comfortable environment.

Meanwhile Grandmother Anna had moved in with Saul the butcher and was well cared for financially, thus no longer a cause of concern. The sole thorn in my mother's side was the danger ridden career I had chosen. She knew my life would be on the line every day.

Realizing Demetri needed her more than ever now that his father had passed on, Shanna gathered a few sentimental mementos and treasured keepsakes, and bid farewell to her mother and Saul.

Through the corner of my eye, I noticed Mom's face light up when she spotted me approaching to say goodbye. Drawing a deep breath, she circled my chest with her arms. Holding me close she paused, imprinting the feeling in her heart as if for safe-keeping before flying off to join her waiting spouse.

It was early August 2001. Life had not yet been interrupted by the 9/11 aggressions, and the beautiful woman she would grow to love, was not yet an important part of her new life.

Military *bravura* goes neither unnoticed nor unrewarded. Therefore, my speedy rise in the ranks of Israel's Special Forces was no surprise. Of particular interest was my ability with a sniper's rifle at a distance, a skill few if any, could match. It allowed me the possibility to take down leaders of Hamas without causing any collateral damage, which in military jargon translates to the usage of people who are incidental to the designated targets, as shields.

Having built a ruthless reputation together with my men, we were feared even in the darkest moments of the night. According to Hamas we were the silent assassins who could strike anywhere, at any time. And we certainly did not intend to prove them wrong.

It was a stressful life, high powered and perilous with human lives often dangling on frail threads. Consequently, whenever possible I would return to my birthplace to spend time with Mother and my grandmother still mourning Saul's passing.

Although their departure for Italy left me sad, I was overjoyed to have the reassurance they would be living in the safety of the Bastone Estate.

I returned to fulfill me purpose. Following a rather complex mission, I realized I would profit from some time away from all the violence, hatred and killings that defined my life on a daily basses. A warm sunny beach on the Mediterranean would be the perfect refuge for the next few weeks.

# VII

I shook my head back and forth to get the water out of my hair, and caught a glimpse of myself in the mirror. Pleased to note how the rigorous training leading to my commission as a Major had paid off. My 220 pound stature was composed predominately of muscles. As I swung the towel around my waste I couldn't help smile. Did I appreciate the attributes that left women staring in admiration? Certainly. Maybe I wasn't very humble, but the truth is the truth.

There were visible signs of several mishaps, but the presence of tiny scars seemed to enhance my sex appeal giving my face a less than perfect, though fascinating appearance.

Hurriedly I continued to dry myself, realizing the day was filled with pleasurable events. Additionally, I wanted to be outside in the warm sun. I was enjoying the well-deserved rest and relaxation or as it was commonly called R&R at the Caesarea Sea Beach Harbor Resort. I swam, played some tennis and was able to release from my mind, even if momentarily, the undeclared war that seemed to expand with each passing week.

This was a time off so to speak and I wanted to take full advantage. The pure white sand felt delightful as the granules nestled between my toes. I dropped the towel and soothed my body, reclining on the soft sands defining the entry way to the Mediterranean. Resting my head on my linked hands I paused all activity, mental and physical to enjoy the beauty of the day and my surroundings. Surrendering to nature, I allowed the hot rays of sun the freedom to penetrate my skin. Then the warmth was gone. I shuddered. What happened to the sun? A dark passing cloud large enough to block the heat must have rolled across the sky.

A husky voice called me to attention.

"Major Levine, get dressed and come with me. There is someone who wishes to speak with you."

Looking up, my glance settled on a pair of dark, almost almond shaped eyes. Rising to my feet I noted a stocky 5 foot 7 inch man with short cropped hair. My guess was that he weighed more than I did. Actually he resembled a solid slab of cement, concealed in a light tan jacket and beige shirt. He had no neck to speak of. His tone sounded serious hence I decided it was best to be accommodating.

"I will be ready in a few minutes," I said, heading off to my room. The messenger followed in my footsteps.

"I'll wait for you here," he grunted, leaning up against the outside of my door.

What could this possibly be about I questioned in silence.

Just a few hours ago I felt so alive and relaxed. I had enjoyed a wonderful conversation with my parents in Italy, sharing the pleasure they were experiencing in their new lives together. Of course, the fact that they were not yet blessed with grandchildren was still a sore point.

There was plenty of time, I thought. Thankfully men had no ticking clocks to worry about. I smiled as I replayed my mother's conversation.

"Maybe it's time to settle down Avi," she said.

"I would Mom if I met a woman like you." She chuckled and I could visualize her olive skin take on a pink hue. I spoke the truth.

But now my brief holiday was about to be ruined by someone or something I had no control over.

Once dressed, I went outside and climbed into the waiting car. The short stocky man drove as if he were in a tank headed for combat. His thick coarse hand found permanent refuge on the horn, causing cars to wisely scramble out of the way.

What the hell is all the rush about? Where are we going? Who is this person I'm risking my life to meet? Who could possible be so important? So many unanswered questions raced through my mind. Could this be a trap orchestrated by Hamas?

I was unarmed except for my physical strength and acquired skills, yet I was about to cross the threshold into unchartered territory. Was this a reckless action on my part?

Careening at breakneck speed with reckless zigzagging at unanticipated intervals, the roller-caster like drive persisted for a half hour, before he pulled into the driveway of a small farm house outside Sea Beach Harbor. Feet on the ground, I composed myself before entering the house. It looked inconspicuous, therefore my curiosity mounted.

Once inside, I was startled to see the hero of the Yom Kippur War, former General Simon Levy rise to a standing position. Beside him, with her back turned toward me, was a female figure. Quickly I reviewed the facts. The General currently filled the role of Ambassador to the USA. Meeting his gaze, I saluted. Even upon retirement, an officer maintains his rank.

"Avi please have a seat," the General said gesticulating toward an empty chair. At that moment the women turned around, revealing her identity. I gulped. Standing before me was Prime Minster Rachel Lagashi. Although a bit more petite in stature than I had imagined, there was a definite air of importance about this high-ranking political woman.

"Major Levine, I have followed your career with a great deal of interest," she announced, lifting her head to make eye contact. "I am certain your mother and father are very proud of you. Demetri and Shanna Bastone are honorable people. I'm also sure your grandfather *Il Fidato* was proud of who you had become," she continued flashing a grin.

She caught me totally off guard. Bewildered by the fact that the Prime Minister referenced my parents and even Grandfather in such a personal way, I remained speechless. After all the powerful leader of the Israeli government had just mentioned Mom, Father and Grandfather by name.

Witnessing my confused expression with demure amusement, the Prime Minister smiled.

"Your grandfather and I shook hands in agreement on many occasions during the early years after the birth of Israel. You must realize that not all the crates shipped into our ports were filled with olive oil. *Il Fidato* lived up to his name—he was a great man, a true friend to Israel when there were very few who were happy or willing to celebrate our existence."

I was amazed by the Prime Minister's candid revelations.

"Now let's get down to business, Major Levine. Let me explain the real reason I sent for you. We have information of a possible attack on the homeland of the United States. We don't know the exact location or date of the planned aggression, but we are sure it will occur soon. If this should come to pass, our country will be in grave danger, because the United States will protect its own borders. We fear that many allies will be forced to take matters into their own hands regarding countries who wish to destroy us.

I have just reassigned Ambassador Levy to head a special group of Israel's finest young men and women. The strategy is not complicated: they will work in teams of two. In addition there will be a man or woman who will act as an emissary, a liaison between the team members and the individuals in charge.

Neither restrictions nor red tape will exist. As far as the targets, they will be either neutralized or eliminated. If you decide to accept the commission Major, you will be the first to join this select group with the code name S.O.D."

There was no need for either consideration or rebuttal. I jumped to my feet.

"Where and when do I start, Your Excellency?"

"I'm happy you're coming on board. You will meet former Ambassador Simon Levy at his residence promptly at 2:00 PM on August 1."

I lowered my head a fraction. "Thank you, Your Excellency I shall be there."

# VIII

It was scorching. Beads of sweat ran across my brow as I neared the entrance of a modest, though well maintained dwelling. Moments later my shirt was soaked from the moisture of nervous anticipation. On the other hand it was August, and I could not expect anything but excruciating heat.

Drawing a deep breath, I knocked. Immediately I was greeted by a seemingly familiar face, yet for a fleeting moment I was unable to identify the individual who beckoned me to enter. Perhaps it was the elevated temps or perhaps I really did not have sufficient dealings with the gentleman to have his name perched on the tip of my tongue.

Following an exchange of several words, I recognized him as the driver who had escorted me to the farm house three weeks prior. Curious, I crossed the threshold. Once inside I wondered if I would receive answers to the many questions that had gone through my mind ever since the first meeting. I was all ears. My efforts were rewarded. Eventually I learned Benjamin was the name of the contact, the man who initially led me into the meeting place where the plan would come to fruition.

My eyes focused on a somewhat time-beaten desk possibly with a story to tell, behind which sat the Prime Minister. A navy and grey stripped arm chair on the left was occupied by the former Ambassador. To his right sat one of the most beautiful women I had ever had the pleasure to feast my gaze on.

"Major I would like you to meet Ziva Mizrahi," the Prime Minister said. "And Ms Mizrahi, this is Major Avi Levine." We greeted each other politely. I was grateful no one was aware of my rapidly accelerating heart beat.

"We have brought you together today to explain, the details of an assignment you will be undertaking if you agree to accept the job. Think carefully before you give your consent, because once you make the decision there will be no turning back. At this time I must emphasize the dangerous nature of the mission."

"Exactly what does dangerous mean, Your Excellency?" Ziva asked.

"It means your lives will be in jeopardy. We cannot guarantee your safety should you accept the mission."

"Do you have any questions Major? Ziva?" Her eyes darted like a spinning ping pong ball hitting both sides of the table.

"I don't," I replied, turning to face Ziva.

"I don't either."

"Good. You will travel together. Benjamin will be your driver and bodyguard.

"There is one other thing, Major. Today is the last day you answer to Avi Levine. Tomorrow you will become Antonio Bastone, son of Demetri and Shanna Bastone."

Ziva turned to face me. From the corner of my eye I noticed her amused smile. Later she confessed just how intrigued she was with the tall, handsome man holding the Prime Minister's attention.

I could also see from her tense facial muscles that she was annoyed my awareness in her regard was practically non-existent, as if she was not even in my presence. Judging from her secure demeanor, I was certain this was a new experience for a woman of her beauty. Undoubtedly, most people, especially men, fawned over her. She on the other hand, rebuked their attentions with poised nonchalance.

Undaunted by her winsome charms, I left her intrigued though somewhat perplexed. Early on she concluded I was different. Apparently she was interested to pursue further.

I had to admit I was captivated by the alluring Ziva. However, much as it was easy to be absorbed by her beauty, I realized I was on a very serious and dangerous mission, one that would not pardon even the most venial distraction.

It was far more important to leave her beauty aside and assess her skills. My strategy was to question her as I would a child. It was essential to find out if she could be of any value in the plans outlined by the Prime Minister. Understandably, the tactic seemed to annoy her.

"Excuse me Major Levine" Ziva began somewhat arrogantly; "tell me—do you speak Turkish, Spanish or possibly Iranian Farsi?" I noticed she didn't even try to minimally mask her anger.

"Major, are you able to mingle with women in casino, hotel and restaurant powder rooms? How about integrating in various villages and the Arab world?

I didn't think so," she cackled, seizing my silence as a response, without offering me the courtesy of a reply.

"Well besides those languages you just mentioned, I'm fluent in Arabic. You see I'm aware of who you are, and your reputation in Israel. While, I may be just a school teacher, don't be deceived by my appearance. I have skills even you don't possess."

Both Prime Minister Lagashi and the Ambassador erupted in peals of laughter.

"I think we have inaugurated S.O.D. with the perfect match." Simon announced. "Major, you will return to your father's estate, and live the sybaritic life of a carefree playboy."

Actually he was not proposing anything new. I had enjoyed this lifestyle until my 17th Birthday. His words enticed my mind into distraction. I wandered back, digging into my memories of Rosa Maria during our last summer together.

"Major—Mr. Bastone you will answer to no one but me and Simon," the Prime Minister said, interrupting my reverie. "Remember in addition to his other duties Benjamin will act as your liaison. Be assured—I have given you my best man; one who will guard you with his life, as he has done for me over the past ten years."

The Prime Minister failed to mention that Benjamin had four bullet holes burrowed in his body, and had come perilously close to dying while in her service.

"Do either of you have any questions?" she asked.

"How do I hide this from my parents?" I said.

"Good question Major. There is no need for concern. Your father and mother have been sufficiently briefed, and are in complete accord."

# IX

Today, few if any, would recognize me as the 17 year old Israeli tennis phenomenon of the past. Forty pounds heavier, multiple scars deeply etched across the surface of my cheeks, and a nose slightly curved from a flying rock that chipped off a bolder when targeted by enemy fire, I bear no physical resemblance to my former self. Furthermore, a smooth, clean shaven look is now replaced with well-groomed facial hair, in particular an almost precision cropped beard and mustache that turned my menacing combatant façade into that of a foreign diplomat. Undeniably Avi Levine was dead and buried.

However, the *demise* of Avi Levine had to be properly announced in the newspapers with a laudable obituary complete with a clean shaven photo of the departed. The picture of an officer with similar physical attributes to mine was posted as the header to an article filled with words of praise from the Prime Minister, and my commanding officer.

Mission accomplished—a stalwart man of elevated military rank, I received a noteworthy eulogy: Rest in peace Avi Levine. Seizing the opportunity, Hamas was quick to assume responsibility for my death, which made it all the more credible.

The next few weeks were busy for both me and Ziva. She made no secret of her sudden onset exhaustion and necessity to retreat to Italy until further notice, for some rest and relaxation. Once sufficiently in possession of her forces, she would return to work.

I made use of the time to get to know Benjamin. The more I discovered about my liaison the more impressed I became. Besides his skills as a protector, the man possessed a wealth of knowledge that would in time prove invaluable. I felt reassured having Ziva on the team, knowing Benjamin could guarantee her safety. It was time.

The Lear Jet with the colorful Bastone logo decoratively sprawled across both sides of its long slender body, smoothly landed at the *Aeroporto Internazionale di Napoli,* the Naples International Airport. Ziva, Benjamin and I hurriedly exited, approached a waiting limo, and were whisked off to our new lives tinted with unimaginable adventures. Not even in the wildest of dreams could such events take form.

The flight was uneventful. When my mother, now officially responding to the name Shanna Bastone spotted me, she sprinted forward, then lunged, covering my face with kisses while wrapping her arms around my waist. Anyone witnessing the scenario would be invigorated by the overwhelming outpouring of emotional energy.

Demetri, aka Father, extended his massive hand to greet the son he often referred to as his pride and joy; then turned toward Ziva.

"You are even more beautiful than I had imagined. *Vieni con me,* come with me, you must be famished after the trip," he said, gesticulating with his hands and eyes to emphasize the house.

"Carmella has been hard at work preparing her most famous dishes to celebrate your arrival. I hope you have a hearty appetite. However, I must warn you—she will be hurt if you do not have at least two helpings of everything."

"Please, don't let my tiny waist fool you, Mr. Bastone. The truth is I eat like a horse."

Immediately, Ziva triggered feelings of affection in my mother. Moreover, the illuminated grin spreading across my father's face confirmed he was sharing his wife's feelings. So far so good, I thought, expelling a sigh.

Once Ziva and my mother had parted our company to freshen up I knew it was my chance to pose the questions burning in my mind throughout the fight.

"Father, where is Rosa Maria. How is she doing? Do you see her?

You know I have to confess that I have thought of her many times since my departure. She is one of those unforgettable women in a man's life."

"I will tell you all about her Avi or rather I should say Antonio, after a hot shower and some good food to fill your stomach."

"Sounds like a good plan to me," I responded, trying to conceal my impatience for any news about Rosa Maria.

Meanwhile Benjamin busied himself transporting the luggage to the same guest house where I had savored the pleasures introduced by a woman, ten years earlier. This place was certainly filled with wonderful memoires. It all seemed so long ago. Sometimes I wondered if I truly lived the carefree life of my past or if it was merely a compendium of boyish day dreams colored with splashes of wishful thinking.

I also pondered just how much information about my new life Prime Minister Lagashi gave to my parents, Demetri and Shanna.

Eventually I learned they were told Ziva would be my partner for the assignment. Together we would help protect the State of Israel. Much more was not revealed. It was however, sufficient to keep them current with the happenings in my professional life.

"We're ready for dinner, Antonio," Father announced. I was happy he was grasping my new identity, though I realized it had to be difficult for a parent who had named me at birth.

"I'm on my way." I mimicked his animated tone, looking forward to delightfully satisfying my appetite in excellent company.

Dinner was a huge success as Carmella made certain there were a variety of menu selections to please every palate. After dessert, Father folded his napkin and placed it across his plate.—a sign the repast was terminated.

"Come my son," he said clearing his throat, "let's get a breath of air on the balcony, and enjoy the beauty of these olive trees. One day they will belong to you."

Reaching into his breast pocket, he withdrew a cigar.

"Your mother doesn't want me to smoke in the house," he said lighting the stogie.

I inhaled at the appropriate moment. "It smells familiar," I said, recalling the sent of burning tobacco from my childhood.

"Let me up-date you. It's been quite some time since you were here."

"OK I'm eager to hear it all—especially about Rosa Maria."

"Shortly after you left to serve in the I.D.F., a welcomed guest arrived from America, Frank Aiello.

"It's a recognizable name, but I can't place his face."

"He is one my biggest distributors in the northeast, and well known in my other circle of friends. In other words, he's well respected by all who deal with him.

One afternoon, while enjoying a swim, Frank spotted Rosa Maria. Of course he was taken by her beauty and captivated by her magnetic smile. He had recently lost his wife to cancer, and was feeling very lonely, in spite of his wealth."

"So did anything happen between them?" I asked. My pulse was racing. I wasn't sure I wanted to hear the answer, and for a brief second regretted posing the question. Sometimes the unknown is more comforting.

"Frank came to me, as was proper, since Rosa Maria was in my employ."

Father paused for a moment to relight his cigar.

"Using my title *Il Fidato*," he continued, blowing a stream of smoke toward the setting sun, "he requested my permission to court her."

"What did you tell him?"

"I told him I would talk to her and her mother on his behalf, and if she agreed it would meet with my complete approval."

"Did they get together?"

"Even though Frank was 20 years older than Rosa Maria, he was still a young man and wanted a son more than anything to carry on the family name. As soon as she heard about Frank's intentions, she agreed without taking time to ponder her decision.

"So she consented?"

"Yes, several weeks later Rosa Maria departed with Frank to begin their new life as husband and wife in the United States. They now have two children: the son he always dreamed of, and a beautiful little girl.

"Do you hear from her? Is she happy? I hope so," I said, not certain what answer I was looking for.

"Rosa has grown to love Frank. After all he gave her everything a wife and woman could ask for. Tell me son, do you still have feelings for her? You knew of course, we were all aware of what was taking place during your last summer here. "

"No, not that way," I said. "But I will always be fond of her, and indebted for her kindness and the life experience she provided. I confess that I often wondered what had become of her."

"Good, so no hard feelings or regrets."

"Don't worry, none whatsoever."

"Now tell me about more about Ziva. Do the two of you have more than a professional relationship?" My Father was a shrewd, wise man with excellent vision!

"I have never met anyone quite like her. She's smart, and from what I'm told by people I respect, she's a great shot, better than good at hand to hand combat. Furthermore, her language skills are equal to mine, though I would never admit it to her. With her looks she would be impossible to work with."

Pondering my closing comment, I chuckled. Difficult to work with, sure, but…who knows, I could be in for an exciting ride.

"I think you've met your match, Antonio. Regarding her looks, I don't believe she has given that a second thought. "

"It will be interesting," I said. "No—make that riveting!"

I always enjoyed my dialogues with Father and now realized how I had missed his company. But life takes us down different paths. Though grateful for my visit and the time with my parents, I knew what lay ahead. I had to get my mind into work mode.

Benjamin, in his infinite wisdom placed Ziva's luggage in one room and mine in another. For himself he chose a room at the far end of the five bedroom guesthouse. Spacious and comfortable for all visitors lucky enough to be invited, the dwelling was equipped with four baths, a large kitchen, and a complete workout room. Once in my quarters memories of my youth and the summers with my parents and grandfather returned, bringing renewed joy. Of course there was the famous rite of passage summer with Rosa Maria: unforgettable even if I should be blessed with centenarian longevity.

I could swear the aroma of our love making still lingered; perhaps on the drapes and certainly on the silk sheets that snugly hugged the bed. Reason told me my imagination was teasing me. But it was fun to believe otherwise even if just for a fleeting moment.

To Ziva, on the other hand this lifestyle was as foreign as the French Revolution. While I reminisced, nourished by thoughts of yesterday's pleasures, she drew herself a bath and soaked away the tiredness. The warm welcome she had received from Demetri and Shanna gave her a felling she had not felt in many years.

It had been a long day. Surrendering to human needs, we both fell fast asleep in a matter of minutes.

The following morning I was in for a humbling experience. My swimming skills, nothing to be ashamed of, were minimized when Ziva hit the water. Watching her swim lap after lap in the Olympic size pool for almost an hour non-stop with the ease of a bird taking flight, left my ego ruffled.

"Enough" I whispered under breath, jumped out of the pool and sat observing her sinewy body slice through the water. Amazing, I thought, she had the refined finesse of a graceful dolphin maneuvering through the Mediterranean Sea. Although she had neither flippers nor a dorsal, her sleek physique seemed custom designed for speed in the water.

When she exited the pool it was with the silent attitude of someone who fully recognized and enjoyed her *bravura.*

"Where did you learn to swim like that?" I asked as she settled in the lounge chair beside me. Much as I tried to conceal my enthusiasm, I feared it was evident I was impressed. Sometimes even unwillingly, we betray ourselves.

Ziva hesitated a moment. Her expression changed to somber. Did I push a wrong button?

"Antonio, swimming was my escape from the pain I suffered after loosing my parents in early childhood," she replied in a soft voice.

Our eyes locked as she turned to face me.

"I have never told anyone about my parents. Meeting Demetri and Shanna and witnessing the love between the three of you left me nostalgic for what I never enjoyed. I was moved by their open arms and gracious hospitality. They treated me as if I was a part of your family—or rather I felt as if I belonged here, thanks to their kind-hearted reception when I arrived. Whatever it was, it gave me a warm feeling—something I don't recall experiencing with such intensity."

I was pleased Ziva had opened up to me. Since we would work together on a serious, life risking mission, it was wise to extend a professional relationship into a personal one. Moreover, Ziva was intelligent enough to recognize the time was right to demolish the barriers she had constructed to protect herself from being hurt again.

# X

Word spread quickly of my return in the company of a beautiful young travel companion. Invitations to events from a formal dinner with the president of Italy to honor his daughter's upcoming nuptials to a Greek shipping heir, to the family christening of a good friend—Don Rucco's newest grandchild, came pouring in, much to the delight of Prime Minister Laggashi. Perhaps initially concerned, she now enjoyed in the serenity that it would all work out.

Welcomed in all social circles, Ziva and I seemed to have broad appeal. This expansive social acceptance set a precedent for us to be sufficiently trusted to obtain the necessary information for our mission.

Nevertheless, prior to the start of the fun and games, Ben and Ziva participated in an intense training program. Rigorous and well-structured, it presented her the opportunity to fine tune her acquired skills to a level few people ever achieved. The dexterity with knives she exhibited surpassed even mine, and her years of nautical training gave her the speed and stamina of a top rated pluri gold medal Olympic swimmer. The added benefit of a gorgeous, well toned slender figure was certainly not displeasing.

To perfect my eye hand agility and visual focus I set up a target range where I spent many days repeating the same exercises. My goal was to increasingly challenge my techniques and savvy with both hand guns and long range sniper weapons.

Soon it would be time to step into my insouciant playboy persona, a role I would play with the alluring Ziva by my side. It all seemed so perfect, except for the danger factor. Then again perfection is just a dream of perception.

I gazed at my watch. Time was escaping at a reckless pace and I still had to finish dressing for dinner with the family. Tardiness was not well tolerated at the table, especially since the exquisitely prepared menu selections had to be consumed as soon as Carmella served them. Furthermore, it was well known that Demetri and Shanna preferred to dine early in order to enjoy long strolls afterward before retiring for the evening.

I walked over to the closet to choose a pair of pants and a shirt. A sudden knock distracted my concentration.

"*Entri*, come in" I said, spinning on my heels to face the door. From the somber look on Ben's face when he entered, I immediately knew some trouble was brewing.

"What's wrong?" I asked.

Suddenly Ziva appeared. Now I was certain something had occurred. My first inclination was on behalf of my parents.

"Are Mom and Father all right?"

"Yes Antonio no need to worry," Ben said reassuring me.

"So what's happening—you look disturbed."

"There is breaking news all over the TV that the United States has been hit by a terrorist attack. They say at a first count about 3,000 people have been killed."

"Where? How did it happen?" I gasped, stunned.

"Two planes crashed into the Twin Towers in New York City. President Bush has declared a national emergency. There is a no fly zone across U.S. territory. It seems another plane hit the Pentagon while a fourth was forced down by the passengers, thankfully short of its target. Unfortunately there were no survivors."

Horrified I turned on the television and flipped through the channels to get to the *RAI 1*, one of the principle state run channels. The *ora di cena,* dinner time *telegiornale* was just beginning to transmit the nightly news broadcast. Although the newscaster was animatedly spewing information in Italian, I was able to understand. Essentially he was repeating what Ben had said, only in more gory detail.

A new terrorist came to the surface with a name that would be on the lips of people around the world for many years: Osama Bin Laden. A photo of the culprit flashed across the screen. A tall, thin man with a scraggly beard, he looked menacing. His message was even more alarming—actually intimidating. Brazen and cold-hearted, he notified the world that this was merely the beginning of the end for all who did not adhere to the Muslim faith and believe in the teachings of the Koran.

"Benjamin I fear the world has changed forever today," I lamented feeling beaten by a man I had neither seen nor did I care to.

I thought back to my meeting with Prime Minister Laggashi and her cautionary warning of impending danger. The threat made against America had come to fruition. Before I could catch my breath, the satellite phone rang.

"Yes *Madame* Prime Minster," I replied. I understand and will convey your message to Ziva and Ben. "

"*Be'hatzlacha* Antonio! And *Be'hatzlacha* to Ziva!"

"Thanks Your Excellency, we sure do need the good luck."

We ended the conversation; I switched off the transmission and quickly notified my parents that the S.O.D. was officially activated.

"Benjamin, you must leave for Israel at once," I said. "You must meet with former Ambassador Levy, and then return with our assignments. I will speak to my father and ask him to set up a meeting with some of his friends who can be of great value to us as we gather information from around the world.

I'll drive you to the airport, and make all the necessary arrangements for a limo to be waiting.

"No Antonio it's better if I rent a car. I want to leave quietly. I don't want people to know about my visit."

"Fine—as you wish."

We parted company, and Benjamin headed to his room to start packing for the journey.

The dinner ambiance that evening was somber, bordering almost on melancholy. My parents, Ziva and I merely picked at the food, excellently prepared as always by Carmella. Reaching for his crystal goblet, Demetri took two sips of the dark red *Bolla Amarone* decanted earlier, and generously poured for the guests.

Except for the clinking of cutlery on the porcelain plates, silence prevailed.

"How do you think President Bush will respond to this morning's attack?" Father said. "And more importantly, how will this terrible delivery of aggression affect you and Ziva?"

"I can't answer Father until Benjamin returns with our orders from the Prime Minister. But it will be a great help to us if *Il Fidato* is willing to summon his friends to a meeting here as soon as possible."

Nodding, Demetri confirmed full understanding of why I had referred to him by his well earned title, *Il Fidato*.

"Does this mean you, Ziva and Benjamin will be leaving us?"

"No, Father, this will always be our home. However, we will be required to go away from time to time to take care of business. Anyway nothing can be done until Benjamin returns, and things cool down. Right now emotions are at an all-time high."

With a vertical swipe of his head, Demetri gesticulated his agreement; "I'll make the calls and advise you when all is ready."

"Thanks Father—much appreciated."

After dinner and a night cap with my father, Ziva and I took a few steps in the garden surrounding the luxurious mansion I would one day inherit. The aromatic landscape, the tuneful chirps of our winged guests, and the magnificence of the starry sky produced a feeling of serenity in stark contrast to the reality of the devastation that had occurred 4,400 hundred miles away.

"In spite of it all, we are prepared for any task the Prime Minister has in store for us," I said, extracting the words right from Ziva's thoughts.

The answer to Father's questioning of President Bush's response would not be verified until years later. Eventually, information provided by covert agencies advising the President resulted in a war based on lies, and false claims of weapons of mass destruction. Unfortunately the authentic focus was concealed under shadows of the faulty allegations.

In reality, the new threat to my mom's former homeland was Osama Bin Laden, a villain who was raised amongst the wealthy Saudi elite. The conniving mastermind behind a number of attacks against the United States, he had been on the FBI's Most Wanted List since 1998.

All the gloom and heaviness of the day's events though worrisome did not distract my attention from the beautiful woman seated beside me. Dressed in a simple white two-piece silk blouse and flowing ankle-length skirt that hugged her curves, Ziva was ravishing.

"Antonio, spending time here with your family and enjoying every day in this idyllic paradise has almost enticed me into forgetting the perilous nature of our purpose for being here together."

I leaned over and patted her hand. "Ziva we know what we have been called to do. And we are well trained."

"*Buona notte*, good night," she said, flashing a smile that could melt through the most rigorous ice age. My gaze followed her as she rose and strolled off in the direction of the guesthouse.

"Aren't you coming," she asked, looking over her shoulder?

"No, I'll sit here a moment longer and enjoy the night."

The cooling breeze from the Mediterranean was too much of a tease to run from. It wafted across the rows of olive trees delineating the Bastone Estate.

Many visitors and friends had been vocal about questioning why Demetri had not replaced some of the trees with flowering bushes and plants to add an enlivening spray of color to the home. However, convinced nothing was more beautiful than his fertile olive trees, he rejected all suggestions.

Gazing at the panorama, I had to admit Father was right. The sights and aromas pleasing my senses were almost other worldly. Additionally, they formed a protective wall shielding all who lived within its boundaries. For me and my parents, the mansion represented a save haven. Here in this peaceful sanctuary, we were untouchable.

I forced myself to rise to my feet and head back to the guest house. Tomorrow would be a big day; therefore it was essential I reserve a generous amount of time to get a good night's sleep. Moreover, there was nothing more to do until Benjamin returned or sent a message from his satellite phone.

The guesthouse was in *quasi* pitch darkness with the exception of a small light from the outside pool. This gleam allowed me to find my way back to my bedroom. Ziva's room was enveloped in total stillness, permitting neither TV sounds nor the minutest flicker of light to give a sign she was awake. In fact all outward manifestations indicated she had probably fallen into a deep sleep. *Brava* Ziva! I wondered, somewhat envious, if perhaps I would be able to enjoy the same luxury. Enough thinking, I thought, I just want to be knocked out. Exhausted, I stripped and slid between the smooth silk sheets savoring the icy feel against my naked body.

Vulnerable, I tried to relax, grateful for the darkness surrounding me. I felt as if the absence of sight and sounds made everything right. Suddenly it all seemed so peaceful—until that is the impromptu interruption.

When my bedroom door opened, the mood shattered. A long angular beam of light shot across the bed, confirming I was no longer alone.

"Are you awake Antonio? I can't sleep," Ziva whispered. I don't want to be alone tonight. Is it all right if I stay in here with you?"

A sliver of moonlight abruptly penetrated the drawn drapes, illuminating her taut body covered exclusively by a short transparent top. Instinctively I pulled back the covers. Indisputably it was a welcoming, invitational gesture on my part.

"Are you sure this is what you want?" she said almost coyly. My mouth dried like the Sahara sands at sunset. A mirage appeared. There she stood with erect breasts and tapered waist nurturing my erotic thoughts. Could her line of questioning actually be serious, I thought.

"And you Ziva?"

"Yes "I want it more than anything in the world," she whispered, slipping out of the shear garment, which did little to conceal her physical assets. Like a shark after its prey she glided into bed beside me, strategically brushing my bulging erection with her cool body.

Was I ever ready! It had been a long time since I made love to a woman: too long. But I had never forgotten Rosa Maria's tutelary words.

> "Go slowly my young lover; gently kiss her eyes, her ears and her neck; stroke her breasts and nipples with delicate pressure until they tingle and stand firm in anticipation of your open mouth ready to lick and suck them. Run your hands down the length of her body until your fingers reach the soft hair between her legs. Open her waiting lips and search for her pleasure spot. When she has been satisfied, her body will be ready to receive your rather large penis."

Rosa Maria had given me useful advice, recommendations which I followed to the letter. In response, Ziva's moans brought me back to reality. Under my fingertips her nipples hardened; her legs spread wide apart: there was no second guessing her wishes. And I did not intend to waste any time.

My hand traveled down her firm stomach over the small mound of hair to the lips now drenched from her passion.

Effortlessly my fingers searched for, and located her pleasure spot. Immediately she gasped.

"There it is! You got it! Don't stop!" Her body sprinted upward to meet the finger bringing her so much pleasure. Suddenly she clamped her thighs around my hand. Her agile back arched just before a vibrating sound blew sweet hot air across my face. Seconds thereafter she smothered my mouth with hers in a seemingly never ending kiss extravaganza.

"Now it is your turn my love" Ziva said mounting me like a horse. Taking my manhood in her hand, she placed the head between the lips well lubricated from her explosive orgasm. Then the gyrations began. Slowly she glissaded down, inch by inch until I was buried deep inside her. Pumping up and down brought her to the realization that she could orgasm again. Her pleasure spot was re-aroused as it smacked against my manhood.

Mimicking her ardor I started to move with heightened velocity until unable to hold back any longer I burst forth in a fulminating orgasm the moment Ziva enjoyed her second climax. Falling forward against my chest she kissed me. I entwined my arms around her in a protective gesture. I now knew the ecstasy my parents shared. I had found my soul-mate.

"Later my love I will do for you what I have done for no man" Ziva whispered, bending over to kiss my resting penis.

Celebrating our first love making feast, we decided to take the next day off. We shunned our routine of a 10 mile jog, before breakfast, favoring instead a few laps in the heated pool. After a quick joint venture shower, Ziva brewed a fresh pot of coffee which I might add we devoured in its entirety.

With neither warning nor apparent stimuli I unexpectedly burst into laughter.

"What's so funny," Ziva asked.

"I was just thinking."

"About what?"

"Well the staff will no longer have any doubts regarding our relationship after they clean up my room. The gossip will surely thrill my parents."

"I hope so, Antonio. I have grown very fond of them: besides their approval is extremely important to me."

"Fear not, Mother already considers you the daughter she never had, and as for my father, his only question was; "What the hell is taking the two of you so long?"

"I have an idea."

"Tell me, I'm all ears."

How about going for a ride after our swim? I'm certain our stable master, Domenico can saddle up two horses for us. Domenico has been with my father for as long as I can remember; taking care of the horses as well as the prize German Shepherds he breeds and rears. The town's people believe he must be part Gypsy judging from the way animals respond to him, especially the dogs. It almost seems as if he has a special method of reciprocal communication with them."

"You mean he talks to them."

"Yes—but the best part is—they talk to him also," I added smiling at the visual forming in my mind.

I extended my hand which Ziva immediately grasped. Together we walked over to the stables to meet Domenico. Anyone observing us would say we were like two school children enjoying a romp on *una bellissima giornata autunnale dell' estate di San Martino*, on a beautiful Indian summer day. Ironically no one would have believed at first glance, that Ziva and I were two of the most ferocious people on the planet.

Dominico greeted me with a hug; trying to lift me off the ground as if I were still the small slender boy who came down to the stables to help him feed the horses. Although Ziva chuckled at the spectacle of watching me being treated like a rag doll, she underestimated the strength of a man who stood six feet six inches tall with a body weight well into the mid 300s.

Grabbing me in a bear hug he succeeded in removing the ground beneath my feet!

"This must be the beautiful lady everyone is talking about," Domenico said, bowing from the waist while removing his sweat stained hat. Ziva smiled in response to the gentle giant's compliment, quickly planting a kiss on each of his bloated cheeks.

"Domenico, can you saddle up a couple of horses for me and Ziva to ride?" I asked trying to override the sudden yelps and barks chorusing in the background.

"What in the world is that ruckus?"

"Antonio, those are my new *cuccioli*. The litter of puppies just arrived this past week. Come take a look at these beauties."

We followed as the gentle giant crossed the threshold into the stables. Once inside, the scenario in front of us was absolutely heartwarming. On the side was a huge red and white blanket on which rested a gorgeous black and silver German Shepherd. Reclining on her side, she was offering sustenance to ten clamoring puppies trying to satisfy their appetites, sucking milk from her protruding nipples. Nine were successful, while the efforts of the tiniest pup were in vain.

"Look at that smaller one" Ziva said concerned. "Is there any way we can help her?" Domenico opened the stall door. Instinctively she ran toward the struggling puppy. However, Mamma Shepherd misinterpreted her intentions. Ears erect, eyes focused on Ziva as if calculating every move, she let loose a deep throaty growl, never disengaging any of her litter from obtaining their nourishment. Protection? Defense? Perhaps a bit of each. But the message was clear.

"*Aspetti aspetti!* Wait Wait! "I will bring the little one over to you. The mother is very vigilant and protective, not to mention possessive of her pups. She will only allow me, and *i Signori* Bastone to get close.

It made sense. She was a new mother and her only concern was the safety of her litter. Domenico reached in and gently lifted the tiny pup. I watched with bated breath as the mother raised her head to survey his actions. Moments later her tail wagged. I let out my breath realizing she was OK with Domenico taking her pup.

Observing her relaxed face, I could have sworn she was smiling and saying; "*Thank you, my friend, for helping my baby.*"

Domenico inserted a small bottle in the pup's mouth and handed her to Ziva who waited with open hands while the little one sucked away. Gazing into the pup's proportionately oversized brown eyes, Ziva and I were captivated. It was love at first sight!

We exchanged a quick glance.

"OK Ziva the answer is yes even before you ask. But please make certain the pup doesn't create any problems."

"Domenico's booming laughter echoed throughout the stable.

Once the tiny Shepherd had finished her bottle, he returned her to Mamma Shepherd.

"She will be fully weaned in about eight or nine weeks. Then you may take her from the nest. Until then just come from time to time and I will let you feed and play with your new pup."

"How does that sound Ziva?" I questioned.

"O thank you so much Antonio," she quipped, brushing my lips with hers.

We returned to the main house to join my parents for lunch. From the girth and radiance of the smiles on our faces it was evident that the news of our bonding was no longer just hearsay. Unhesitatingly Shanna reached out to Ziva, encircling the young girl in her arms. Pulling her close she whispered in Hebrew;

"Welcome my daughter, love and cherish Antonio as much as I and his father do."

Tightening her arms around Shanna, Ziva gave free reign to the steady flow of tears running down her cheeks.

"Fear not for he is my life."

Demetri's sneeze interrupted the moment.

"Any news from Benjamin?" he asked.

"Not yet Father, but I need to talk to you about some financial matters. Money from the Prime Minister is available, but I'm not sure how long it will take to actually get it. I would like to have access to some funds as soon as possible. Whatever amount you loan me will be repaid immediately," I assured him.

My father laughed; "Son it is obvious you are clueless about your own personal finances and just how wealthy you are. When you were born your grandfather followed the advice of a close friend and invested fifty thousand dollars to acquire shares of a certain stock. That friend is Warren Berford and the stock is Kurtshir Hadewic. Therefore, your net worth is about $47,000,000, give or take a million."

My jaw dropped. I was in shock! Was this true? I had not the slightest inkling regarding any inheritance left me from Grandfather's estate.

"Antonio, I will make all the arrangements for you to have access to those funds as you need them."

Life was full of surprises. Every corner turned unveiled an unforeseen circumstance—what was next?

# XI

The anticipation of Benjamin's contact either by phone or in person was one of the most stressful challenges Ziva and I had to confront on a daily basis. While we waited, we ran five miles to dismantle some of the anxiety mounting with each silent second. Our course was a round trip path to and from the tiny village nestled in the valley on the outskirts of the Bastone Estate.

Once completed, we headed to the firing range to keep our skills sharp and fine tuned using the plethora of fire-arms Father made available. Afterward, to deplete the last vestiges of nervous energy still lingering, we went to the gym for an exterminating work-out. I guess it is safe to say we were in superb physical condition.

To reward our efforts we finished the program with a dip in the pool. The soothing water never failed to help us unwind, relax and heal our aching muscles. Since Benjamin had not given a sign of life in two weeks, we kept trying to ward off the effects of excessive worry with our rigorous morning workouts. But how long would we be able to maintain this massacring rhythm? Yes youth was on our side; we were however, not indestructible.

Finally the much anticipated ring of my satellite phone pierced through the evening's quiet. The caller announced Benjamin was scheduled to arrive the following day. Reclining beside Ziva, I repeated the message in just a few short words. Together we pondered the nature and implications of our first S.O.D. assignment, though neither of us deemed it necessary to vocalize our thoughts.

Although it was a restless night despite our exhaustion, we refrained from any discussions; perhaps believing that even the slightest attention allotted the issue would possibly create negative scenarios. Instead, lost in our thoughts we awaited the dawn.

Benjamin arrived just minutes after the sunrise, unpacked his one bag, brewed a pot of strong coffee, and tore into an Israeli bagel carried over from the homeland. Posing the tattered bread on the circular table, he opened a small worn leather pouch, extracted three files and placed them beside his plate.

"Now we begin," he announced, shifting his gaze between me and Ziva in quick staccato intervals.

"Paper work?" I said playfully.

"Antonio these three folders contain the identities and necessary information pertaining to men who have three things in common: a lust for money, a thirst for power, and a deep seeded hatred for the State of Israel."

"Not very nice guys are they?" I muttered.

Benjamin was too busy sorting the folders to offer a comment. I noticed that two folders were identified with a large E on the covers whereas the third had a big N. The letters were code to differentiate between the fates of the men whose names would soon be revealed.

I opened the third file marked with the letter N, which stood for neutralize, and read the name William H. Hartford, III. My memory may be a bit hazy, though I know he is the senior senator from South Carolina.

"Benjamin, is Senator Hartford next in line to head up the powerful Foreign Relation Committee?"

"Yes and he's important because this committee is responsible for allocating financial aid to Israel and other countries."

"Well he certainly doesn't make a secret about his feelings for Israel. If I'm not mistaken, his speeches, interviews to the press as well as television interventions not only document his sensibilities, but introduce a platform with conditions for action."

"Antonio, the Senator would do everything in his power to cut off all aid unless Israel agrees to fulfill specific conditions. However, in complying he knows the safety of citizens may be jeopardized."

"Do you know that for sure?"

"Well, the Prime Minister supplied information regarding the Senator's strong ties to the oil rich Arab world, O.P.E.C. And we all know the oil cartel holds the fate of many nations in its greedy hands."

I scrutinized the documents, which clearly outlined the details of the ultra-religious Born Again Christian Senator, whose depraved inclinations would sicken even the most macabre character.

As his power intensified, likewise his practice of pedophilia heightened. Unfortunately the Senior Senator from South Carolina was gluttonous for the supple flesh of adolescent girls. With the passing years, he began to satiate his appetite consuming the innocence of younger and younger prey.

His misfortunate victims hailed from the Mideast to China. To his credit was the ability to conceal his criminal antics from both family and friends. In fact, the general consensus proclaimed him a religious man committed to God, family, and his career.

The information was mind-boggling. I reread certain paragraphs several times.

"I think we may need to call upon some of Father's American friends," I said, casting a glance first at Benjamin, and then my beautiful partner, before closing the file.

"Dare I inquire about the contents of the other two folders?" Ziva asked.

"Here we go," Benjamin responded, reaching for the second file identified with a large E. Emptying the contents of the folder on the table, I noticed the striking photo of a bearded man. His complexion was marred by an array of pock marks, sparing neither his upper cheeks nor forehead. I could only imagine what lay beneath the thick coarse facial hairs.

Exaggeratedly close set eyes, emphasized the off kilter proportions of a prominent nose, the tip of which sat close to his salt and pepper mustache. He answered to the name, Yazeed, proud of its Arabic literal translation—*God will increase.*

Suffice it to say, he took the directive verbatim, actually believing his *increase* was imminent. From a starting point supplier of outdated weapons to a few impoverished third world countries, Yazeed eventually branched out to become a major dealer for the most sophisticated weapons. The individuals he dealt with were unfaltering and thankfully so, as he was well aware that if he floundered, he'd pay with his life.

The Institute for Intelligence and Special Operations, known as the Israeli Secret Service, Mossad had obtained information that Yazeed had met with Mansor Raftab, a man slight of stature, though a powerful leader, none-the-less.

Recently, Iran had been boasting about their creation of a nuclear facility built to produce high grade uranium for, according to Raftab, "peaceful purposes." It was no secret this diminutive man's grandiose schemes were designed to shift the balance of power in the Middle East. His goal to destroy Israel was known worldwide. Therefore, entering the nuclear power phase was the first step toward meeting his objective.

A bright ruler mistrusting all, Yazeed lived a guarded existence whenever he left the sanctuary of his private quarters. Vanity and an insatiable lust for women were his failings. Unable to resist a beautiful lady, he lived with the illusion that he was irresistible to every female he coveted. Additionally, his folly led him to believe he was the best poker player in the world. As irony would have it—he actually was an excellent player, who had beaten many of the best Texas Hold'em champs from around the world.

"The poker table, my love will be our way to take Yazeed down," I said centering my eyes on Ziva.

"I think you might be right," she responded, sharing my thought. "Take him down in his element!"

"Let's see what the third file contains," I suggested.

Folder number three contained the photo of a dark-skinned, clean shaven, handsome young man with deep set brown eyes and a smile that accentuated a perfect set of stainless white teeth. However, pictures can be deceiving: despite his movie star appearance, Mr. Zarin Doust was the most dangerous man of the trio.

Doust was born with a silver spoon in his mouth to a successful entrepreneurial father, owner of the largest import-export business in Iran, and a well-respected investment broker mother, an ace at managing the portfolios of some of the wealthiest Iranians in the country. Needless to say, Zarin, the only child of the affluent Doust couple, was reared sparing little if any luxuries. A brilliant student with a gift for finance, he was expected by those who knew him to one day not only assume the leadership of the family business, but expand it in the global marketplace.

Undoubtedly Zarin would comply with his father's wishes, though not in the manner expected of him. In college he had met a group of religious zealots whose beliefs included, but were not limited to the ousting of the Shah. Taking it further, he propagated the replacement of the deposed Iranian leader with an Islamic Republic under Ayatollah Khomeini. This regime would bring about a return to the true teachings of the Koran.

Next on the 'to deal with' agenda were the Zionist who controlled Israel, the followers of the Pope with their false god, and last but not least the American *bon vivants* with their decadent way of life.

According to the information in the folder, it was reported that Doust headed a lucrative operation with reported revenues totaling tens of millions of dollars—all while destroying countless lives.

Zarin Doust was the largest drug dealer in the Middle East, perhaps the world. His power base was widespread with merchandise imported from Afghanistan, Turkey, Mexico, and China. His business controlled the refining of beautiful flowers and poppy seeds into the lethal toxins that careened through the veins or sucked into the lungs of men, women, and worst of all children addicted to his evil source of pleasure.

I had read enough.

"Zarin's wealth is funding the terrorist groups attacking the United States as well as many other countries," Benjamin said, closing the file. "He must be stopped."

"I agree—I think we all agree," I replied, catching Ziva's nod of consent. "Who do you think should be our first target?"

"I believe Yazeed presents the greatest threat," Ziva said. Benjamin confirmed unanimity. We were all on the same wave length.

"I agree. The Senator's chairmen appointment will not occur until January 2002. This will allot us sufficient time to plan and execute a strategy. Furthermore, a great deal of preparation will be needed before we target Zarin."

# XII

Thankfully it was reconfirmed: all three of us agreed on the order in which each of the three targets would be handled.

"The Prime Minister has asked me to emphasize the danger you will be facing," Benjamin said in a soft but firm tone, as he rose to his feet.

I was fully aware of the risk I was taking in accepting the mission, and was certain Ziva had no illusions either. We both knew that under normal circumstances, Mossad would be called upon to take care of these problems. However, we were living in different times, which called for diverse methods in handling the menacing situations that threatened our nation.

"Senator Hartford is a perfect example of what the Prime Minister and former Ambassador Levy are referring to," Benjamin said. "Since America is our greatest ally, there can be no evidence, not even a minimal hint attributing either Mossad or Israel's connection to this downfall.

Both of you are fresh, unsoiled identities with neither histories nor reputations. Furthermore, you hail from the world of the rich and famous. However, if either of you has the misfortune to get caught or worse yet killed, there is nothing Israel can do about it."

The message was clear, straightforward and certainly not sugar coated. Reaching for his brief case, Benjamin removed a large white envelope.

"Inside you will find a new Turkish passport, as well as a summary of your newly scripted past life," he announced, handing the envelope to Ziva. Although the facts are true, the places and locations cited are fictitious.

Antonio, since you already have both Italian and American passports, and since Major Avi Levine is dead and buried, there is no concern about you. In fact your man of mystery persona will serve to enhance your playboy mystic."

The three folders were returned to the leather pouch and placed in a safe behind the built in bar in the den of what had become their permanent home.

"Before we start making plans for Yazeed, we must introduce Benjamin to our new friend" Antonio said.

"Come," Ziva called gesturing to Benjamin, "You will meet our friend as well as the walking mountain named Domenico."

We walked toward the stables in silence. I noticed that Benjamin's face exhibited a puzzled look. Maybe he was just deep in thought. He certainly had good reasons.

Meeting us half way, Domenico strolled over, in the company of a medium sized dog. Wildly wagging her tail was a way to express the joy she experienced in meeting new friends, who she hoped would love to play with her and satisfy her appetite for treats.

Trying to restrain any outward manifestations of delight, Benjamin knew it would be his job to walk and feed the newest member of the team. However, once the playful pup planted several licks on his face and began nibbling the tips of his ears, all the tough guy restraint in the animal's regard, collapsed. On the other hand who could resist the charming antics of such an adorable and loving four-pawed friend?

"Well it's time to give her a name," I announced. "We can't continue to call her puppy. It's so impersonal. Do I hear any suggestions?"

"Actually I have thought about it ever since we agreed to raise her," Ziva confessed smiling.

"Let's hear the selections—what names were you considering?"

"How does Cuoco sound? It means cook in Italian. Also, it will be a tribute to Carmella. I'm certain she would be pleased we thought of her."

Before anyone responded, the pup let loose with three throaty yelps, instantly interpreted as her official approval for the name chosen. The decision was made and our friend and colleague was christened Cuoco.

"We can break the news to Carmella," I said, chuckling, "it's almost l'ora di cena, and I'm famished from all this brain-work!"

Taking Ziva under the arm I escorted her to the dinning room. As always, no one was disappointed. Following another superb supper, Ziva did the honors to inform our wonderful chef about Cuoco. Hearing our decision, she giggled in delight like a young school girl handed a new doll.

"*Grazie* Carmella," Demetri said rising from the table. "Another delicious meal." With quick determined steps he headed for his office. Moments later he returned carrying a large white envelope.

"Antonio here you will find all the information regarding your finances," he said, handing me the envelope. "The interest alone amounts to a little over fifteen million dollars. As you can see, there is no need for concern—you will not have any financial problems.

You will also notice the names and contact information of all the banks and the advisers handling your investments, in addition to the numbers of the different accounts. I think you will find it all clear and well-organized. If for any reason you fall short, notify me and I will transfer whatever funds you require."

"Thanks Father, this certainly reassures me."

I opened the envelope. It was as my father had promised. All the information was clearly written. Grateful for my photographic memory, I scanned the file, imbedding all the names and numbers in my mind.

"Do you have any questions?"

"No Father it looks great."

"As per your request, some of my friends from Italy and the East and West Coasts of America, have agreed to meet here the first week in November, assuming this works with your schedule."

"Thanks Father, the timing is just about right. By the way do you know anyone of relevance in Monte-Carlo?"

Demetri smiled, "Prince Robert, and his late father, Prince Tainier have been friends of the Bastone family for many years. Will they do?"

"Can't debate their fame," I said.

"Actually we own a villa there. Your mother and I enjoyed much of our special time together in that beautiful country."

"Why am I not surprised," Ziva said.

# XIII

To occupy a seat around the dining table at the Bastone estate would be the dream of every individual engaged in law enforcement. Dinner guests, enjoying the generous offerings of food and wine were often the infamous *Capi*, heads of all the major crime families from both sides of the Atlantic, animatedly conversing in Italian and English, or more accurately put in their unique intermingling of both languages, known as *Italish*.

Only one man, *Il Fidato* had the power and clout to summon these *Capi* on short notice. When Dimetri had in mind a meeting, his illustrious guests would arrive in a heartbeat. Seated at the head of the table as was customary, Father suddenly rose to his feet, wine glass in hand. Saluting his visitors, he thanked each by name for traveling such a distance without the slightest inkling of a motive for the convergence.

"Most of you either know or have heard of my son Antonio," Demetri began. "Well, honoring his request, I have invited you to my home for this dinner meeting. Antonio will now remove all the mystery and explain why you are here."

"Thank you, gentlemen," I said. "I realize you all have professional obligations, and busy schedules, so please know I appreciate the time you have sacrificed to fly over for this meeting. As you are all aware since 9/11 everything has changed both in your world as well as in ours. For reasons I cannot discus at the present time, I have been selected to work toward neutralizing or eliminating those individuals whose principal goal is to destroy life for all who oppose their beliefs.

Make no mistakes regarding the sinister nature and intentions of these people. In reality they are lavishly funded evil men, paid to kill all who stand in their way. This my friends, simply stated is a fact of life.

These individuals have networks expanding throughout the Middle East and beyond. They are involved in every business, from slave trade, blood diamonds, and weapons, to all categories of drugs.

Of course no honor code exists among these ruthless men. Children, wives or any family member for that matter, are all fair game to the jackals."

I had everyone's full attention. No one ate or drank.

"I am asking you, and your organizations to keep your eyes and ears open.

Most of you control either the docks or the transportation networks throughout the United States, Italy, Turkey and places I am perhaps unaware of."

Whispered traces of laughter from the men united around the table, confirmed I had spoken the truth.

"We must all agree to halt the rise of this small but very powerful group of fanatics who are intent on destroying all that you and my father have worked for. And we must help our governments in secrecy; *sub rosa*, without their knowledge.

My job is to gather pertinent information, to use against them. This is not a complicated plan: nevertheless, please feel free to discuss among yourselves before deciding. I must caution you about the serious risk and irrelevant monetary gain. Are there any questions?"

Heads shook in unison.

"If any of you wish to speak with me or my father, we will be available to listen to your concerns. In the meantime I thank you again for your time and attention. Good evening Gentlemen."

Father and I left the dining room, walked out to the patio sipping the last remnants of wine we had taken from the table. In silence we waited for someone to approach with a question, suggestion or concern.

Nervously I tapped my foot. I could see Father's jaw contract.

Would anyone step outside to talk to us? After what mistakenly seemed like hours in the minds of anxious men, Frank Aiello approached.

"Demetri, Antonio please come inside and join us."

Father and I exchanged questioning glances; then trailed in his footsteps as he led the way back into the dining room.

"I have been chosen to act as spokesperson for all those who at one time or another have been helped by *Il Fidato*," Frank proclaimed, raising his glass.

"Demetri, your son is now considered part of all our families. We will do whatever is needed to assist him in any way possible."

The gentlemen rose to their feet, clinking glasses. "*Salute* Demetri *e* Antonio!—to your health!" The toast was short, to the point and unmistakably clear.

"All information from the United States will be passed on to me and in return I will inform Demetri," Frank announced prior to ingesting the last drop of wine in his glass.

"I will do the same on this side of the Atlantic," Don Rucco added.

"Are there any questions?" I asked.

"How much can one man do?" Don Rucco questioned?

"*Bravo,* good point. There are two basic things to remember. One, if you sever the head, the body will die. We have no restraints regarding our methods. Two, I am not operating alone. Other teams such as mine are in training as we speak. Is that clear? Once again the head nods were unanimous.

"Once more, please accept my thanks for coming all this way to meet with us, and for the respect you have shown Father in your response to my request."

"How about another round of drinks?" Father asked visibly proud of my performance in front of his influential associates. No one refused, nor were they expected to.

Although Father's friends were unquestionably not strangers to the Bastone Estate having crossed the threshold into the dining room upon numerous occasions, both Shanna and Ziva knew their presence was not convenient at certain times and in specific circumstances.

Moreover, convinced of their powerful gray eminence status behind the scene, neither one took offense or was unwilling to follow protocol when the old school Italian men were in reunion.

After the night cap, the men departed, but not before filling the room with compliments for Carmella's exquisite meal, and Father's excellent selection of wine. Frank paused for a final word.

"Demetri, this was an interesting meeting. Be assured we will do everything we can for Antonio. All he as to do is ask."

"Thanks Frank, I know I can count on you. Now tell me about the family? How are Rosa Maria and my little *figliocci?* I bet my godchildren are growing up fast."

"Yes the children are getting big, and Rosa is just fine. You know—very happy. And Dimetri, my friend, I am forever grateful for the new life you gave me."

"Please tell them they are always in my prayers," Demetri whispered, giving Frank a goodbye hug. "*Ci vediamo presto*, see you soon," I shouted from the patio.

# XIV

The Lear Jet touched down softly on the runway of the *Aéroport Nice Côte d'Azur.* Although I often wondered why a rich nation like Monaco did not have an airport, I absolved myself from trying to resolve the dilemma, created in my own mind. I had to admit the noise and pollution factor once eliminated kept the glorious principality quiet and elegant. Furthermore, the Nice landing was good enough and by no means inconvenient.

After the landing gear came to a halt and the engines shut down bringing the craft to a complete standstill, we disembarked and walked several yards before climbing into the glistening black Royals Royce Phantom V Limo. The plane, pilots and the limousine, along with the chauffer were provided compliments of my father whose generous offerings were ours for as long as needed.

Once comfortably settled in the Rolls we were driven to one of the beautiful villas owned by the Bastone Corporation. Overlooking the crystalline blue sea and coastline from a hill, the panorama from the patio was breath-taking.

"Don't worry about the bags," Benjamin said, "I'll take them inside."

Ziva and I remained transfixed by the fairy-tale ambiance into which we had been cast.

"I'll unpack your things Antonio."

"Thanks."

"Benjamin please leave my bags in the room, I'll unpack later," Ziva shouted from the patio. I knew her long enough to realize she preferred to handle her own belongings.

Although Demetri wished to provide a full staff to accommodate his guests, I politely explained to my father that we all agreed it would be better if Benjamin assumed most of the household chores. Agreeable to our wishes he complied, but mentioned that he and Shanna had engaged the culinary services of a local woman during their time in Monaco.

"Antonio she is a fantastic cook. By the way her name is Françoise."

"OK Father—I'll keep her in mind and share your recommendation with Ziva and Benjamin."

"She may come in handy one day." I could see his mischievous smile, through the telephone wires. "Anyway the kitchen should be fully stacked. Also I assume the villa has been cleaned and there are fresh sheets on the beds."

"Yes Father, it is as you ordered. Everything looks perfect. We will be just fine."

Exhausted and famished from the travel, Ziva and Benjamin joined me in the dinning room for some *canard à l'orange*, duck in orange sauce, which we washed down with a bottle of superb wine from Father's prized wine cellar.

"Perhaps we should turn in. I'm beat from the traveling," I said, wiping my lips and placing the napkin across my plate.

"Good idea," Ziva chimed in.

"We'll need a lot of information in order to find Yazeed. Tomorrow will be a long busy day. Let's head to bed."

I grabbed Ziva's hand and led her into our designated bedroom, while Benjamin checked and doubled checked the house from north to south and east to west, until he felt reassured there was no imminent danger or threats lurking in any hallway or corner. After all he considered me and Ziva not only his charge but very special friends. Therefore, our safety was his priority.

"Goodnight Benjamin," I whispered over my shoulder; "we'll see you in the morning."

"He looks a little sad—don't you think?" Ziva asked.

"He misses Cuoco," I replied, "but she is still too young and just in the preliminary stages of her training to qualify for our team. I am not worried because Benjamin knows Domencio will take excellent care of her."

"Still he must miss her terribly, just as I do."

"You're sentimental my love."

As soon as our heads landed on the luxurious *Pratese* dressed, pillows, we departed the world, casting off even if momentarily, all our cares.

Nine hours thereafter, Ziva opened her eyes, smiled coyly and kissed me gently on the cheek. Though conscious I pretended to be still asleep as she tried to free her long slender arm from under my bulging bicep. Successful, she rose stark naked and headed for the bathroom. Her beauty and physical perfection left me eternally in want for her delicacies.

The sound of water splattering on the marble shower floor was my cue to get out of bed. When I heard the echo of Ziva's melodious purr, I knew she had set the appropriate temperature, and had just stepped under the warm stream. Reaching the door I peered in just in time to catch the crystalline spray cascade down her perfectly rounded beasts, her tiny waist and long tapered legs. I never doubted she believed she was not showering in privacy.

Ziva was still young and relatively inexperienced to truly understand the meaning of love until she met that special gentleman, me, who had made love to her in a way like no other. Having crossed the point of no return, she would never again regard love as she did yesterday.

Fully awake I was ready to start the new day. Turning off the shower, Ziva stepped out careful not to slip on the wet marble, grabbed a super-sized towel hung on a warming rack, wrapped it around her shoulders, and rubbed until she was dry.

Walking into the bedroom she put her lips on mine and greeted me with an electrifying kiss, far more potent than three cups of the darkest caffeine laden espresso on the market. I had to admit Ziva looked absolutely smashing even at this hour of the morning.

The aroma of fresh pressed coffee permeated the room. Jumping to my feet I returned Ziva's kiss, targeting her nose in lieu of her lips and ran for the shower allowing the ice cold droplets to awaken my brain and get my blood circulating, before the flush of warm water would calm the shivers.

"Are you hungry?" Ziva asked; "I'm starving!"

"Me too," I shouted from the bathroom.

"Hurry and get dressed my stomach is growling like a famished bear."

"Mine too," I said chuckling at the metaphor. "I'm ready—let's see what's on the menu."

I hear voices coming from the kitchen," Ziva whispered as we neared the entry, "I think Benjamin has company this morning."

Seated at the table sipping a cup of coffee with Benjamin, sat a very attractive petite women, probably in her mid-forties. Both stood at attention when we walked in.

"Antonio, Ziva, I would like you to meet Françoise, your father's housekeeper. "Upon learning of our arrival, she graciously came over to see if there was anything we might need."

Benjamin seemed different. Was it an attitude? Was it the unfamiliar circumstances? Or did the presence of this sweet lady result in a quickened heart-beat? Undoubtedly something had changed his demeanor.

"*Enchanté de faire votre connaissance, Monsieur* Antonio, it is a pleasure to finally meet the son of Demetri and Shanna Bastone," Françoise said bowing her head. "I heard so many wonderful things about you. *Monsieur* is this beautiful woman your wife?" she asked fixing her gaze on Ziva.

Since neither Ziva nor I spoke French, Parisian born Benjamin utilized his mother tongue to translate Françoise's question.

"Well thank you Françoise, the pleasure is all mine," I said, as she walked toward us extending her hand.

I winked my response while my sexy girl looked at me wide eyed.

"It might not be a bad idea to have someone your father trusts help take care of the house as well as prepare some meals—assuming you and Ziva are in agreement," Benjamin volunteered.

The smiles running across our faces gave the answer he was hoping for.

"That will be wonderful," I said. "Father spoke exceedingly well of Françoise. She has been highly recommended. Let's see if she is available, and if so, for how long?"

When Françoise was informed of our wishes she clapped her hands, darted over to us, and gave each of us a bear hug.

"*Mille fois merci*—thank you so much" she said excitedly. Gazing at Benjamin I was just in time to catch his beaming ear to ear grin.

Benjamin had another surprise for us. Extracting a large white square envelope from his hip pocket, he handed it to me.

"This arrived this morning from the Palace."

"Let's have a look."

I opened the envelope, slipped out the gold embossed stationary and noticed it was a handwritten note signed by *Son Altesse sérénissime le Prince souverain de Monaco,* His Serene Highness Prince Robert. The invitation requested my presence with Ziva, at a small reception he was hosting this evening, if we had no previous engagements. Of course the courtesy of a reply was *de rigueur* as the French say, required by etiquette.

A telephone number was listed, inviting guests planning to attend to phone their response. Since an invitation from Prince Robert was rarely regretted, I quickly dialed the number. The voice on the other end advised me to hold for a moment. At the sound of the Royal gentleman's greeting I tapered my breathing for better auditory clarity.

"Antonio I hope you're calling to accept my invitation," Prince Robert said in perfect English without any traces of his *Monégasque* birth.

"Certainly, Your Highness, Ziva and I would be delighted to come."

"I am looking forward to meeting the son of my good friend, Demetri Bastone, and of course the beautiful Ziva, who I have heard so much about."

"It will be our pleasure. My father and mother send their regards and hope all is well with you and your family. "

"We shall speak again, Antonio."

"By all means—*à bientôt*—see you later."

"Well that is a rather exciting surprise—dinner with the *Monégasque* Royals! What will I wear?" Ziva exclaimed, not realizing her voice was audible to all.

"Please tell *Madame* not to worry—I would like to help her if she wishes," Françoise said, turning to Benjamin for his translating services.

"*Merci* Françoise," Ziva responded, following her intuition. "I will happily accept your assistance."

# XV

"Benjamin, why don't you stay home this evening and help Françoise," I suggested, turning in his direction. "Considering our destination, I doubt we will be in any danger. Moreover should an unpleasant situation arise at the Palace, their security force is more than equipped to handle it."

"Fine Antonio I'll remain here this evening. But if..."

"No but if—don't worry at all. There is no need for concern. Just enjoy the evening."

"Thank you."

Actually Benjamin was looking forward to spending time getting to know more about Françoise. Somehow she had ignited his fancy and he was curious to uncover if she was married or romantically involved with someone. Although this would be a good opportunity to dive into her life, he still felt a little uneasy not trailing behind us to the Palace to keep an eye on me and Ziva. However, he complied with my wishes and retired to my quarters to select my outfit for the night's event.

Benjamin volunteered, of course with Françoise's consent, her wishes to assist Ziva with her fashion choices for the event. Grateful for the kindness, I was certain my beautiful partner would share my sentiments.

Later in the afternoon following a brief siesta, Ziva received a visit from her honorary *dame de compagnie*, lady in waiting.

"May I ask what you are planning to wear to the royal dinner?" she asked.

"Sure Françoise come in and I will show you" she replied, pointing to an outfit sprawled over the chaise lounge. I decided to wear this black two piece pants suit with a row of rhinestones running down the front of the jacket and along the side of one pant leg. What do you think?"

"*Mais non Madame!* No no, a lady does not wear pants when meeting *Son Altesse Sérénissime le Prince Souverain de Monaco*" she said breathlessly, first in her native tongue, then in heavily accented broken English.

Walking over to the armoire she hurriedly rummaged through the selection of garments neatly hung on soft rounded satin hangers.

"*Non non non,*" the chorus of nos was almost comical, but Ziva maintained her calm, observing Françoise, with an air of amusement.

"*O-la-la, oui oui oui !* Yes yes yes." Pulling a full length emerald green gown from the closet she fixed her gaze on Ziva. "Beautiful" she exclaimed, pointing first in the young woman's direction then toward the dress.

"*O oui* Françoise, this gown is *exquisité*. I will be thrilled to wear it. *Merci* for your help. I'm certain Antonio will approve."

I had to admit that approve was a rather inadequate word to describe anything about Ziva. In fact when my eyes focused on her, dressed like an empress, I thought I was experiencing my first mirage. Stunning in the gorgeous *haute couture* gown, she seemed more a figment of my imagination than a real flesh and blood women. Speechless, I was floored.

"You look absolutely dazzling, ma *chérie*. I doubt I have ever seen a woman as spectacular as you are this evening."

"Why thank you Antonio," she muttered, visibly flushed.

"You better get used to such compliments. I'm certain there will be many more."

"O Antonio you are far too gallant."

"Not at all—just being truthful. Are you ready to head over to the Palace?"

"Yes I'm ready."

"I am going to take the Ferrari Enzo this evening instead of the Rolls. Father left both cars for us."

"It doesn't matter to me as long as we arrive safely."

Feeling a bit constrained in my double breasted Armani tux and impeccably pressed shirt held firm by Father's cherished studs, I sat beside Ziva as we drove to the Palace. The scene could have easily been borrowed from a modern day Bond film, featuring a playboy who doubles as an international spy in the company of his sexy accomplice. I smiled at the thought, unwilling to share it with my beautiful lady.

"It is truly splendid here don't you think?" Ziva asked as we rode though the picture perfect streets of Monte-Carlo.

"Yes almost seems as if we are characters in a fairy tale. We are nearly there—see there's the Palace. "

"It looks like a fortress."

"I read a little history about it. Actually it was built in the 12th century as a Genoese fortress. Here we are."

I pulled up to the entry of the Palace and stopped in front of the valet. He opened the door as I ran around to help Ziva exit from the low slung passenger seat. The tall slender sentries posted on either side of the entrance stood at attention, flawlessly motionless.

"*Bonsoir Monsieur et Madame*, the valet greeted as I placed the key in his open palm.

"Ziva, are you ready to take on our first assignment?" I whispered, squeezing her hand. A deep breath, a wink and a coy smile had to suffice as a response. The deep breath is a great idea, I thought, following her example.

Once inside, we were escorted into a large ballroom vibrantly decorated with extravagant arrays of beautiful flowers, undoubtedly from the neighboring Sanremo. The Ligurian costal city on the Italian Riviera was world renowned for its extraordinary flowers.

We mixed in with the roughly fifty exquisitely dressed guests, intermingling and sharing polite pleasantries. Jeweled female hands sporting glistening diamonds, emeralds and rubies lifted crystal goblets ever so delicately to impeccably colored lips. Their gallant cavaliers, trapped in starched evening shirts offered the *petite hors d'oeuvres* to their ladies while adroitly juggling their own cocktails.

The guests were either milling about or seated at small tables positioned along the perimeter of the room.

"If this is the Prince's concept of a small reception, I'd be curious to see what a large affair would look like," Ziva whispered. Before I could comment, a tall, distinguished gentleman parted company from a circle of friends and approached.

"*Bienvenus*—Welcome! I'm delighted you were able to attend," he said, extending his hand. Radiant and genuine, his broad smile was a far cry from the bogus party smirks seen more often than not. Recognizing the Prince, both Ziva and I came to attention. Was it an intimidating moment? Not exactly, because the open, gracious demeanor of *Son Altesse Sérénissime* was that of the boy next door who had invited us to a friendly get-to-together.

"*Madame*, your photos do not do you justice," he announced, turning to Ziva. "You are exceedingly more beautiful in person. Among the old photos my mother left me there is one of Ava Gardner. Your resemblance to her is striking. The next time we meet I will show it to you."

"Thank you, Your Highness your words are very kind. Your mother, Princess Grace was truly a special lady, revered globally for her philanthropic endeavors, in addition to her exceptional beauty. Who can ever forget the shock of her unexpected passing, and in such an untimely manner? It was a terrible tragedy and a great loss for all mankind."

The Prince bowed his head in thanks and in reverence to the memory of his departed mother.

"Antonio, before I introduce you to my guests who I might add can't seem to take their eyes off the most enchanting couple in the room, allow me to inquire about the welfare of your parents. How are Demetri and the lovely Shanna? I have not seen them in a long time."

"Both are doing very well Your Highness, and send their best wishes for your health and well being."

"Please thank your parents for me, when you speak to them."

"May I present you to my guests?"

"Certainly." Ziva's quick response preceded mine.

Extending both arms in an invitational gesture, the Prince smiled. Ziva and I accepted, and arm in arm we walked toward the curious on lookers. Interesting facial expressions betrayed their surprise and bewilderment. If I could vocalize their thoughts, I'd say the question burning their tongues was an inquiry regarding the identities of the stunning newcomers, apparently in a close relation ship with the Prince.

"Don't worry," the Sovereign reassured, "you will not be expected to remember all the names of the people you meet this evening."

In silence I chuckled. How could I possibly tell him I would forget neither a name nor a face at the reception? It was just not part of my game plan.

I had to admit that the identities of the beautiful people sipping drinks and nibbling on *hors d'oeuvres* were rather impressive. The list consisted of Spanish royalty, a Romanian Count and his consort, German business tycoons, the American Ambassador to Greece, two actors filming an action movie on location (both had their eyes glued on me) and an international selection of wealthy real estate investors interested in acquiring or selling properties to the rich and famous.

Much to our amusement, there was a group of Arab Sheiks on a sybaritic journey of pure unfettered pleasure, set on enjoying a holiday of wine, women and high stakes gambling at the legendary Casino de Monte-Carlo. As expected, once in their visual range, the hedonistic gentlemen could not take their eyes off Ziva, probably speculating either in the quiet of their minds or to each other, what price she would command for an evening of sensual bliss.

Since they could build castles in air to their hearts' content to no avail, I was not the least bit troubled. Proud because she was exclusively my woman, I smiled, realizing according to their perspective, I was a poor man!

The evening literally flew by. Just as I had hoped, we were treated like a red carpet couple. The Sovereign introduced me as the son of his longtime friends Demetri and Shanna Bastone, King and Queen of the olive oil world who was on a visit to Monaco in the company of my beautiful companion, Ziva. With the stamp of approval from no less than his Royal Highness Prince Robert II, our place in high society was assured.

Questions and invitations arrived quickly from everyone and anyone of importance.

"How did you meet? Where are you from? What do you do for a living? Where are you staying? How long will you be in Monaco?"

The barrage seemed endless, as if we were in a court of law, being interrogated by a prosecutor. Our heads were spinning. Nevertheless, gracious and courteous, Ziva and I answered the questions as rapidly as they were posed, until the Prince, surveying the scene, came to our rescue.

"*Mes amis, le dîner sera servi sous peu*—my friends, dinner will be served shortly," he announced in French and English. "Furthermore, Antonio and Ziva are thrilled you wish to become better acquainted, but please give them a little breathing space."

Talk about Prince charming coming to the rescue—our gallant host was a life-saver, and we were grateful. I made a mental note to extend my thanks, circumstances permitting before the evening's end.

Ziva occupied the seat of honor to the right of the Prince and I was seated in close proximity. Leaning back in his chair, he drew my attention. Realizing the charming Royal wanted my ear, I too leaned back to meet him.

"Antonio," he whispered smiling, "your father requested you be given the Royal treatment, and as we both know, he is a man whose wishes are granted. I hope this doesn't disappoint."

"It could not have gone any better, Your Highness," I replied, returning his smile. "You have been truly gracious. And just for the record, I have every name of every guest not only connected to the face, but imbedded in my mind."

"I should have known better, Antonio. After all you are the son of Demetri!"

We enjoyed a chuckle before straightening our chairs to savor the meal. After the sumptuous dessert, espresso and parting words, the Prince received eye witness evidence of my photographic memory, as I greeted each guest by name, leaving them all somewhat surprised.

# XVI

Exhausted from her housekeeping chores, Françoise departed for an evening's rest, leaving Benjamin alone with his thoughts in the dimly lit kitchen. Realizing he would never fall asleep until he was certain Ziva and I were safely in our room, he was determined to spend the night there if need be. To him honor and integrity signified incomparable loyalty and dedication.

Though his head, weighty with concern nodded, he anxiously awaited the sound of our voices before shutting his eyes. In the short period during which we had been together, Ziva and I had become more than just an assignment from the Prime Minister. Actually we had taken the place of the family he no longer had, but continued to yearn for.

Benjamin had enlisted in the Army at seventeen and worked himself up to the rank of Tank Commander. Decorated for heroism during the Yom Kipper War, he was proud to have the medal pinned to his chest by General Levy, an officer who never forgot the heroic soldier. Years later, when Rachel Lagashi, a rising star in the political world reached the status requiring high level security, he remembered the tough young Tank Commander who had logged many hours as a helicopter pilot, and wondered what paths he had taken.

Summoning his administrative staff, the General requested updated information on Benjamin Anker. Quick and alert, his liaison discovered through a telephone call that the man in question was now an instructor with Special Forces.

"He is perfect and fills the job description," the General said turning to Rachel.

"I'm not as certain as you are, Sir. What else do we know about Mr. Anker?"

"Enough to realize he's suited for the job!"

In spite of the Prime Minister's initial objections, Benjamin was assigned to protect her at all costs. Perhaps the four bullet wounds scarring his body were the testimony the General needed to validate his qualifications. The decision was made. Benjamin proved his worth during the more than ten years he kept Lagashi out of harm's way. Ironically at her request, he was now assigned to guard me and Ziva in the same fearless and devoted manner in which he had protected the Prime Minister.

When informed of his new charge, a smile appeared on the lonely man's face. Difficult as it was to believe, Benjamin had not been with a woman for a long time. In fact, he had never experienced a serious relationship. His work had been his lover, friend, and constant traveling companion. Observing first hand the love and affection between me and Ziva, as well as my father and mother, saddened him. Along with the melancholy came the realization of just how much he had forfeited for his country.

Although consenting to the regrets game was not part of Benjamin's plan, he swore he would walk this path again should he have a chance to repeat his life. However, meeting Françoise caused an exhilarating reaction.

Benjamin was captivated! But was it too late for him? The feelings and stirrings were present, undoubtedly. His heart went into speed mode when in her company. Beads of sweat careened across his deeply lined brow every time she addressed him in conversation.

Yet the questions surfaced: Who is Françoise? What did he know about her? Was she married or emotionally involved with someone? And if all conditions were possibly a go, would she reciprocate his feelings?

The screeching sound in the driveway as I navigated the Ferrari toward the entrance of the villa snapped his mind back to reality. Relieved we had returned, unscathed, he slid the chair away from the table and rose to his feet. The anticipation of a well-merited night's sleep was his sole compensation for the last few hours spent in the company of his sometimes silly thoughts. But a man entangled in the web of a beautiful woman often becomes powerless.

The questioning continued. Of course a woman with such unique beauty and culinary talents would have a husband or at the very least a lover. Was his heart racing for naught?

Ziva and I entered the house chatting and laughing, commenting about the Prince's reception and the people we had met.

"Benjamin—you are still awake!" I said, startled to see him on his feet just several hours before the onset of dawn.

"I was curious to hear how the evening went. Wouldn't be able to sleep with you and Ziva out of the house."

"The reception was just lovely," Ziva said before I could get in a word.

"Yes it was perfect," I added. I guess we are now part of the upper crust international *Monégasque* high society."

"And Antonio has been invited to play in a high stakes poker game with our new friends the Sheiks from Saudi Arabia," Ziva announced, proud of her lover.

"That's great—perhaps it will get us a little closer to our target," he said, swiping his left eyebrow with his index finger. I noticed the traces of lingering sweat that had settled on his forehead. I hoped our outing had not caused him undue worry.

"How uncanny Antonio—this evening Françoise asked whether we would be here for the big Texas Hold'em tournament in about three weeks."

"I'm not sure. Players like Yazeed prefer no limit cash games. I just don't think he will be interested in a game were any amateur can get lucky and win. His ego would not withstand such a blow. I believe he will only play where he feels he has an edge. If he doesn't play I won't be participating.

I'm going to spread the word that there is an extremely wealthy, but terrible, Texas Hold'em player at the Casino de Monte-Carlo and hope he takes the bait." Both Benjamin and Ziva chuckled at the ploy. I interpreted their reaction as an unofficial approval.

"By the way how are things going with you and Françoise?" I asked. Is she working out for you? Are you satisfied with her services around the house?"

"She's fine," Benjamin mumbled. "There is no need to look for a replacement."

"Good, I'm happy to hear that."

Oddly, Benjamin seemed to be avoiding eye contact with us. I didn't know if Ziva had picked up on it. Actually it was not only obvious, but inconsistent with his behavior. Whenever he addressed anyone, he always looked them straight in the eye. In fact he repeatedly cautioned me against trusting those whose gaze roamed away from the target during a conversation.

Eventually I mentioned it to Ziva.

"I noticed it also and found it weird. It's not in his character."

"Well let's not read anything into it for the moment. If it happens again, I'll handle it."

"I'm beat—all I want to do is crawl between the sheets and fall asleep in your arms."

"Now that sounds like an excellent plan, Ziva."

"Then let's put it into action!"

Ten minutes, thereafter, we were in a deep all pardoning sleep.

Together with the first rays of the sunrise, the strong aromas of fresh pressed coffee, and just baked biscuits permeated the house, stirring us back to reality.

"I think Françoise arrived," I said eagerly anticipating breakfast. "If I know Benjamin as I think I do, I'd say that before she slips into her uniform, she will be served a sumptuous meal."

"Talk about a sumptuous meal—let's not waste any time, I'm starving," Ziva whispered, kicking off the light silk quilt. "I want to see Françoise's reaction to breakfast."

We quickly dressed and headed to the kitchen.

"*Qu'est-ce que tu as fait*—What have you done Benjamin?" Françoise asked jokingly.

"It's nothing—nothing at all" he mumbled under breath. I caught the first inklings of panic swipe across his face.

"I just thought I'd get things started to make it a little easier for you."

"This is not started—this is finished!"

Witnessing the scene I had to chuckle. Here Benjamin stood defenseless like a disobedient child caught with his hand in the cookie jar. A full grown adult, a war hero, a man who had faced death innumerable times, Ben now faced a petite docile woman who seemed to have the power to intimidate him.

"I am sorry it won't happen again. Doesn't your husband make breakfast or any other meal for you while you are working?"

"That would be impossible since he passed away over ten years ago!" she said, with a sigh.

"Benjamin—are you trying to find out if I'm spoken for?"

"Françoise I was just..." he stammered, unable to complete his thought.

"Well let me make this easy. The answer is no, I'm free and single and yes, I would love to go out with you if you ever have the time."

Tough guy Benjamin was captured totally off guard without a word of reply.

"Next time I will make coffee and biscuits for you if you don't mind," she said. A nod accompanied by a full tooth smile conveyed his feelings.

As an epilogue to the Benjamin—Françoise scenario, we enjoyed a delicious breakfast, folding our napkins only when every morsel was consumed. Undeniably we had plenty of fuel for a long days work.

Later in the evening Benjamin and I sat at the dining room table, meticulously cleaning the weapons, previously stored in the wine cellar. We each chose a specific weapon. I worked on the Ruger 22/45 pistol while Benjamin preferred the Glock 17C, even though it was somewhat larger and caused a slight bulge under his jacket when strapped on. The Ruger however, is easily concealed even if I'm wearing a tuxedo, which seems to be most evenings.

"How do you plan to lure Yazeed to Monte-Carlo?" Benjamin asked interrupting my thoughts.

"I have given much consideration to this."

"So I assume you have a specific plan?"

"Yes. I have decided to set myself up as a very affluent pigeon, ready to be plucked."

Benjamin remained pensive for a few seconds. Was his silence a sign of disaccord with my ploy or merely an interlude to process what I had said?

"Tell me Antonio, how did you become such an expert card player?"

"My outfit passed the time playing poker between missions. It didn't take me long to determine I had a gift for reading body language and facial expressions. Today this is known as a *tell*. The more I played, the better I became. Eventually I discovered that my proficiency at calling hands with no margin of error whatsoever far outweighed the joy of actually winning the game.

When Texas Hold'em became the rage, I fine tuned my skills and looked for greater challenges. The men in my outfit, as well as others at the game table said my eyes turned ice blue like hardened diamonds when I understood I had the winning hand. That was my *tell*."

"Knowing you, I doubt you would allow others to read you," Benjamin said.

"Of course not! I immediately started wearing dark glasses to hide my betraying flaw."

I was certainly not in this to be defeated. Loosing at anything is not my style. In fact, it became a challenge I absolutely had to win. From time to time when I heard of a large cash game, assuming the timing was right, I'd sit in and share the winnings with my men.

I remember after one game I was approached by a beaten player, an older man, obviously an American in a huge ten gallon cowboy hat who inquired if I was a Pro. I told him who and what I was.

"You're a natural, Avi," he said in his south west drawl. "A type like you can make a fortune playing full time. If I were in your shoes I'd give it serious consideration."

"Thanks but the military is my life, though I'll admit a good card game is a great way of easing the tension of warfare."

"If you ever change your mind and decide to come to the US, I'd be happy to back you," Mr. Ten Gallon Hat proclaimed, handing me his card. Glancing down before sliding it into my pocket I noticed it read, Boyle Drunsen, The Texas Dolly. At the time the name meant absolutely nothing. As far as I knew he was an American tourist on vacation with his family; a father and husband who had tired of the sightseeing experience and was looking to get involved in a bit of action to liven up his trip.

"You know Avi, you have a special gift that cannot be taught. I have seen this kind of talent only once before, but that man has passed away."

A compliment is always a joy to receive, even though I had no idea from whom it was originating. I had only the name, Boyle Drunsen in my mind. Soon after while following the televised Texas Hold 'em tournament, I noticed seated at the table wearing his trade mark ten gallon hat was none-other than Boyle Drunsen.

The commentator presented him as the two time World Series of Poker main event champion who had spent a half century collecting prestigious titles at the tables. Evidently he had been inducted into the poker Hall of Fame. This info gave even greater merit to his compliments.

"After Boyle's praise maybe you understand why I'm a successful poker player," I said laughing.

Benjamin nodded his agreement. "I think you're making a big mistake, Antonio. Yazeed will never accept a challenge if you play the part of the pigeon. On the other hand if word got back to him about a young playboy, undefeated at the table, who had taken Monte-Carlo by storm, he might just bite. If you remember when we examined his profile you decided we would use his ego to bring him down. Yazeed would never come for just the money; he has more money than he can spend in two life times. Besides beating another bad player is insignificant to him. Instead, the possibility of bringing a rising upstart down to earth might wet his appetite."

"*Bravo* Benjamin. You hit the nail on the head. In lieu of playing the pigeon, I'll go for the hawk."

# XVII

Françoise strolled leisurely into Ziva's bathroom and drew a warm aromatic bubble bath, before heading into one of the guest rooms, to take care of her own hygienic needs. Hurriedly undressing she slid into the shower adjusting the flow to as hot a spray as she could possibly endure without suffering first degree burns. The clouds of vapor from the moisture went unnoticed. Distracted by her thoughts of Ziva, she realized she had developed an affinity for the beautiful young girl.

If she didn't waste time under the soothing hot spray, she would be able to check on her once again before retiring. Yes, Ziva had Antonio, but he was conscientious about satisfying her other needs—those only he could gratify. But she could be there as a lady in waiting and perhaps confidante should the situation dictate. Certain a pleasurable evening had been planned, Françoise wondered when I would return to my waiting companion.

Minutes later, I walked into the bedroom just in time to catch Ziva entwine a plush oversized monogrammed bath towel around her shoulders.

"I have news from my mother and father," I exclaimed, animatedly like a little boy wanting to share praise from a teacher.

"I hope all is well."

"Yes—They are leaving for Israel. Grandma Anna's friend the butcher suffered a fatal heart attack and they wish to be with her during the seven days of Shiva following the internment. My guess is they will try to bring her back to live at the estate now that there is no longer any reason for her to remain there. Besides she is at the age where she should not be living alone."

"That sounds like a good plan. By the way, speaking of changes, would you mind, my love, if Françoise stayed here in one of the guest rooms?"

"Any special reason," I replied teasingly.

"Actually yes—I have grown very fond of her in the short time she's been with us, and I find the thought of her going home to an empty house every night rather disturbing. Besides, she is teaching me French and in return I am forcing her to be more vocal in English. But if you feel her staying here could cause us some problems, I won't insist."

"Interesting idea, I wonder if I should consult Benjamin," I replied laughing.

Ziva giggled, "This man who would kill at the drop of a hat for either of us, has taken bullets for the Prime Minister, yet when in her presence he turns into a love sick puppy."

I could only agree with her considerations, having also witnessed the amusing metamorphosis of Benjamin.

"I assume you are in agreement with Françoise staying here. Actually it will only be while we are in residence.

Chuckling inwardly, I nodded in agreement. The feeling in my gut told me it would probably be much longer than that.

"I received a call from the casino manager announcing a high stakes game scheduled for tonight. If you feel up to it, I think it would be great if you could join us. I'd certainly love it. The leering Sheiks from Prince Robert's party will be there, and I'm more than certain you'd be a fatal distraction in one of your sexy dresses."

"You really think my *gluteus maximus* will get them to take their eyes off the cards?"

"Just come and I promise you the focus will be on your bubble butt. Lured by the delicacy, they will be drooling like toddlers in an ice cream shop. So do I hear a yes?"

"OK Antonio, I'd love to join you," Ziva said, emitting a hearty laugh over the metaphor I had just created. "If you don't mind, I'd like to speak with Françoise about our idea, and ask her if she would like to live in the house during the time we are here.

"And now for your reward."

"What reward—what are you talking about?" I asked.

"For being such a good boy and agreeing about Françoise you shall be well rewarded when we return this evening," Ziva chanted undoing the belt on her robe to allow me a quick peek at the pleasurable offerings.

Lunging forward, I engulfed her in a full embrace before aiming for her lips. Reaching between her long well toned legs I whispered, "why wait love? I can see you are ready for me." She spread her legs to be more accommodating just as I steered her toward the bed. It was a perfect moment. I caressed her breasts until she began squirming in pleasure, or was it impatient anticipation?

Unable to hold back any longer I entered her body, thrusting firmly, rhythmically as she swiveled and lifted her hips beneath me. Would it happen? Would we enjoy a passionate simultaneous climax? When her shrieks of joyful culmination harmonized with mine I knew the mission was accomplished. Resting side by side, we cuddled for awhile. I had learned early on that women desired this tender sequel to love making. I was right! In recompense she flashed that special indescribable smile—exclusively mine to savor.

"Antonio, I hate to break away, but I better return to the shower or we'll never be ready in time," Ziva whispered, swiping my cheek with her index finger. "Then I want to go to the kitchen to find Françoise."

"Sounds like a good idea."

A perfumed freshly showered Ziva, dressed in a soft Frette bathrobe, stepped into a vacant kitchen. However, the lingering aroma of sautéed mushrooms told her the master chef was not far away. In fact a closer look revealed she had stepped out on the balcony. Tip-toeing not to interrupt the moment, she found Françoise staring at the moon, dreamy eyed. Humming a tune unfamiliar to Ziva, she swayed back and forth without upsetting her arms, tightly folded across her slim waist.

Ziva tapped her gently on the shoulder to avoid the startle reaction.

"I wish to have a word with you, Françoise," she said quietly. I'd like Benjamin to be here also."

"*Il y a un problème*, is there a problem *Madame?*" the petite woman asked casting a worried glance.

"No not at all—relax," she responded smiling.

When summoned, Benjamin came quickly as anticipated.

"Hello ladies. Is there something I can do for you?" he inquired politely. "Is everything OK?"

"Yes—don't worry, all is well. I just want you to be here when I speak with Françoise. I need your translating services."

I noticed her expression turn serious. Perhaps the sudden intervention of Benjamin intimidated her.

"Benjamin, Antonio and I would love Françoise to live here full-time whenever we are in residence. If she is willing she can have one of the guest rooms. Of course she will receive a raise."

With obvious joy in the tone of his voice, Benjamin conveyed the message to Françoise who ran to Ziva shouting *oui oui* yes, yes, in French and English while wrapping her short delicate arms around the tall girl.

"*Merveilleux*—wonderful! Benjamin will you please pick up Françoise tomorrow and help her take over whatever she needs?"

Before a response could be heard, I stepped into the kitchen. Judging from the trio of full tooth smiles I had the reassurance Ziva's suggestion was received with delight.

"I see everyone is happy," I said. *Brava* Ziva! Now it is time for us to go to work.

Ben, please take out the big car, make sure it is washed, and ask Françoise to help my beautiful girl get ready for tonight. We plan to arrive at the Casino no later than nine, because I was informed by the manager that the game will begin shortly thereafter."

I knew for a fact that tardiness is neither accepted nor tolerated.

"Money will be no problem. Prince Robert has put an unlimited line of credit at my disposal. The buy in is $250,000 per player. There will be eight in the game; our three Arab friends, me, an American, and a young toy-boy dipping his hand into his cougar girlfriend's bank account."

"That adds up to six," Ziva said.

"Well last but most important two businessmen from Yazeed's native country of Turkey will be joining us. I have a feeling they are collaborators. Anyway they are the players I must take down if I want word of my skills to reach Yazeed."

"Yazeed will hear—don't worry Antonio," Benjamin reassured.

"I'm not concerned at all. Thanks to Prince Robert, the casino manager provided all the information necessary. I was on the phone with him while you and Ziva were speaking with Françoise. It's going to be an interesting evening."

# XVIII

Silence cut through the steady undercurrent of the Tower of Babel chatter. All eyes turned toward us when I entered the casino with my ravishing Ziva keeping pace beside me. Benjamin trailed a few, respectful steps behind. The slight bulge on the left side of his jacket indicated the reason for his presence.

Earlier Prince Robert had briefed me about the protection rule: each individual or group was permitted no more than two body guards. No exceptions would be considered. If the rule was violated for any reason whatsoever, the transgressor would be banned from the Casino de Monte-Carlo and every other casino throughout Europe and the Mideast.

I was not concerned. In the company of Benjamin and Ziva, I felt reassured any less than desirable situation could be handled.

The casino manager rushed over to greet us, performed am exaggerated bow while kissing Ziva's hand.

"*Monsieur* Bastone the funds are available as soon as you are ready to play," he whispered.

"Show me to the table," I said.

"*Oui Monsieur,*" he chirped escorting us to a private room. Immediately my eyes surveyed, and then memorized the scene. Seven gentlemen impeccably dressed were seated, focused on stacking their chips. I was invited to sit between the American and one of the Turkish businessmen. My dark glasses did little to obstruct any movement or behavior around the table.

Without delay the cards were shuffled and dealt; the starting blinds were posted at one and two thousand dollars, and would be increased every hour with no rising limits. I knew my fate tonight depended on how successfully I managed my time in order to get a read not only on the board, but on the other players. Getting a correct read involved a mixture of science and psychology, a tricky skill to master. It would be a while before I could maximize on my talent. Professional players knew a discriminating eye. And they were well aware of the role of unwavering attention. It was an essential requisite. Thankfully I possessed both.

Within a couple of hours I was reading the players hands. The accuracy of my read seemed to illustrate I was actually standing behind them in full view of their cards. Judging from the facial expressions, I believed the Arabs seemed to have neither a disturbing nor worrisome hand. When dealt inopportune cards, they'd break into peals of laughter, and applaud like little children at a fun movie, whenever they won on a bluff.

In contrast, the American, undoubtedly a pro, was a rather tight player, who would not stay in unless he had a strong hand. On a quest to demonstrate his card playing abilities to his rich cougar, the toy-boy certainly did not covet loosing. However, easily distracted, he was unable to remove his gaze from Ziva. Meanwhile his benefactor, Lady Moneybags, grew exceedingly more irate with every passing second.

My take on the Turks proved to be correct. Interestingly, their game strategy was based on team effort. Signals were sent via chip movements to convey either the strength or weaknesses of their hands. It took me a total of fifteen minutes to break their code. Patience: it was essential to the outcome of the game that I wait for the right hand to take them down.

"Antonio I'm going to the powder room to freshen up," Ziva whispered.

Nodding I followed her through the corner of my eye just in time to catch the Sheik's son give in to the temptation to rest his sweaty palm on her *derrière*, arrogantly assuming the thrill was his to seize.

In a split second as the invasive hand reached the target, the pleasure stealing *bon vivant* was prostrate, screaming and writhing in agony, clutching his obviously broken wrist.

Turning my head in the direction of the bedlam, I smiled. "Damn she's good," I whispered to myself! The young man's father did not disturb himself from the table. His body-guard and two casino employees escorted him out of the room. I was so proud of my Ziva. She could certainly take care of herself, all without forfeiting her beautiful sexy look.

Four hours thereafter, the game was put on hold for the players to take care of physical needs; stretch their legs, visit the guest lounges and feed nervous appetites. Benjamin joined us at the bar.

"How's it going?" he asked. Since he was not allowed near the table, he had no idea who was ahead.

"I'm up roughly $125,000, the Turks about $350,000 and Louis, the toy-boy, is on his last leg. Actually he should be gone in the next few hands unless the gambling gods smile on him. Our Arab friends are down the balance. I think the American is up more or less, $25,000 give or take a few thousand."

"Things are heating up now," he replied.

"Yes—let's see what happens when we reconvene. Are you tired Ziva? Why don't you let Benjamin take you home? It's been an exhausting day and I don't know how long this game will take."

"No Antonio—don't worry I'm just fine. Actually I'm enjoying watching you play. By the way Benjamin and I spotted the two armed Turks seated outside the gaming room."

"OK Ziva, as you wish," I said flashing a smile. I knew it was pointless to argue. I'd never win.

Gazing at my new Jaeger-LeCoultre timepiece Father had recently given me, I noticed the break was officially over.

"Time to go back to work," I announced. I headed to the men's room, splashed several handfuls of cold water across my face, reached for the towel dangling from the attendants hand, gave him a $50.00 tip and returned to the game room, where I was informed the American decided to call it a night. The game was down to seven players.

The blinds were now at $2,000 and $4,000. Pretty boy Louis seemed refortified and went all in on the third hand. Unfortunately for him, his insignificant pair was no match for my duo of Queens. With only six players left, I knew time was running out and I did not want the Turks to call it a night and walk away with the winnings.

I suggested the blinds be raised to $5,000 and $10,000 and hoped my cards matched my skills. Most of the top players play only 15 to 20% of the cards they're dealt, including the hands they bluff with. Breathing deeply I focused on winning.

Within an hour two Sheiks went down, one to me the other to one of the Turks.

"Well we're almost there," I thought quietly. "Just one more Arab to defeat and I'll be pitted against the two Turks as planned."

Cards are unpredictable—sometimes they award victory and other times they snatch it. I noticed the remaining Arab player seemed to have a change of luck. His cards were coming in favorable, and there was nothing I could do but wait. Patience, I always told myself especially in apprehensive situations may render a sweet harvest.

Then in the blink of an eye, the Arab made a fatal mistake. Believing he was on a hot streak, he opted to go all in with nothing more than a jack and a four. The bet was almost $300,000. Immediately the Turks dropped out. Tension mounted. The Arab kept nervously clearing his throat: a tactic? Or just nerves?

I glared at my hand. A Queen Five off Suit, (Q5), often identified as a pre-flop hand, sobered my expectations. Normally I would discard this hand. I called the bet upon reading the Arab to perfection. Now it was in the lap of the poker gods. When the Arab threw down his Jack, and I the Queen, I noticed the veins in his neck swelled and pulsed. Something was happening!

After all the cards were dealt, my Queen High stood tall assuming the rank of winning hand.

"How could you see me with the two pieces of shit you were holding," the red faced Arab screamed, throwing his cards across the table in disgust. No poker player would play a Q5, the Granny Mae.

"Just lucky I guess," I mumbled while raking in my winnings. Rising from the chair he slid his hand beneath the folds of his robe. Seated at the far end of the room, Benjamin jumped to attention, reached inside his jacket and rested his open palm on the handle of the Glock.

I ripped off my dark poker playing glasses and focused my steely blue eyes on the devastated loser.

"If you do not wish to lose more than just money, I would advise you to remove your hand from inside your robe, preferably, empty."

The Arab paled to corpse status, spun away from the table and stormed out of the room, spitting threats. He was totally unaware that Benjamin, Ziva and I understood every irate word.

Only three players remained in the game, me and the two Turks. My plan rolled into dawdling mode as first one, and then the other were dealt good hands. There was still nothing I could move on until after a change of cards. I found myself staring at a pair of Aces. Should I slow play them to set a trap? The response arrived quickly.

The next three cards on the flop were an Ace and two Deuces gifting me with a Full House. I cast a sidelong glance at the Turks. My gut feeling pinpointed to a very strong hand from one of them. This indicated either three Deuces and two Aces or four Deuces. Instinct was the name of the game, and it leaned toward the four Deuces. Early on I had learned to trust my gut feeling.

When the Turk's partner raised the bet, I folded. The look on their faces assured me I was right.

"I could have finished that infidel," he said to his partner in Turkish, confirming I had not erred in my judgment.

Careful not to unveil her language skills, Ziva translated their conversation.

Eventually, Lady Luck brought me the long awaited hand. Holding the Nine and Ten of Hearts the dealer laid down the six, seven and eight of the same suit, dealing me an unbeatable Straight Flush. The betting started with the first Turk followed by my raise. Ultimately the sign I had been hoping for came from the second Turk who convinced he had the winning hand, bet it all.

The silence in the room intensified. No one around the table drew a breath. The tension in their jaws was at maximum level. Eyes dared not blink. Lips were tightly sealed. I intercepted their thoughts. They hoped I had a strong enough hand to stay in until they were ready to pounce.

The next two cards failed to pair any of the cards already on the table. I opened with a large bet. Their surprise was unmistakable. Both opponents were certain I held an Ace High Flush. Sealed lips turned into smiles after I made my play. First one, then the other called "all in," nervously awaiting my response while prematurely counting the money they had won prior to my decision.

Breaking the suspense after a few minutes, I pushed all the money piled in front of me, to the center of the table.

"I call" I announced.

One of the Turk's jumped to his feet, hurling his Four and Five of Hearts Straight Flush on the table. Instantaneously his accomplice congratulated him on his victory over the young playboy. Shattering the moment of glory, I laid down my Nine and Ten of Hearts revealing an unbeatable hand.

It was a high security alert moment. I noticed how their faces exhibited first disbelief then fierce rage followed by menacing threats. Escorted out of the casino, they shouted a pelting downpour of curses in the foulest language.

I requested management to put the money on hold for me, and handed the dealer $10,000.

"The fish has been baited" I whispered; "let's see how long it will take him to bite."

# XIX

Dawn was beginning to squirm through the darkness when Ziva, Benjamin and I, exhausted but content crossed the threshold into the villa. Françoise stood wide eyed, anxiously waiting to greet us, curious to hear all the exciting details about the casino evening. As always, the buttery aroma of her delicious preparations set our mouths watering.

Ziva and I headed for the table where sliced crusty bread, sweet puffed croissants, and a kaleidoscopic selection of her own home made fruit preserves were ready for the taking.

"*L'omelette au fromage,* the cheese omelet will be done in five minutes," she announced.

"There is no need to translate," I said grinning at Benjamin. "The fragrance says it all."

"I'll fill Françoise in with all the evening's details while you and Ziva enjoy the meal.

There was no contradicting on our part. We savored breakfast. Meanwhile Benjamin gave Françoise in her native tongue, a step by step account of the events, concluding with the news of our decision to postpone our departure two weeks.

"Antonio wishes to continue playing at the Monte-Carlo Casino to enhance his reputation as a Texas Hold'em player to be reckoned with," Benjamin announced.

Françoise's smile broadened, not so much because of the reason triggering the postponement, but for the fact she would be living with us for a longer period. I think she was beginning to regard us as family, though her feelings for Benjamin, fully reciprocated were of a non-familial nature.

A sudden rustling caught our attention as the sun burst in through the kitchen window. In synchrony our heads lifted. To a bystander we would have seemed like marionettes manipulated by the nimble fingers of a master puppeteer.

What was that unfamiliar sound, we questioned silently? To the untrained ear the barely audible echo we each heard could have originated from a small animal, or perhaps the wind blowing a loose twig against the side of the villa. However, though unexpressed verbally, Benjamin, Ziva and I suspected it might be someone trying to trespass inconspicuously. We neither shared our concerns, nor felt a need to.

Meanwhile oblivious to what was happening in the garden of the home she grew to love as her own; Françoise busied herself clearing the plates from the kitchen table. As she removed the cutlery and glasses she softly lifted her voice in a lovely French tune, the lyrics of which were understood exclusively by Benjamin.

"*Merci* Françoise," I said rising from my seat; "breakfast was delicious and the serenade quite charming."

"*O Monsieur*" she replied, blushing, "*vous êtes trop gentil,* you are too kind."

I winked my approval, stretched like a cat awakening from a nap and extended my hand for Ziva to accompany me. Quick footed, Benjamin, sprang to his feet, and distanced himself from the windows, pulling a startled Françoise with him.

In the blink of an eye, a burst of gun fire shattered the front door lock with an ear-piercing clamor. Two men crashed through, glaring at us with dilated pupils.

"Death to the non-believers," they shouted in Turkish.

I bolted toward the intruders slammed my left forearm down on the arm of the trespasser closest to me then smashed the palm of my right hand under his chin, snapping his head back. Without consenting a moment to catch his breath, I finished him off with a firm side hand chop across his carotid artery, immediately cutting short the scream of pain emanating from his lips. Glazed eyes filled with hate just a few short seconds ago were now vacant of all signs of life. The other aggressor was not quite as fortunate. His silence resulted from a bullet logged between the eyes, when with his hand around the Glock, Benjamin trumped the dream of attaining whatever glory the now deceased man's "employer" had promised.

Quick and observant, Ziva immediately recognized the prowlers.

"Antonio these were the two body guards in service to the Turkish businessman in the card game the other evening."

"Why am I not surprised?" I replied, proud of Ziva's ability to identify the intruders. "We should have realized his point of view. After all being defeated by a playboy would be difficult to digest. Unfortunately this does create somewhat of a problem. I don't want Yazeed to be aware of what we are capable of doing."

"Exactly" Ziva chimed, followed by a nod of agreement from Benjamin.

"I see we are all on the same page."

"Always Antonio," she whispered.

"We can soften the blow by calling the police, reporting a break-in and claiming money and some of my jewels were stolen during the heist. In the meantime you and Benjamin should get rid of the two bodies. Once news of the robbery gets out, the Turks will think these two double-crossed them and took off with their newly acquired treasure."

For a young woman, Ziva was quite an impressive character. How well we had been matched!

"If, you'll excuse me now," she said, I would like to calm Françoise so we can get the place cleaned up

"Sounds like a plan to me, *ma chérie*. Now I know why I love you so much—brains, beauty, and a sexy body to die for. You have it all!"

Ziva laughed. "Get to work boys, or the police will be here before we're ready."

Benjamin and I ran to one of the guest bedrooms, yanked the sheets off the bed and returned to the "crime-scene." Spreading them on the floor, we rolled the two would be assassins in the sheets and stashed the hurriedly wrapped bundles into the trunk of the Rolls Royce.

Let's go Ben—I want to get rid of the cargo!"

Benjamin jumped into the Rolls. We drove down to the docks and fastened the bodies with weights we found on the pier.

"This should do it," I said satisfied with our package wrapping *bravura*."

"Looks pretty good Antonio—let's do away with them."

One at a time, the corpses were slipped into the welcoming water below. The tide, our most reliable accomplice would soon carry them deep into the Mediterranean Sea for some hungry sharks to feast on.

"Mission accomplished," Benjamin announced.

"Now back to the ladies. I think they will need us today."

"Why just today," he chuckled. They always need us."

We enjoyed a laugh despite the tense circumstances before heading back to the villa. We rode in silence, accompanied by our solitary thoughts. In the quiet of my mind I wondered how the girls were taking the day's events, unaware Benjamin was entertaining similar concerns. My worries were centered more on Françoise who did not have the training, expectations and quick reflexes Ziva did.

When we entered, I spotted the ladies, cuddling large sifters of cognac. Françoise appeared composed, an accomplishment I attributed to Ziva's influence in conjunction with the 1994 Pierre Ferrand Ancestral cognac they were sipping. Upon seeing us, our housekeeper/chef rose to her feet wearing a wide-eyed expression of wonderment. I knew she would be seeking answers; certain only Benjamin could oblige and clear up the disturbing unknowns.

Minutes later, prompted by Benjamin, in broken English mixed with French, Ziva contacted the police.

"My villa has been burglarized," she shouted, as soon as a person responded.

"Tell me what happened, *Madame*?" a deep throaty voice asked.

"We were out having a picnic breakfast and when we returned we discovered thieves had broken into the villa. My jewelry is gone.... money is missing and the place is a mess!"

"*Madame*, what is your name and address—be calm—we will be there shortly."

I smiled to note my beautiful Ziva was also a convincing actress. In the interim, Benjamin took Françoise aside.

"Please be patient. I will explain after the police leave. You will have all the answers. If they question you, just tell them you didn't see or hear anything."

# XX

Chief Inspector Carletti, upon learning the burglary occurred in the Bastone Villa, gathered four of his top men and rushed off to the crime scene. The tall muscular Carletti with a seemingly sprayed Riviera tan, and full head of dark, silver streaked wavy hair, was well aware that Prince Robert was a close family friend of the olive oil barons. Undoubtedly this was a high profile case that merited urgent attention.

Soon after the authorities were notified, I received a call from the Prince.

"Antonio, please accept my apologies for this terrible disturbance. Thankfully no one was hurt. Please be assured that all will be done to apprehend the invaders."

"Thank you, Your Highness; we are relieved it is being handled so quickly."

A locksmith and a crew of contractors were soon at the entry, ready to replace the two front doors and locks destroyed by the gunfire. When the Chief Inspector and his men arrived, Françoise greeted him with a hug and double kiss. Benjamin, Ziva and I stood at attention, somewhat puzzled by the exhibition of familiarity. The silence was pronounced: questions and answers would perhaps come later.

I responded to all the Inspector's inquiries. After listening to my account, he and his colleagues were speechless. Monte-Carlo's police force boasts a ratio of one officer for every hundred residents. Additionally, the entire principality is covered by a 24/7 video surveillance system. Rarely if ever were such violent crimes committed and when they were the culprits were quickly taken into custody.

This time, Inspector Carletti scratched his head in disbelief. He and his squad were clueless.

"*Monsieur* Bastone, I don't know what to tell you. We have no idea who masterminded or executed this robbery, nor why they would use a firearm to shatter the locks in broad daylight. But in view of the violent nature of the break in I'd say you were very fortunate to be out of the house."

Although Inspector Carletti had attained top tier status in the police, he remained puzzled by it all.

"I too question their motives and manner of entry," I said. "Perhaps they were aware of our late night casino game last evening and believed we were totally comatose. Furthermore, my guess is they hoped blasts of gunfire would disorient and scare us into revealing the location of the safe and other valuables.

Had it not been for Françoise who prepared a picnic brunch and suggested we shower, slip into comfortable clothes and spend the morning filling our lungs with fresh air, their plan may have succeeded. And who knows, one or more of us may have been seriously if not fatally wounded."

"Yes you are fortunate," the Inspector said, shaking his head. At least no one was hurt. What exactly is missing?"

"Well it seems that their rummaging paid off. They found a rather substantial sum of cash and some jewels Ziva had not yet returned to the safe," I said.

Chief Inspector Carletti continued to shake his head incredulous as I gave a perfect, well scripted rendition of the crime. Thankfully he bought our account, confirmed by Françoise's rhythmic nods of agreement to everything I said.

"*Monsieur* Bastone, I will go to the casino, prowl around, ask some questions and try to discover if there were any wary or questionable types either loitering suspiciously or just hanging around until late in the evening. We have seen enough here."

Once Inspector's Carletti's men finished their search and examination for clues they departed.

"Again *Monsieur* Bastone, I offer my humble apologies for this awful experience. I will notify you as soon as we have some news."

"Thank you Inspector, I'd appreciate your interest in this case."

Once they departed, Françoise prepared a quick snack of cold chicken and fresh vegetables. After eating, she suggested we retire for a much needed nap. Too exhausted to offer resistance, we obliged, knowing we owed her a lot of explaining once we regained our composure.

Without spending any energy on pre-siesta small talk, I drifted off as soon as I shut my eyes. Two hours later I was recharged and ready to take on any project, including presenting an explanation and answering Françoise's questions.

Shortly after sunset, Ziva, Benjamin, Françoise and I reconvened in the living room. I never expected the ensuing conversation.

"If you don't mind," Françoise began, rising to her feet, "I'd like to tell my story."

"Sure" Ziva said, gazing at her with a smile. "Tell us."

Benjamin sat wide-eyed, unable to predict what was about to happen.

"I apologize for my poor English. If I need help, I'm certain you will help me Benjamin."

"Of course Françoise, if you get stuck, switch to French and I'll translate."

"Thank you. I'd like to talk about my late husband. He was a well respected member of the *Sureté Publique*, who had earned the rank of *sergeant* in the Monaco Police Force. Benjamin, you remind me of him in many ways.

Outwardly gentle and gracious toward others, he was a man of steel who would never hesitate to protect or defend a person in distress, and would sacrifice his life for his loved ones.

That was my Armand—a heroic type. In fact the day I met Benjamin I was startled by the resemblance: the same physical size, and a similar facial configuration and features. The likeness was so striking that on several occasions I almost slipped and called him Armand!" Visibly emotional, she paused just long enough to catch her breath.

Benjamin's face flared to beet red as he translated her words.

"One night" Françoise continued, I was working late for Antonio's parents, so my Armand stopped at a local pub for a drink and a quick bite to eat. A robust man seated nearby had overindulged in alcohol and became abusive to the waitress. His petrified wife sat frozen in silence beside him, powerless to exercise any control over the situation. Seeing the girl in distress, my Armand intervened, as a member of the Police Force, and suggested the man go home and sleep it off if he didn't want to be arrested and charged with disorderly and offensive behavior.

Casting a downward glance at Armand, the burly man misjudged my husband, committing the same mistake as others. Sneering in response, he was surprised when a rock hard fist slammed into his fat gut. Doubling over in pain, he vomited soiling his pants and shoes. Understanding the severity of the situation his wife pleaded with my Armand not to arrest him promising she would take him home to sober up.

Unfortunately Armand was betrayed by his soft gentle side, and agreed to her request. He did however, issue a warning, cautioning against any repeat behavior. 'If it happens again,' he said, 'I would not be so pardoning: the man would be apprehended and charged.'

Two nights thereafter, while leaving for work, my Armand was fatally shot twice in the back as he walked to his car. A tall heavy set man was spotted leaving the scene but, *malhereusement*, unfortunately it was the only description the police furnished. After months of investigating and interrogating the large man who had the run in with my Armand, the police had no hard evidence to make an arrest."

"Were they able to at least identify the suspect?" I asked.

"Yes—we found out the man's name was Paul Tarrow. But it was useless. He swore he was at home with his wife on the day of the crime.

And she backed his alibi. No weapons were found and the case was put on hold even though Armand was one of their own.

A month later after *Monsieur* and *Madame* Bastone had departed, a strange occurrence took place. The police learned that Mr. Tarrow was at his favorite bar enjoying a drink when a petite young redhead wearing a short skirt and high stiletto heels approached him. Some official reports of the incident claim she was wearing a wig. However, all agreed she was heavy handed with her application of make-up, creating a look that gave her a brassy appearance. Witnesses reported they left the bar together. The following morning Paul Tarrow was found dead with his throat sliced open from ear to ear.

The police spent a couple of weeks searching for the killer, but unable to find a suspect based on circumstantial or direct evidence, the crime was identified as an unsolved homicide and filed under cold case."

Benjamin, Ziva and I sat on the edge of our seats not daring to speculate on any follow ups.

"So the murder remains a mystery," Benjamin said.

"Yes and no," Françoise responded.

"Yes and no—well what does that mean?" Ziva asked puzzled. All eyes were on Françoise. No one was prepared for her response!

"I was the petite red head with the heavy make-up," she said.

Benjamin cleared his throat several times. Embarrassed he muttered, "I'm sorry." I could see that Françoise's admission had shocked him.

"There was no way I would have allowed an assassin to take the life of someone I loved," she continued." '*Vie pour vie, oeil pour oeil, dent pour dent'—c'est justice rétributive*, a life for a life, an eye for an eye, a tooth for a tooth—it's retributive justice and written in the Bible's Book of Exodus. Therefore, I had a right to settle the score. I would do the same for all of you. You are family to me and if someone does harm to any of you, in any way, I would seek revenge."

Holding on to the back of the chair, Françoise walked around and sat, shaking like a frail autumn leaf caught in a sudden breeze. Tears streamed down her flushed cheeks, certainly not in remorse, but to honor the memory of her dear husband. Patting the traces of her sorrow with trembling fingers, she waited for a response from the people she had grown to love and trust; people to whom she had just confessed her darkest secret.

Would they understand? Would they be horrified? Would they banish her from their service—or worse, turn her in to the police? Was she foolish to have confessed her deed? Would she live to regret this soul-baring moment?

Ziva sprang to her feet, walked over to Françoise and knelt at her knees. With an enveloping embrace she cuddled the distraught woman; then stroked her face as one would a defenseless child, answering all her questions while dismissing her most dreaded fears.

"Françoise we consider you one of us. You are family. Nothing you have done in the past will ever change that."

Although Françoise did not understand every word Ziva spoke, her feminine intuition conveyed the message. In return, she hugged Ziva as tightly as she could with the little strength she possessed.

Rising to his feet, Benjamin, took her hand in his, whispering his support while removing his handkerchief. I watched as the two connected, breathing a sigh of relief. Of course I was neither willing nor capable of either chastising or repudiating Françoise for her decision to defend Armand's honor by taking the life of his assassin. We all understood and shared her feelings.

"Now it is your turn to come clean," she said fixing her gaze on Benjamin. "I have a feeling there is more to you than three wonderful people with a love for the Texas Hold'em, on holiday in Monte-Carlo."

"How much can I tell her," Benjamin whispered in Hebrew. She has seen too much already and I feel I need to give her an explanation."

"You can tell her that we are on a mission to rid the world of selfish individuals, whose only goal in life is to accumulate wealth from the pain and suffering of others, without respect or concern for human life. At this time I would not inform her of our connection to the Prime Minister and *Il Fidato's* friends. Less is always better, and sometimes too much knowledge creates disadvantages for all."

As Benjamin carefully repeated my words to Françoise with a simple uncomplicated delivery, my gaze met Ziva's. The eye contact was sufficient dialogue to express our feelings. I nodded and the love of my life read my gesture like a book.

"Only if she is willing and feels there is no reason to remain here," I said in a barely audible voice. Ziva smiled.

"Benjamin, ask Françoise if she would like to work for us full time, which would involve accompanying us on trips. Wait, let me re-phrase that. Instead of offering her the option to work, ask her if she would like to join our family."

Benjamin's face lit up like a meteor igniting the evening sky. His unmasked sigh revealed a feeling of relief for the possibility of a new life, in lieu of the sickening sensation in the pit of his stomach whenever he pondered having to bid farewell to Françoise. I could see he was agitated—most likely involved in silent negotiations with his Creator, bartering for a positive response.

"If you'd prefer to take some time to think about…"

"No Benjamin, she replied, cutting him off in mid-sentence, I would be more than thrilled to join the family."

"Ben," I said, "I think Françoise could use another handkerchief."

"*Oui, oui*" she replied, smiling in spite of the steady drizzle sliding down her cheeks. "But these are different tears—these are tears of joy."

In her quiet moments, prior to drifting off to sleep, Françoise had been dreading the day we would leave, fearing she might never see us again. It would be far too painful to suffer once again, the agonizing loss of the only people she trusted and loved. Moreover, she was well aware of Benjamin's special feelings for her, fully reciprocated the moment her eyes met his. Never would she have predicted either her ability or willingness to give her heart to another man.

We all sat composing ourselves after Françoise's unexpected tale.

Who would have ever thought such a nurturing, petite and sweet woman would be capable of such a pre-meditated vindictive act.

When the phone rang I jumped to my feet. Upon hearing Inspector Carletti's voice, my pulse accelerated.

"*Monsieur* Bastone, we cannot seem to locate the two men who work for the Turkish businessman," he recited all in one breath. "I'm afraid they are no longer in Monaco."

"That is rather suspicious behavior," I said.

"Yes—I think you are correct in your assumptions. They were in the casino the evening you won a sizeable amount of money, so in a sense they had a motive."

"They must have left soon after ransacking the villa"

"My guess is they bribed a cargo ship captain into allowing them passage to some far away port."

Apparently Inspector Carletti bought my story, I thought smiling.

"Where are the other Turks?" I asked.

"They were advised of their *persona non grata* status in Monte-Carlo and asked to return to their own country. Once a visitor is defined unwelcomed he or she is expected to depart immediately."

"Great work, Inspector. At least we have the assurance they are no longer among us. Thank you for all your efforts. I will certainly inform Prince Robert of your efficiency in handling the situation."

"I'm sorry I could not recuperate the money and jewels stolen."

"Our major concern is always safety. And knowing the thieves are gone certainly reassures us."

"If you notice any suspicious behavior or individuals please give us a call."

"I will and thanks again Inspector."

After I hung up and related the conversation to Ziva and Benjamin, I phoned my parents to up-date them on the latest events, including the addition of Françoise to our team.

Actually Demetri and Shanna were overjoyed with the news. Françoise had been their part time employee dating from the tragic death of her husband, and they had both grown very fond of the sweet grieving widow.

During the conversation I learned some rather interesting news from my father. Frank Aiello had sufficient information to stop the arrogant low life South Carolina bastard Senator William H. Hartford III in his tracks! I certainly didn't need ulterior prodding. He was a danger in need of removal and I was more than ready to take him down. It was time to move forward.

"I wonder if it's best to forge ahead on Frank's information, instead of just waiting for Yazeed to take the bait if indeed he ever would," Ziva pondered aloud. Benjamin nodded in agreement. Once in possession of Father's news, he shared her feelings.

Ziva and Benjamin were in for another surprise.

"While speaking with my father, I discovered Françoise, that you are fluent in Spanish and Italian. This elevates you to tri-lingual prominence. Sometimes you just never know the talents of another."

Benjamin turned in her direction.

"Why didn't you mention your language skills?"

"You all spoke either English or another language unknown to me. Once I realized you not only understood French, Benjamin, but spoke it so beautifully, I felt having you translate would give me a chance to know you better. I am truly sorry for my omission and beg your forgiveness. Please do not hold this against me or discredit my integrity. But if you have second thoughts about my joining you, I will..."

"Nonsense Françoise, don't even go there," Ziva said, interrupting her mid-sentence.

"*Naturalmente verrai con noi*—Of course you will come with us," I said in Italian. "How long do you think it will take to get your affairs settled?"

"*Due o puo darsi tre settimane al massimo*—two or perhaps three weeks—not more."

I was surprised to hear her near perfect Italian.

"Good this will give me some time to make arrangements for our trip to the United States as well as give me the opportunity to visit my family in Italy. In the meantime I suggest we benefit from some relaxing leisure time and enjoy this beautiful country."

"Great plan—I'd love to get a tan and swim a few laps. I think I might be spreading a bit. Easy life and too much fabulous food," Ziva said, flashing a smile at Françoise.

Synchronically shifting our gazes to my absolutely gorgeous girl, all three of us erupted in hearty belly laughs.

"Does that mean you all agree with my attributes spreading?"

"Undoubtedly," I responded, leaning over to plant a kiss on her cheek.

"Since we are back on the fitness kick, it will be the tennis courts for me," I announced.

The pro at the prestigious Monte-Carlo Country Club in Roquebrune, Cap-Matin, had extended an open invitation for me to play there whenever I was itching for the courts. Since it was only a two mile drive from Monaco I decided it was time to work on my serve.

Benjamin why don't you help Françoise settle her affairs, so we can leave as soon as possible."

"Antonio, as much as I would love to give her a hand, my job is to protect you and Ziva. But I cannot fulfill my obligations if I am not in you presence 24/7."

From the tone of his voice, and his taut jaw, I knew the message was please don't argue with me—this is not open for discussion.

"*Bravo* Benjamin—You are right as usual my friend; sometimes I forget that we have a rather unique life style."

# XXI

Françoise busied herself tying up loose ends, and moving into a comfortable place of closure in preparing herself to leave behind a familiar life and surroundings. While she settled her affairs, Benjamin, Ziva and I spent some quality time, relaxing and involving ourselves in activities we enjoyed but frequently avoided due to recent time constraints.

I was thrilled to discover I had not forfeited my tennis game especially since the Pro at The Monte-Carlo Country Club was not an on par match.

"Antonio you're quite good with the racket," he said wiping the sweat from his brow. "Why didn't you turn pro and join the tour circuit?"

"Because, I knew I would never reach *numero uno* status, and not having the honor of being classified the number one tennis player in the world, was a, let's say failing, I could never accept. Instead, I joined my father in running the family business."

"Do you have any regrets?"

"Absolutely not! I am where I am meant to be. However, I always enjoy a good tennis match, both in the role of spectator and player. Also it's a fun way to relax, distract myself and keep in shape."

Tennis and running were my stress busters, whereas Ziva preferred swimming. While awaiting Françoise to conclude her business, she did laps in the pool under a glistening sun that turned her Sephardic skin a rich chocolate brown, enhancing her natural beauty.

We spent our evenings at the Casino where I might add my poker playing skills sharpened and my reputation as a force to be reckoned with spread like a plague. International poker champs as well as one of the leading tournament players of all-time seized the moment to challenge my cunning at the table. Many VIP players departed leaving their monetary assets in my hands. Yet, in spite of my newfound fame, Yazeed offered no sign of recognizing my rising star status, which gave us impetus to change our plans.

While we unwound and enjoyed life, Françoise scurried about closing bank accounts, notifying her land lord she would not renew her lease, and bidding farewell to a handful of close friends who had stood by her side during the difficult times. Sorting through her possessions she spent her energy separating the treasured things she would take with her from all the other things she deemed worthless, both financially and emotionally. She did take the time to pack up and distribute to the less fortunate, many garments and possessions—all while tending to the nutritional needs of her new family.

The days passed quickly and eventually the time was ripe to depart the beautiful enchanting Monaco. I phoned Prince Robert to express my gratitude and appreciation for all that he had done to insure our stay in Monte-Carlo was sublime. He went out of his way to please, and it was more than evident as well as appreciated.

Françoise organized and checked the things she felt should remain in the villa for future visits. We sat pensive. Hardly a sound was heard, except for the twittering birds. Once everyone's check list was completed, I locked the doors. Benjamin surveyed the grounds one last time.

"Everything looks good out here," he said concluding his inspection. I'd say we're ready to head to the airport."

"Let's head for home. I actually look forward to a relaxing flight on Father's jet. It will be great to see my parents."

Once the landing/take off gear was withdrawn and the plane started climbing to the clouds, Benjamin shut his eyes while Ziva and Françoise huddled together chattering in their newfound shared Italian language. In the quietude of my mind, I found myself racing through the past several months, reflecting over all that had transpired and changed. We arrived, a trio and were returning a quartet! The selection of Yazeed as our first target was thwarted due to unforeseen circumstances.

Chief Inspector Carletti was a shrewd professional. Furthermore, eradicating Yazeed in Monaco may have placed Prince Robert in an awkward position, especially following the break-in and robbery at the villa. We neither needed nor coveted another mysterious crime.

The flight to Italy was smooth. Within two hours we began the descent to the private jet airport in Naples, Italy. Exhaling, I noticed how serene and happy I felt to avoid the congestion, chaos and frustrating security measures adopted at large commercial airports. Moreover, the girls were thrilled with the no weight luggage limit and no waiting to retrieve the bags from a conveyor belt running non stop until you personally yanked them off one by one, often risking a muscle sprain.

*Benvenuti a Napoli!* Listening to the welcome to the City of Naples in Italian, my thoughts switched to Grandma Anna and how I longed to see her sweet maternal face. I was also excited by the up-coming presentations of Benjamin, Ziva and the newest member of the team, Françoise. Soon another constituent would be joining the group—Cuoco. I smiled at the thought of the cute little puppy. By now she should be almost fully trained and ready for action. What a powerful team we will be—surely indomitable.

Gazing out the window while the plane glided to a gradual halt, I noticed a huge man, whose dimensions left me questioning if he could fit into the limo. Somewhat familiar in his demeanor, the distance left me unable to pin point his identify. Nevertheless, I assumed he was on my father's payroll and waiting to drive us to the Bastone Estate.

When I deplaned I was pleasantly surprised to see Domenico, eager to greet us. The delight didn't end there. Nearing the vehicle, I opened the door while our chauffer helped Ziva and Françoise settle in after stacking their luggage in the trunk. Thankfully Domenico was a well muscled man because indisputably those bags were rather heavy.

Aiming for the passenger seat I was stopped in my tracks—it was not vacant! Poised like an exotic empress sat Cuoco, snout slightly elevated and pointed forward, wagging her tail in pure rapture. No longer soft and pendulous her ears stood erect like two missiles perched on firing stools, fuelled and ready to be launched.

As soon as she spotted or rather sniffed me, she literally flew through the open window, gyrating her hips while slamming her paws on the ground performing a personally choreographed dance. When she added an aria of barks and yelps to question where we had been and why we had abandoned her, I chuckled realizing months of rigorous training had suddenly vanished into thin air.

Too tempting to resist Ziva jumped out of the car, ran around to Cuoco and the two embraced, each shouting a greeting in their own native tongue. A few soft words and I succeeded in calming the girls. It was now Benjamin's turn to greet and be greeted. Even though he liked to claim he hated Cuoco's warm moist tongue brushing against his face, he did not hesitate to turn his head, in a blatantly willing move to receive the standard double cheek Italian kisses, aka licks.

Three down and one to go: it was time for the introduction of our most recent affiliate.

"Françoise, meet Cuoco," I said pointing to the pup.

"Cuoco, this is Françoise."

Thus began the sniff-fest which culminated in a few pelvic wiggles, a wide tail wag and a sudden jump, though somewhat impolite, followed by a lick on her nose. Stepping back, she extended her paw and welcomed a rather startled Françoise into the family as the audience laughed in delight.

Meanwhile, Domenico's alto greeting boomeranged and echoed, conveying his unmistakable joy to have us back home. In an instant with the same passion and enthusiasm he shared with Cuoco, his muscular burly arms enveloped me and Ziva. For a brief moment it appeared as if he was returning from the supermarket with his prize possessions—two brown bags filled to capacity with the day's provisions. However, in lieu of fresh vegetables and exotic colorful fruits, he toted me and Ziva. Once freed of his embrace, Domenico focused his attention on Françoise. Removing the at least two sizes too small hat from his massive head, he bowed slightly, meeting her gaze.

"*Buongiorno e benventua Signora*" he said, wishing her a good day and a warm welcome.

"*Grazie Domenico, sono contenta di essere qui,* thanks, I am happy to be here, she replied in his native tongue, a gesture which brought a huge grin to his weathered face. "I have heard so many things about you so I'm thrilled to be able to finally meet you."

"Now that Cuoco and I are well acquainted with the entire family," he replied beaming, "let's go to the villa. The family is eager to see you and hear about your trip."

# XXII

As expected, Carmella had prepared all our favorite foods. Mixed in with the best Italian dishes were sumptuous delicacies that would make any Jewish home proud.

Grandma Anna and Carmella had formed a friendly kitchen alliance despite the language hurdle. Nonetheless, the culinary strategies better know as recipes, seemed powerful enough to transcend all barriers.

Although Demetri was restless for some immediate alone time with me, he realized his beautiful Shanna would be furious if prevented from having her own time to catch up on the events, happenings and mundane gossip from Monte-Carlo.

I made certain Mom and Father were happy and smiling, assuring both they would receive equal time with us. With a few of the more interesting things left unsaid, Ziva and I wove a wonderful tale about Prince Robert and all the beautiful people we met at the Palace.

"Best of all was Antonio's success in the casino. I think in just a short time, he has gained quite a prestigious reputation—one that perhaps takes years," Ziva boasted, filling in the details.

Both Mom and Father seemed to delight in her enthusiasm, though I noticed their gazes kept returning to Françoise. I filled in the missing blanks and ran through a brief summary detailing how and why she is an important part of our little family.

Much as I was certain my father had been briefed on the latest events that had occurred in the villa, I wasn't very sure my mother had received the same precise information, including the news from Frank Aiello centered on bringing down the Senator from South Carolina.

At the conclusion of the hug-kiss-fest we sat down to feast on the rather strange menu combinations served. Following the meal, Mom pulled me aside.

"Your father and I noticed a special bond between Benjamin and Françoise," and I'm not alluding exclusively to a friendship."

"Yes, you and Father are correct as always in your assessment of the situation. I do believe there is a budding romance there."

"I'm happy to receive your confirmation—it is really important to have a worthwhile love interest in life—just as I do!"

"Father is a lucky man."

"And I a lucky woman."

Since it was a lovely evening, Father beckoned for me to join him on the patio for some private talk.

"Take the wine with you," he suggested as I sipped the homemade red drink, unwilling to part with such divine nectar.

"It is time for us to speak, Antonio. Let Ziva, Benjamin and Françoise busy themselves with other things. I'm sure they have much to talk about."

"Undoubtedly," I replied, chuckling over an imagined conversation between Ziva and Françoise.

"Now down to business: Prince Robert advised me of the break in. He said the whereabouts of the two Turks remains a mystery. But I know better—in fact I'm certain you and Benjamin sealed their fates even before the first shot was fired."

I placed my glass on the table, leaned in toward Father, and gave him a run down of the events occurring on the morning in question.

"We also changed our plans regarding Yazeed."

"Wise move Antonio."

"I didn't think it was a good idea to deal with him in Monaco after what had taken place with the break-in."

"Word has come to me through my friends on the docks that he is presently buying up raw material for Mansor Raftab whose dream is to build a nuclear facility for Iran. So whatever needs to be done regarding the Senator—take care of it quickly. Yazeed has been given unlimited funds to work with and even my powerful friends cannot interfere with his plans to acquire all the material Raftab will need to start his journey toward controlling the Middle East."

"That's a lot of worthwhile information."

"Yes Antonio it is important to tell the others."

Immediately I summoned Ziva, Benjamin and Françoise and notified them of the information my father had received from overseas.

"Time is essential regarding Senator Hartford's elimination as head of the Foreign Relation Committee. We must act quickly," I said. "He's a stumbling block.

Benjamin, call the Prime Minister as soon as possible. Ask her to give you the latest, up-dated information so we can put our plan in action. In the mean time I'll work with Father and we'll see what our friends from the shady side can add to the mix."

Recognizing the urgency of the situation at hand, Demetri immediately phoned Frank Aiello and left a pressing message with an urgent call back request. While they waited for him to return the call Benjamin arrived with good news.

"A fund raiser for the families of the 9/11 victims has been scheduled in Palm Beach Florida, two weeks from tomorrow. Well guess who has a home there? If you answered our friend Senator Hartford, you'd win the prize! Also there will be a celebrity Tennis tournament with a $25,000 participation fee, and a fashion show to garnish the fancy of trendy style conscious men and women."

At the mention of a tennis tournament I sat upright in my chair. This was too good to pass up.

"Best of all, our friend the Senator will be chairing the event," Benjamin concluded smiling.

When Frank returned the call an hour thereafter, I responded after the first ring. Following several sentences of social pleasantries, we switched to business.

"Antonio a shipment of fresh meat from Yemen is due for arrival in Florida within the next ten days," he said.

I knew "fresh meat" was the Senator's term for those special girls who would gratify his degenerate pleasure seeking appetite.

"I assume they will be sent directly to his estate," I responded. "Also we must find a way to set up video equipment in his bedroom with outside feeds."

"Not so easy" Frank said; "the Senator has a crew of well-trained men who guard his home and office like hawks—24/7. And don't forget—he has the most high tech surveillance equipment on the market."

"Don't worry; I'll handle it. I have access to people whom I am not at liberty to speak of who can crack any code or surveillance equipment in existence. I just need to know the date, time and place of the merchandise delivery."

"I give you my word—you'll have that info as soon as possible."

"Good I'll wait to hear from you."

"OK-My best to your father and mother. Rosa Maria and I are looking forward to seeing you again here in the USA. We're happy you're coming. By the way Rosa is eager to meet Ziva."

Certainly, Rosa Maria had told Frank about the summer we met; she was a new employee for my parents, eager to please, and I was a young hormonal spurting adolescent, impatient for an amorous adventure. Dusting off the memory of the exhilarating experience, I wondered just how deep her soul baring conversations went. Did she reveal all, or did she keep part of the truth concealed in a secret, just she and I shared?

Frank was a vital player. Moreover, I was fully aware beyond shadow of a doubt reasonable or otherwise, that without his powerful connections the mission would not be successful. Therefore, furthest from my mind was the wish to piss off the Don. After all he was the man backing me up. Discussing was not an issue. Ziva and I would surely accept his invitation for a visit. There was no other acceptable RSVP option.

"Frank my warmest regards to Rosa. Ziva shares my enthusiasm about coming to America, seeing you all and spending time with the children."

"Thanks Antonio."

As soon as Frank and I parted company, I walked over to my father's favorite chair, which as expected he occupied while scanning the day's journals. The aura of smoke mingled with the pungent scent confirmed he was puffing on his cigar.

"Father," I whispered not to entice a startle reaction; "I'd like to play in the Palm Beach Celebrity Tennis Tournament: can you please take care of all the necessary arrangements. Also please call some of your designer friends. I know Ziva would love to be in the fashion show.

"I'll be on it first thing in the morning."

Before retiring I detoured through the kitchen to get a glass of water. Benjamin seemed to have the same need to satisfy. Perhaps it was the salty *Parmigiano* we munched on after dinner with the last sips of wine.

"You're thirsty too," I said greeting him.

"The cheese, I think, he murmured laughing. "Listen Antonio, the Prime Minister received the same up-dated info about Yazeed. She also indicated that whatever was needed to take down the Senator would be at your disposal. Obviously she too would like to see the Senator quickly eliminated as Yazeed is Israel's primary concern. She's fretful that a direct hit by Mossad might create too many adverse reactions, internationally. Israel can not afford blame for any more violent covert operations."

I nodded in agreement, fully understanding the Prime Minister's apprehension. A blazing fire storm of negative publicity had erupted following the assassinations of several prominent nuclear physicists working for Iran.

The following morning I summoned my teammates for a meeting in the guest house—my new headquarters.

"I have some up-dated news today. We'll be leaving for Palm Beach in about a week. Reservations have been made at the Breakers Hotel for our accommodations. Two suites will be available during our stay there. At the moment there is no plan for the elimination of Senator Hartford in the political arena. Do I hear any ideas?"

"The Israelis have developed a relaying video and audio device the size of a nail head. I took the liberty to order several. They will be arriving via courier along with some other pieces of the most high-tech surveillance equipment on the market," Benjamin said.

"Great—but we have to plot a way to gain access into the Senator's bedroom," Ziva added.

"I have an idea. Let's assume my father decides to send him a gift, a piece of jewelry."

"Jewelry? What kind of jewelry? Cufflinks?" Ziva questioned.

"You can't give a tie pin—nobody wears those any more," Benjamin chimed in laughing.

"No—no cufflinks or tie pins. I'm thinking something more pertinent to his career, like an American flag pin he can wear on all his jacket lapels. It'll be different—in 18 carat gold with precious stones. At the top of the flag pole, we'll install the device. We might not be able to get a video, but a recording of his voice engaged in his lurid pleasure would be just as valuable and serve our purpose."

"That's clever Antonio," Ziva said gazing at the man she adored.

"Glad you agree. Benjamin, when do you expect the package to arrive?"

"I believe the courier will get here sometime in the late afternoon or early evening tomorrow," Benjamin replied.

"So is everyone in agreement with the idea to give our Senator a precious flag pin?"

"Yes, yes and yes." The response from Benjamin, Ziva and Fran-çoise was unanimous.

"Good, I'll phone my father's jeweler and give him the order to make the piece. I'll ask him to insert the device at the top of the flag pole as if it were part of the design. Then we'll hope for the best. If this fails we will have no choice but to eliminate him. I know this is not in keeping with the Prime Minister's wishes, but I see no other course of action."

"I could try to seduce him, lure him to his bedroom and leave it there," Ziva suggested.

"Absolutely not," I yelled flashing my infamous steely blues eyes in her direction.

"I will not allow you to place yourself in a compromising position without me or Benjamin by your side. It is out of the question. Furthermore, you are far too old for his tastes," I added teasingly. "Besides I doubt his bodyguards would let you anywhere near him without running a full body scan. Perhaps, the only person they wouldn't check would be the Senator.

I'll call the jeweler right now and ask him to come over first thing in the morning. I don't want to lose any time. We have a plan and I want to put it into action as soon as possible."

At 10:00 a.m. the next morning, Salvatore, Demetri's personal jeweler arrived, curious to discover the reason behind the urgency. He had received a call from *Il Fidato,* barely minutes after the sunrise, requesting his immediate presence at the estate.

As soon as the jeweler tapped the door knocker, I was on my feet, ready to greet him and get down to business.

"*Signore* Antonio, *Il Fidato* spoke of urgent business—how can I help you?"

"Salvatore I'd like you to design an American flag lapel pin on an 18 carat gold base. The flag itself should be made of rubies, sapphires and diamonds."

"*Sarà una spilla bellissima,* it will be a beautiful pin, *Signore* Antonio."

"Time is of the utmost importance. I'll be leaving the country in three days and must have the pin. Can you satisfy my wishes?"

"*Signore* Antonio," Salvatore began, smiling, "when your father expresses a wish, I oblige. For *Il Fidato, tutto e' possible,* everything is possible. You will have the *spilla* in your hand, *dopo domani,* the day after tomorrow, and that is a promise."

"*Grazie* Salvatore," I said, accompanying him to the door.

"*Signore* Antonio, "please tell your father my Gina is doing well. The doctors reassured us she will make a full recovery from the trauma she has suffered. May God bless him always. He is a great man!"

"*Grazie Salvatore, sei molto gentile,* you're very kind."

Father never ceases to amaze me. Who knows what feat he accomplished this time! Since my curiosity was unsatisfied, I made a mental note to ask him.

*All'ora di pranzo,* as the clock struck 1:00, *a* taxi came to an abrupt halt in front of the main entrance to the residence. A slightly built man, his pale complexion exaggeratedly pasty against the up-turned collar of his black jacket, stepped out. Elegantly dressed in casual attire, he carried under his right arm, a distressed, well worn leather envelope fastened by two larger elastic bands.

"This is the Prime Minister's man," Benjamin said. He will help us take down the Senator."

"*Shalom,*" Shanna said as he crossed the threshold into the living room. Though his name was Shlomo he specifically requested to be addressed as Sam.

"Sam may I offer…"

"No thank you *Madame,* I'm not hungry," he responded, unexpectedly anticipating her offering. "But a hot cup of tea would be much appreciated if it won't put you out of the way."

I noticed Benjamin's lips curl into a faint smile. Later he explained that the slender man, gracious in his demeanor who seemed like a perfect gentleman, incapable of swatting a fly, had been involved in more dangerous Mossad missions than any other living Israeli.

"Let's retreat to the guest house," I suggested. With the exception of Grandma Anna and Carmella, we all walked out onto the patio and headed towards the guest house."

"Sam, do you have what we need?" I asked. Peering up at me through his glasses, he nodded and handed me the envelope.

Hurriedly I opened the leather case. I noticed a small box nestled in the corner. I reached over and quickly extracted it. When I opened the lid I discovered a trio of tiny pieces, individually enclosed in tissue. Unwrapping the packaging, my eyes focused on three devices, similar in size and shape to tiny nail heads. In the center of each was a strategically placed white dot. I stared at the contents mesmerized.

"Sam, are you sure these will do the job? We have only one chance to succeed. If not we will be forced to consider more drastic measures for the completion of the mission." My somber gaze divulged the serious nature of the situation.

"Yes Mr. Bastone," he reassured, setting down his cup of tea. Though soft and short, his response was firm. "Both the Prime Minister and former Ambassador Levy briefed me on the creation of S.O.D. and the important mission to keep Israel neutral and free from any involvement in this and any future operations. My mission is to assist in any way possible, especially since I developed the device you are holding in your hand."

Given that Sam and I spoke exclusively in Hebrew, only Ziva and Benjamin understood the full content of the conversation. I explained to him the plan we had devised and how we would utilize the jewelry, once fitted with his device.

"This should work perfectly," he replied. I can easily insert one of the components into the design of the flag. Don't worry; it will be totally hidden from the untrained eye."

"Great—that's all we ask."

# XXIII

The stress level was climbing as we retired to our respective bedrooms. The severity of our mission played heavily on our nerves. We knew we had to succeed. No margin error or failure was permitted.

Although the Palm Beach departure was imminent, much still remained on our *to do* list prior to boarding the jet. I needed to get my tuxedo cleaned and pressed after the Monte-Carlo events, and Ziva had to choose a gown for the Ball preceding the fashion show and Celebrity Tennis Tournament. Unlike me, there was no way she would wear the dress worn at Prince Robert's reception. I chuckled, realizing she shared that trait with my mother and most probably a high percentage of elegant well-heeled ladies, globally. Men sure had it easier, at least in this camp.

I did feel however, that a new dress shirt would spruce up my tux. Since I was tall and muscular I never had success with off the rack suits and on the counter shirts. But as always, *Il Fidato* had the solution.

A patron of bespoke tailoring, he phoned Caraceni, a world renowned artisan whose designers and tailors had suited Prince Tainier and generations of Kings from Italy and Greece, as well as show biz greats Humphrey Bogart and Cary Grant, all impeccably dressed gentleman with distinctive styles. When *Il Fidato* called, people came—likewise a group of Caraceni's finest tailors.

Father was assured three tux shirts of different styles and fabrics would be waiting for me the moment I arrived at the Breakers. Two tailors would be available for any alterations or imperfections in the fit.

Of course *Il Fidato* thought of Ziva. After speaking with Valentino, he was promised the designers best seamstresses to take her measurements and present several of his exclusive *alta moda* creations prior to the Ball. Of course Benjamin and Françoise were not excluded from the sartorial extravaganza. Both Caraceni and Valentino were asked to prepare garments for the pair since neither had wardrobes of that caliber.

It was a busy evening, with everyone scurrying about taking care of last minute details, making certain all were on track as planed. Shortly before retiring, both Mom and Father kissed me goodnight, whirling my memory back to childhood.

"Good night, sleep well and *sogni d'oro*, golden dreams," Mom whispered before turning to leave. It was a rather strange evening, though I could not decide why.

Once settled in our room Ziva and I surrendered to passionate love making as if it was our first time in each others arms. Benjamin and Françoise consummated their relationship, though except for a confession in full confidence to Ziva, no official announcement was ever made.

Françoise was moved to tears in Benjamin's arms. His reputation and violent experiences were in contrast with his gentle, loving approach in bed. I guess love does conquer all. In common we all shared that special joy felt among people whose appetites for *amour* and fulfillment were satiated. The *dénouement* unraveled as coddled in the finest bed linens the Bastones' could acquire, we drifted into blissful sleep colored exclusively by golden dreams just as Mom had wished.

Fall was gifting us with much desired mild temperatures especially after the first unseasonable inklings of early frost in late September, abruptly followed by a prolonged *Estate di San Martino*, Indian summer. However, considering it was the 22nd of October, an unobstructed sun continued to illuminate the countryside. Minutes earlier I had received a message that Salvatore eagerly awaited my arrival in the guest house. Recognizing his talents as a jeweler he was certain he had designed and created a superb lapel pin. Nevertheless, until he received a much longed for *bravo* from *Il Fidato's* son, he remained somewhat anxious. In fact the uncertainty prohibited him from truly savoring the treat offered on a beautiful silver tray: Grandma Anna's baked *rugelach*, a Yiddish crescent shaped pastry filled with raisins and apricot preserve, accompanied by Carmella's aromatic fresh brewed espresso.

I arrived promptly at 9:00 AM, greeted Salvatore with a broad smile and firm handshake.

"*Tante grazie*," for your efforts and quick turn around time," I said before previewing the piece.

"I think you will be pleased, *Signore* Bastone," he replied, gently lifting the cover on the tiny black box nestled in the palm of his left hand. In spite of the slight nervous tremor detected entirely in his thumb and index finger, I noticed his eyes glowed with pride as he handed me what he believed was one of his finest creations.

My heart raced. This was truly a question of life or death. The success of the mission rested on his *bravura*. I lifted the pin out of the box and transferred it to the palm of my hand. It looked minute, but dazzled.

"*E' perfetta Salvatore. E' bellissima!* It's perfect—it's beautiful. You did an excellent job, Salvatore. Michelangelo could not have created a better masterpiece!"

No greater praise can be attributed to any artist or artisan than to be not only mentioned in the same breath as the greatest of all Italian Masters, but praised as highly. Salvador bowed humbly, and then straightened to his 5 foot 6 inch height, beaming like a full moon in mid-July.

"Please tell your father it has been a great honor to have been summoned in your hour of need," he said parting company.

Before I could satisfy his time, efforts and expenses the sprite diminutive man bolted out the door, singing and gleeful as if he had selected all the correct numbers and won Italy's high stakes *SuperEnalotto* lottery.

I returned to the guest house dying to show Ziva, Benjamin and Françoise, the masterpiece pin.

"Here it is," I announced, lifting up the cover.

"It is beautiful!" Ziva gasped. "I don't want to give it to the Senator. He's not worth such a gorgeous gift."

Benjamin and Françoise voiced their agreement.

"It is our only means to a successful mission. But don't worry, we'll come up with a plan to get it back before all hell breaks loose," Benjamin reassured. "We have to be careful no one discovers the high tech nature of the pin. Sam did an excellent job. He has demonstrated a phenomenal creative genius in incorporating the necessary *toys*, all without visibility to the naked eye. Yet our own eyes and ears will sit on top of the flag. What a gem—the precious gem that will bring the Senator to his knees!"

We enjoyed a brief moment of anticipated celebration before Ziva and I took Salvatore's work of art over to the main house to show Demetri and Shanna.

"Mom, Father, this is the pin Salvatore made."

"It's a flag waving in the wind," Mom said. Look at the flawless stones in the direct light. The reflection gives the piece movement."

"Salvatore has truly surpassed his own *bravura*," Father added.

"It is a bit larger than other flag lapel pins," I said, "but the work is so fine. Unmistakably it's one of a kind."

"I'll say it again," Ziva said; "it's so beautiful, I hate to give it to him. We must devise a plan to retrieve it once the mission is accomplished."

"Why not commission Salvatore to make a second piece with non-precious stones and have Ziva get close enough to the Senator to pull a switch?" Shanna suggested.

'That's a great idea Mom—now why didn't I come up with that solution? Father, can you take care of this with Salvatore? Things are hectic at the moment, and I'm afraid we will not have the time to spare. Anyway we all know that for you he will move mountains. By the way, one day you must tell me about his Gina."

"Antonio don't worry, I'll phone Salvatore immediately and have the pin delivered to you as soon as it's completed. As for Gina—well I did what most men in my position would have done, or at least I would like to think I did."

I'll admit that Father's parting comment baited my curiosity: but all in due time. We had pressing business to take care of first.

"Wish us luck. We will truly need it this time," I said. The Senator is pretty shrewd. He's no fool. But since this is our first mission, we cannot fail the Prime Minister. The fate of Israel could depend on us."

After saying our goodbyes and receiving well wishes from my parents, Ziva and I returned to the guest house. Our parting was quick, as busy people could not afford the luxury of lingering for light conversation. Nevertheless, neither of us caught the tears streaming down Shanna's cheeks, nor the sudden tremor as Demetri wrapped his arm around his wife's waist.

"Fear not *amore mio*," he whispered, you know our son is a giant among men. He will protect all of them—*E' il figlio di Il Fidato!* He is the son of *Il Fidato!*"

# XXIV

Silence permeated as immersed in our own thoughts we glided through large foamy white clouds, firmly buckled in the comfortable reclining seats of *Il Fidato's* preferred jet. The Palm Beach International Airport was just several hours distant. Father had arranged for a limo and driver to accompany us to the Breakers. Although I was certain one of Frank Aiello's trusted men would be doing the chauffeuring honors, once at the hotel, Benjamin would take over, fulfilling the role.

While it was not spoken, and although Ziva understood that Cuoco was not yet ready to join the team, I knew she mourned the pup's absence. Benjamin on the other hand, entertained reveries of his beloved Françoise, marveling over the virtuoso of Fate's performance in crossing their paths. Meanwhile, the woman who had captured his heart was busy thanking God for sending her a wonderful gentleman as well as a new family. In the quiet of her thoughts she prayed for their safety.

In spite of my own auspicious destiny with Ziva, I took advantage of the situation to focus exclusively on the Senator, reviewing over and over the plan for his destruction. It had to be absolutely glitch free—as always error was not an option.

The flight was smooth and relaxing allowing the hours to tick by like minutes. Soon the pilot and crew were announcing the imminent arrival in Palm Beach. Just as the sun dipped beyond the eye's vision field, the landing gear was lowered and the wheels hit the runway. Father had made some phone calls prior to out departure, consequently, we would be escorted into the airport and through customs easily and quickly.

The limo driver was waiting to accompany us to the Breakers. As I had imagined the Hotel had a luxurious, European flair from the Mediterranean decor, furnishings, and colorful hand painted murals to the exquisite deluxe amenities compliments of a well-trained staff whose goal is to indulge, pamper and please with their quintessential service. A stroll through the lobby revives historical memoires of oil magnate Henry Flagler's 19th century concept for elite accommodations on an island resort. He more than succeeded!

Once we completed the check-in protocol, we headed to our respective suites.

"Let's meet near the pool in about an hour," I said to Benjamin and Françoise."

Both nodded their approval. Ziva of course would never forego a dip in the pool and after a lengthy international flight a leisurely swim would be a relaxation booster. Father had booked the Imperial Designer Suite for us, which as anticipated did not disappoint. It was absolutely beautiful, designed in cream with mandarin color accessories by Badgley Mischka. Entering the eye darted instantly to the amazing ocean view: merely the *antipasto* to the lavish offerings.

Hanging in the bedroom closet were four *haute couture* Valentino gowns designed solely for Ziva. Nearby on the dresser were five Caraceni shirts and a varied selection of Hermes neckties, pocket squares and cummerbunds all custom made.

"Father certainly went out of his way to make certain we look fabulous," I said, lifting one of the cummerbunds and slipping the silk sash around my waist.

"Look at these exquisite gowns—how will I be able to choose one?"

"It really doesn't matter Ziva. Tomorrow evening, my love, we will make our selections and undoubtedly you will be the belle of the ball. Talk about bespoke tailoring!"

In keeping with our plans, we unpacked, sipped some refreshing mineral water, chilled to perfection, slipped into our swim wear and headed poolside to meet Benjamin and Françoise. When Ziva dropped her robe and walked to the edge of the pool, the deck silenced. In a split second her long taut body was cutting through the blue waters without the slightest ripple or resistance. I marveled over how invested in swimming she was. Once life returned to the pool deck and the stilled tongues vibrated in words, we all got our feet wet.

Movement plus the water massage felt curative and soothing following endless hours in flight. Afterwards we had dinner at Echo, the Hotel's Asian restaurant.

"The sushi is excellent," Françoise said, posing her stainless steel chopsticks across the plate.

"Well their claim of 'capturing the yin and yang' are authentic," Ziva added. Dining here is really a serene and enjoyable experience."

"Tomorrow will be an eventful day," I interrupted. "We must retire early to be in full form."

"I'm ready for a night cap," Benjamin whispered, extending his hand to Françoise in a chivalrous gesture.

We departed and returned to our respective suites. Minutes later, like middle school students we were fast asleep.

The following day we kept a low profile, enjoyed the pool, a bit of sun and a light lunch at the Beach Club Restaurant. Later we dedicated our efforts to preparing for the big night. Dressed to perfection in our splendid custom designed wardrobe, compliments of *Il Fidato*, we met Benjamin and Françoise in the lobby prior to the start of the Ball.

Needless to say, Senator William H. Hartford, III was the center of attention at the fundraising gala in the opulent Venetian Ballroom. All was proceeding according to plan. A tall handsome man with salt and pepper hair, and a deep tropical tan, he was dressed in a black double breasted tuxedo tailored to perfection. His demeanor resembled that of either a fashion icon or the consummate politician.

Pundits speculated he would be the Republican presidential candidate in the next election. Approached by the far right wing of the party he had been reassured the necessary campaign funding would not be an issue. The dilemma however, was centered on his willingness to forego the power he would have as head of the influential Foreign Relation Committee, as well as the luxury to gratify his degenerate appetite in the confines of his own room. His inflated ego left him with the obnoxious certainty he would if elected leave for all posterity, a great presidential legacy. Still, the decision to jump into the ring would require much soul searching.

Once again the room froze. Silence permeated. Cocktail banter stopped. Drinks remained immobile between jeweled fingers. All heads turned toward me and Ziva when we entered the ballroom. It should not have surprised me.

Like a graceful swan my beloved pranced into the arena on my arm. Elegant and breathtakingly gorgeous, she gave great honor to the snow white form fitting silk backless gown she had slipped into just moments ago. The ruffled trimmed hemline literally danced with every muscle in her body. To top it off, her glowing bronze tan and glistening black hair produced a striking contrast.

Standing tall beside her in my black Armani tuxedo, I was proud to be wearing *Il Fidato's* black opal studs and cufflinks.

I noticed Senator Hartford immediately. With a swift wave he summoned his aide.

"Stephen who is the couple that just arrived," he asked, gesticulating with his chin pointed in our direction.

The slender young man with the rimless glasses reached into his inside pocket and removed a long narrow brown book.

"The man is Antonio Bastone," he said, raising his eyes from the open page. His father, Demetri is the Italian olive oil king. Antonio is his sole heir and from what I understand, he's quite an adept tennis player. The woman, known simply as Ziva, is from Turkey. By all accounts, she is his girlfriend. Would you like me to dig deeper into their back grounds?"

"No, no—it is not necessary. They are certainly an eye catching duo. I just wondered why I had not seen or met them before. Stephen, please ask them to join me. I would like to welcome them personally to the fundraiser."

As requested, Stephen approached and introduced himself, smiling.

"Mr. Bastone, Senator Hartford would like to meet you. Would you join him for a drink?"

"Certainly Stephen, it will be our pleasure.

As soon as he turned on his heels, I leaned over to Ziva, "The game begins" I

whispered in her perfumed ear. I loved that she loved to drench herself in any of her three preferred Jean Patou scents—1000, Joy and Sublime! Taking her arm we walked in Stephen's footsteps to meet the Senator while he held court on the opposite side of the ballroom.

Nearing him I realized he was rather distinguished in appearance. Face to face with the target, I clasped his hand in my palm and gave two firm shakes. In a heartbeat his gaze switched to Ziva. I knew exactly what was spinning in his mind. Lamenting not having met Ziva ten years earlier, he could only fantasize gratifying his pedophile craving with her as his teen, love object.

"Mr. Bastone we are honored to have you and Ziva join us for such a worthy cause. May I ask if your trip to Palm Beach was enjoyable?"

"Thank you Senator, we are please to be here. And yes, our flight from Italy was rather pleasurable."

"I understand you're quite a pro on the court. Would you be interested in teaming up for tomorrow's doubles match."

"It would be my pleasure, Senator. My father and I have great admiration for you and your political platforms."

"Mr. Bastone, please thank your father for me," he responded, visibly thrilled by my unmerited praise in his regard. "Not everyone shares your sentiment."

I reached into the pocket of my trousers. In the blink of an eye, a rugged, hefty man materialized, invading my space. The familiar bulge in his dinner jacket similar to Benjamin's, confirmed he was a bodyguard, trained to catch every suspicious move.

I turned just in time to see the Senator's two raised fingers. Instantaneously the guard stepped back a pace and withdrew. His reaction time was commendable. Caught in an awkward situation, I do believe Hartford never felt I represented any imminent danger or threat. I was the olive oil man's son, with a great serve, fast legs and a gorgeous girl-friend—a fancy European playboy who would be a worthy contributor should he decide to make a bid for the presidency. Appearances are deceiving, I thought, grinning inwardly.

Of course I pretended nonchalance and ignorance in the light of what had just occurred. Withdrawing my hand I held the shiny silver case, engraved with the initials W.H.H. I had retrieved from my pocket.

"Senator, my father requested I offer you this small token of our admiration, should I have the good fortune to personally meet you."

"What a thoughtful gesture. Please thank your father for me," he said opening the case.

When his eyes fell on the sparkling label pin, his surprise and delight were more than evident.

"Mr. Bastone this pin is beautiful. How original. I have never seen one like it. I must pin it to my label immediately."

"Senator, please allow me the honor," Ziva said, lifting the box from his hand before he could remove the pin.

"Certainly—be my guest," he replied lifting his lapel. "I'm speech-less, which is a rare trait in a politician," he added laughing; "but I promise you and your father that I will wear it always and with great pride. You will never see me without it."

Both Ziva and I shared and instinctive unexpressed thought, later confessed: that's just what we are counting on. Meanwhile, Benjamin, Sam and Françoise sat in a Florida Power and Light service truck parked about a half block distant from the hotel. If I could see their faces I'm more than certain they were smiling and raising their thumbs in a sign of triumph.

Meanwhile in the van, a happy trio applauded. "As you can see the video is working fine and the audio as well," Sam said, removing the ear piece from his sweating head.

"We never expected a video—what an additional bonus," Ben-jamin added.

The trap was set. Once the rat came out to play, we'd have our culprit.

"I bet Antonio and Ziva are curious and eager to hear how well the pin functions," Françoise said.

"Let's head over to the Ball. I'm always nervous when they are not in my direct visual field."

"Benjamin, you worry too much. They are safe at the Breakers—it's probably guarded like a fortress this evening."

"I know, Françoise but I feel better when I am in their company."

I breathed a sigh of relief, fully aware everything the Senator would do from here on in would be common knowledge.

I felt secure as long as Hardford wore his pin. This was the most important part of the mission. It went well and in celebration I wanted to take pleasure in a dance with my beautiful love.

# XXV

Before the dessert was served, news of the Fundraiser's success echoed throughout the Ballroom. Apparently the event had netted over $550,000 from benevolent donors and an international conglomerate of generous philanthropists.

Aside from the money raised, I had to admit, Ziva and I had made our debuts into the glorious and swanky vanguard of American High Society. Similar to the enthusiasm that greeted us in Monte-Carol, we were once again thrust into the limelight as glamorous newcomers on the playground of the super rich and famous.

Questions were asked regarding how we had met and why until now we were absent figures on Palm Beach: queries posed predominately to satisfy the curiosity of the upper crust: inquiries that were in reality mere meaningless drivel. However, gracious in our wonderful host country, we obliged, smiling at all the appropriate times.

Several hours thereafter, my fingers felt numb from all the handshakes and Ziva lamented her face hurt from the incessant smiling. Therefore, when the Senator approached I seized the moment for clarification.

"I don't know how you do it" Senator Hartford. "This is all new to me and Ziva. We're not accustomed to being on a campaign trail in evening wear. A myriad of people to meet, countless names to learn, so many hands to shake, and so much small talk. It's almost overwhelming. After all I'm just a small businessman from Italy."

"Mr. Bastone, I rather doubt anyone would identify your company as small," he replied, throwing his head back in a hearty laugh. Furthermore, you might as well get used to it. You and Ziva were a smashing success. If I were you I'd prepare for a host of other invitations. And now if you'll excuse me, I'll say goodnight. I want to be well rested for tomorrow's match."

"I understand perfectly."

"Are you guests at the Hotel?"

"Yes—it's beautiful here. Reminds me of a fancy Italian villa. The 16 and 17 century Belgian tapestries are museum quality. And of course we love the high ceilings and gorgeous chandeliers in the lobby. I think they're from Murano. It's very well decorated. Are you staying at the Hotel?"

"No—I have a house here in Palm Beach. Whenever I can I fly down; it's great to be able to get away for some quiet time."

"It certainly is lovely here," Ziva said in parting. "Have a restful sleep, Senator."

"Thank you. See you in the morning on the courts."

After our goodbyes I was anxious to return to the suite, tug open my tie, and peel off my garments. Whoever designed the tux concept, elegant as it may be, committed a grave over sight in the comfort department.

Once free of our confining garments we savored our favorite energizer—thirty minutes of passionate love making.

"That's better" I said. "This is the best part of the evening."

"I'm looking forward to tomorrow's tennis match. Can't wait to see you whip Stefan on the courts."

"There were so many people there this evening—too many. I think I'd rather face enemy fire than that a hoard of high society types," I moaned.

"Who told you to be so tall and handsome? You had every woman eying you with lust in their hearts, and some men too," Ziva said laughing.

"Don't think I didn't see all the men looking at you—fantasizing about you," I shot back.

"Antonio—I guess we're a pretty hot couple!"

"Not much we can do about that!" I quipped. "I'm going to phone Benjamin. I want to hear if the pin worked."

As soon as I stepped out of bed, my cell buzzed.

"Antonio, we're in the lobby. We'd like to see you for a moment."

"We're on our way, Benjamin."

We slipped into some causal clothes and headed for the lobby. Benjamin, Sam and Françoise were waiting as promised.

"Let's go outside," I suggested. "It's a beautiful evening."

When we previewed the video and briefly listened to the audio we were overjoyed. Not only was the flag pin a beautiful piece of jewelry, but the device worked to perfection.

"Antonio I already heard some racist comments from the Senator's mouth, comments that would be rather embarrassing, though I don't know if they would be strong enough to end his career." I'll spend the night in the van, just in case his pedophile appetite flares."

"Good idea. We might get lucky," Ziva said.

"OK Sam—we'll see you in the morning," I added taking leave. "Well done!"

Ziva, Benjamin, Françoise and I exchanged good night wishes and headed for our suites, proud of the successful unraveling of the first part of our mission.

In the morning, as I was preparing for the match with Senator Hartford, a thunderous knock interrupted my concentration on the tennis strategies I was about to play.

"One moment," I shouted, grabbing my shirt.

"Antonio—good news," Sam announced as I pulled open the door. Grinning and excited he entered, frantically waving a disk over his head. "We got him! We got him! Last evening after the ball our friend returned to his home where two very young girls from the Middle East were waiting for him to engage them in frolic and fun. And he did not spare any pleasure seeking antics. We caught it both on video and audiotape. He was in such a rush to gratify his depraved needs and strip naked, that he threw his jacket over the nearest chair. What a stroke of good luck! It seems that the pin ended up in the perfect position to capture all his activities."

"That is incredible news Sam," I exclaimed, thrilled he was able to get so much so early on.

"Antonio there is enough eye witness testimony here not only to end his political career but to get a conviction."

"Great job, I said giving the slender man a hug. Well done my friend. You may return to Israel reassured your family and the nation can sleep a little easier tonight."

Thanks Antonio, it was a pleasure to be able to work for you. Please give my warmest regards to *Il Fidato* and your beautiful Mother."

I walked Sam to the door, returned, phoned Benjamin and awaited his arrival. As soon as he walked in I played the disk. Several minutes later, with mouthing nausea in the pit of my stomach, I switched it off. Not one to easily suffer side effects from life's wanton realities I had to admit the visual and audio were repugnant. Once I caught my breath I planned the strategy.

"What happens now," Benjamin asked, noticeably affected by the loathsome scenario.

"I am going to make three copies, one for CNN, one for MSNBC and last but not least one for the Senator's diehard supporter, Rupert Murdock's Fox News."

"Hi Benjamin how are you and Françoise this morning? Sleep well after your exciting night in the van?" Ziva asked entering the room fresh out of the shower.

My God I thought, she looks so sexy and alluring, even with wet hair and an oversized bathrobe camouflaging her delicacies.

"Call Françoise tell her to come over so we can all have breakfast together."

"Great—We are wonderful Ziva, thanks: and you will be ecstatic when you see what Antonio has in his hand."

"Let's wait for Françoise, and then we can all look."

"I'll see if she is ready and we'll meet you here in 20 minutes."

"Make it 30," Ziva said giggling. I have to get ready also.

"You look beautiful even as you are."

"Thanks Benjamin, aren't you charming this morning."

"No Ziva," I said, he's not charming—just truthful."

"You boys are making me blush!"

"OK—let's get ready and not waste any time. Remember I'm in a match with the Senator, in a couple of hours," I reminded them.

When Benjamin departed Ziva and I turned our attentions to selecting the morning's outfits. Mine for tennis and her's for tempting and tantalizing the fantasy of every man alive. We busied ourselves getting ready. I was however, somewhat concerned about the flag pin. As of the present moment we did not have a replacement to substitute the original. This was a vital component that would guarantee the successful completion of the mission.

Time for thoughts and reflections was not much of a luxury these days. A sudden knock on the door interrupted my concerns. In walked Benjamin and Françoise, looking rested and relaxed like a couple of tourists enjoying a Palm Beach holiday.

"Are you ready for breakfast?" I asked.

"We're famished," Benjamin responded.

I phoned room service after interrogating my guests on their menu preferences. Since my tennis match was imminent I ordered a glass of sweet Florida orange juice and lightly buttered wheat toast. There wasn't much time for a long leisurely breakfast. The celebrity tournament was due to start at 10:00.

It was a hot sunny day and the tropical climate did cause some discomfit among the more mature players. Billy Crystal, featured on the billboard as the evening's performer was participating as well as many former high ranked pros and red carpet celebs. Seeing Stefan Bjornberg's name on the program was thrilling. I wondered if the former number one Swedish Pro would recognize me.

The turnout was phenomenal, consequently the tournament was open for public viewing and moved to the Delray Beach Tennis Center to accommodate the over 8,000 spectators.

From the Breakers, the little over twenty-two mile drive to the

Delray Tennis Center clocked in at 31 minutes. I left the hotel with time to spare for some warm up serves, asking Benjamin to do me the honor of escorting Ziva and Françoise. Certainly there was no resistance to my request.

"Maybe the package will arrive," I said, in parting, still pondering the substitute flag pin we were waiting for.

When I reached the courts I noticed the Senator warming up with some other players. I wondered how much energy he had left after his long night of lecherous debauchery with the young girls.

As I neared the courts, my eyes focused on the Senator's navy warm up jacket. There in full view under the blazing mid-morning sun was the shimmering flag pin. If only luck would be on our side and Benjamin would arrive with the substitute pin, the switch could occur right in the locker room, officially concluding the mission in glory.

"Good morning Senator," I said, waving my racket.

"Morning Antonio—Are you ready for the match?"

"Yes I'm looking for a little *love* on the court," I said referring to a win from the opponent's zero score. Of course I was being sarcastic, though obviously, and thankfully the pun flew right over his head.

We started hitting some balls to each other. The weather was marvelous, a radiant sun sat in a deep blue cloudless sky, another perfect day in paradise, as coastal Floridians love to say.

As expected, Senator Hartford was not my worst teammate. Moreover, he was in surprisingly good condition for a man of his age in a career not overly compatible with physical fitness, except of course for his extra curricular activities.

Within minutes, Stefan Bjornberg joined us accompanied by his partner, an affluent real estate developer with a firm determined handshake.

"You're Antonio Bastone," he said smiling. We were once opponents on the tennis court! I remember you—you're a phenomenal player. You came dangerously close to beating me!"

"How nice to see you again, Stefan," I responded. "Here we are once again on the courts!"

"Why didn't you go on tour? I was certain you'd be ranked as one of the top three players by now."

"Life sometimes throws unexpected curve balls, and in a heartbeat, destiny changes."

"Something specific?"

"Yes—I had a misfortunate accident and suffered a severe rotor cuff injury that ended any hopes for a tennis career. Afterwards, I dedicated myself full time to my father's business. No remorse and no regrets."

"That's wise. It we can't accept a circumstance or situation we must try to change it. And if it is impossible we must make the best of it and find other paths."

"I fully agree Stefan and that is precisely what I did."

"It's so nice to see you again—good luck on the court."

We exchanged a friendly handshake and parted, just as the Senator approached.

"Seems like you and Bjornberg are friends. May I inquire where you met," he asked.

I informed him of the tennis match years earlier, in Italy, but did not mention I was there just for a summer holiday. As far as I was concerned that was sufficient information.

"It's time to pick up the rackets," I announced as the other players hit the clay. Gazing in the stands for Ziva, Benjamin and Françoise, I noticed not many people had showed up. Perhaps tennis was not a crowd drawer in South Florida.

But rash judgments often have little if any value. Within minutes of the initial serves, once it became evident that the quality of tennis was far from dilettante, the stands started filling up. In less than 30 minutes they were overflowing with fans and spectators.

Bjornberg and his partner, a business tycoon, quite adept on the court were heavy favorites to win the match. Between my competitive nature and that of the Senator, the tournament soon switched from a fun charitable event, to a fierce battle of egos. Hartford did not have a penchant for loosing, and needless to say, neither did I.

The match was quickly tied after the first couple of sets. It was hot and adrenalin was pumping through my body. I kept my stride angle wide and my extended arm rotation angle broad, in spite of my injury. Sweat poured down my face as I sent a fast spinning kick serve across the court. Though probably not a 130 mph record *à la* Federer or Djokovic, it was surely at a three digit speed. Wiping the beads of perspiration from my brow, and racket, I glanced up to where I knew Ziva would be sitting. What a refresher—there was my smiling gorgeous girl, flanked on either side by non other than *Il Fidato* and his beautiful wife, Shanna.

I bowed my head in acknowledgement as Father suddenly swept his hand up to the inside pocket of his navy blazer, flashing a grin. The pin I thought, muffling a scream of delight. Father brought the pin. Now in front of my three VIP fans, I had to win the match. I knew what was required: I had to rotate my hips to further empower my serve.

Stefan was my opponent. Thankfully I was in excellent physical condition and quite a bit younger. Having the maximum of energy, flexibility and strength on my side, I won the match, a victory, pleasing Mom, Father and the Senator.

However, in savoring the blissful moment, Hartford failed to notice the prevailing silence, except when it was shattered by hundreds of different cell phone rings suddenly echoing around the stands.

"How rude," the Senator murmured, walking toward the court side chair where his jacket was poised, neatly folded. Lifting the navy garment, he slipped it on, turned and took several steps in my direction. Extending his hand, he clasped mine in a hearty shake. Squeezing, I tried to cancel from my mind, the vile images presented earlier on the video.

"Well done," an alluring female voice echoed, planting a quick peck on his cheek. While Ziva complimented the Senator's prowess with the racket I maintained my pressurized grip. Accordingly, between Ziva's unexpected reaction, and his hand on the verge of being crushed, it was not surprising to witness Hartford squirm. He was unquestionably at a disadvantage.

A silence of the grave returned once the cell phone calls had been answered, immediately after the win. Betrayed by a heavy breathing the politician found incapable of muffling, he shifted his gaze away from mine. I unshackled his hand from my hold, smiled and wished him a good day. He retrieved his jacket, and swung it over his shoulders, never noticing his flag pin was slightly off its original mark.

"Once again my beautiful darling deserves applause," I whispered; "one down and two to go."

I winked over at Ziva who smiled her approval. Incontestably we shared a magnetic connection. Walking over to her, I noticed the Senator's chief aide rushing toward him. From the disturbed, almost contorted expression crossing the man's face, I didn't need a sharp intuition to surmise a tempest was brewing.

The impromptu assemblage lasted all of a minute, ending with an ashen complexioned Senator fleeing the courts, leaving behind his prized rackets. As his limo pulled away I noticed he dusted his brow with the back of his hand. Something worried him!

"That was an interesting exit," I said climbing into the car.

"The pot is in full boil," Ziva replied.

Mom and Father joined us in the car for the return ride to the Breakers.

"I must admit I was somewhat surprised to see you in the stands."

"Antonio this was too important a job to leave to chance. That pin had to arrive on time. Besides my concern for the successful outcome of the mission, your mother and I always enjoy spending time with you and Ziva."

"Yes, it does seem like a luxury these days," Mom added playfully.

"For some reason I am famished," I announced.

"I wonder why" Ziva said, encouraging his humorous rebuttals.

"Let's have lunch in the suite, my love. Benjamin and Françoise are freshening up. This way we can turn on the TV and see the havoc our fabulous gift has brought the good Senator."

"I'm in favor, Antonio."

I showered while Ziva made arrangements with the kitchen staff. Nothing disappointed. Room service set a beautiful table. While overcome with the delectable aromas from the Breakers master chefs, we watched a noted politician's life crumble into slovenly shards. The media, partisan or otherwise broke the story. TV, radio, Internet, newspapers, all portrayed the wildly spinning carousel of depraved deeds. There was neither compassion nor empathy—and why should there be? By days end Hartford was a dirty household name, and his new gig was dishonorable Senate resignation!

Soon after the Attorney General from Hartford's home state of South Carolina launched an investigation to discern the criminal charges needed to seek an indictment from the grand jury. With the exception of Fox News and the New York Post, assuming the possibility of tainted evidence defense, the media was broadcasting news of an imminent high profile case. Meanwhile, the Senator's damage control PR staff announced the airing of an interview on Fox News to clear up the bogus rumors.

The existence of probable cause was determined; therefore in following legal protocol, search warrant in hand, the F.B.I. investigated the Senator's homes and computers, gathering evidence. Undoubtedly they were aiming for a conviction!

Once Hartford's files crammed with compromising pictures and e-mails confirmed the validity of the discs, the allegations evolved into accusations. Soon even Fox News demanded the Senator's resignation. The graffiti on the wall was more than legible—the man was guilty of lascivious behavior with minors. In spite of his protestations of innocence and entrapment—he was a criminal.

Several months thereafter, the Senator reappeared as a breaking news headliner when his wife surprised him *in flagrante*, in the act of committing a perverted deed. Enraged, disgraced and ashamed, she pumped four bullets into his chest and two in his groin. The retaliatory reprisal was successful—fatal.

Paying homage to the man and politician at his burial stood the preacher and several feet behind, the grave diggers.

Filling his vacant seat as Chairman of the Foreign Relations Committee was Senator Jill Bradley from New Hampshire, a well respected longtime friend of a small Democratic country in the Middle East.

# XXVI

With our Palm Beach mission successfully accomplished, we prepared for a return to Italy where Benjamin, Ziva, Françoise and I would start plotting a strategy to take down our next target, Yazeed. First on the agenda was a call to Frank Aiello. I wished to simultaneously offer thanks for all his efforts, and to extend an invitation to him and his family to join us at the Bastone Estate.

Unfortunately, due to Frank's reputation, there were too many eyes trailing him in New York. Furthermore, my intention was to set up an *incognito* face to face meeting. I was sure, however, that in combining business with pleasure, I would accomplish my goal.

"Frank," I said after his hello, "how about flying out with the family? It would be nice to get together and catch up. What do you say? Can you clear your schedule?"

"Antonio my family and I would be honored to accept you invitation," he replied. I could hear the joy in his voice.

"Wonderful, Frank, will you let me know when you plan on coming?"

"Yes, I have some important matters to take care of first. But I will call you as soon as I have some free time blocked off."

"I'll await your call. Give my regards to Rosa Maria."

As soon as we ended the conversation, I informed the others of Frank's imminent visit with his family.

"How nice," Ziva said.

"Yes I agree," I replied, taking a deep breath. "It sure feels good to be home."

"Not only to be home, Antonio, but to have completed our first major mission so successfully. I think we're all jubilant."

"I heard from the Prime Minister's assistant. He mentioned she is overjoyed we annihilated a bad link to Israel. This is satisfying. Let's take some time to unwind—then we'll meet to discuss a strategy to eliminate Yazeed."

In one of our conversations Frank Aiello had mentioned Yazeed's connection with the Russian Mafia. In fact he was victorious in obtaining enriched Uranium for the Iranians. Meanwhile, my father was determined to reach out to his Saudi friends to seek their help in obtaining information to pinpoint Yazeed's present whereabouts. If possible he wanted to get an insight into his plans and scheduled activities for the upcoming weeks.

Recognizing the *bravura* of the Mossad in retrieving information, I suggested Benjamin return to his Israeli homeland to gather some additional clues, first hand. Though Françoise would not be pleased by his absence, she understood the importance of his assignment. Joining the team meant she would have to accept some challenges and compromises, like it or not. Nevertheless, willing to embrace her new culture, she continued her tasks always with the gracious smile that captivated Benjamin's heart.

In the interim Ziva unwound engaging Cuoco in a game of ball throwing and fetching. Judging from the frenetic tail wagging and animated giggling, it was obvious both ladies were enjoying the inter-action, despite the fact I was Cuoco's preferred companion. Alert, astute and obedient, our pup was fully trained and eligible to join the team.

Shortly after sunset, dinner was served to the family. We reunited around the large African Blackwood—Mpingo dinning table, a gift to *Il Fidato* from a Kenyan aristocrat he befriended. After the five course meal, and preceding his habitual night cap in the garden, Father phoned Prince Muhammad Din Laud granted the late hour. Italy was one hour behind, but the Prince had a widespread reputation as a night owl. Consequently, there was no danger of either disturbing a deep sleep or halting a dream in progress.

Delighted to hear from his old friend, the Prince inquired about the health of the Bastone family before beginning an exchange of friendly pleasantries. It was a good tactic to put each other at ease, and set a light tone for the conversation. Father wanted information without blatantly asking for it, and expected the Prince to volunteer whatever confidences he had heard, if indeed he had any.

"How is your father, King Al-Kaziz? I hope his health is as good as his flourishing oil fields," Demetri said, laughing.

"All is well with my father," he replied after a short pause; though he is concerned about Mansur Raftab's influence on his people. He's just a common piece of camel dung."

Listening attentively, Father merely uttered "Raftab is a bag of hot wind, and a small one at that.

"Demetri—we cannot and should not take this character lightly. As we speak he is gathering material with help from that Turkish son of a whore, Yazeed. The plan is to build a nuclear arm. With this weapon Raftab could gain control of most of the oil fields in my country as well as in Yemen and elsewhere."

"Should this occur, Israel and the United States would not take it lying down—there will be war," my father replied.

"King Al-Kaziz is one of the most powerful men in the world. Who is this Yazeed? Why is he a threat to Prince Muhammad? After all he is merely an insect underfoot, a scorpion crawling in the scorching dessert sand. Your father is a powerful man—why can't he just crush him?"

The Prince remained silent for several seconds, perhaps searching for a response without demonstrating fear.

"Demetri, Raftab is the largest supplier of weapons to most of the Middle East as well as many third world countries. Killing him is no easy task. Moreover, he is a necessary evil because we use him from time to time."

My father was clever. His feigned ignorance in Yazeed's regard appeared to be an advantageous approach. However, he knew he had to tread cautiously if he wanted to obtain information that would be of value to me without waving any red flags.

"Where does Yazeed spend his leisure time?" Father asked chuckling as if delivering a half-hearted joke. "I want to be sure I will not choose the same vacation spot."

"I have been told he favors the French Riviera. His love of beautiful women and gambling make it the perfect place for this son of a donkey to relax and indulge in some fun."

"Too bad! I love that region as well, but for very different reasons. Maybe I'll have to redesign my vacation plans," he said jokingly. "Well I won't take up more of your time. It was nice to speak with you. Please extend my best to King Al-Kaziz. With God's help perhaps your troubles will come to an end, one day."

"Thank you Demetri—always a pleasure. My regards to your beautiful Shanna and to Antonio."

I was glancing at my watch wondering about the conversation between Father and the Prince when my phone rang.

"How are you, Your Excellency," I said upon heading Prime Minister Lagashi's greeting.

"Very well thank you. I think congratulations must be extended to you and your team for a job well done. I am more than pleased with the outcome of your mission."

"Thank you, Your Excellency. We now have to deal with eliminating Yazeed. Actually I can use your help to identify his current whereabouts. I'll get back to you as soon as I have some information."

Ending the call I noticed my father had returned. Curious to hear the outcome of his conversation with Prince Muhammad, I turned sharply on my heels to face him.

"How did your call go? Any helpful news?"

"I learned Yazeed has made the French Riviera his European playground. If all goes as planned, someone should notify you of his schedule."

I had to admit Monte-Carlo and the whole French Riviera coast made sense to me. And why not—it was beautiful, sunny, coddled by the glistening Mediterranean, elegant, fun, and filled with young gorgeous women, ostentatious bling and great gambling. It was a perfect Mecca to accommodate a sybaritic lifestyle.

Within the hour we had three reliable sources supply all the necessary information including Yazeed's noon arrival the following day. He would be accompanied by three women and several bodyguards.

"Now if you'll excuse me," Demitri said, "I'd like to join your mother for a short walk in the garden, before we retire."

"Thanks for your intervention Father. Enjoy the walk."

As soon as he departed, I approached Ziva, Benjamin and Françoise, who were seated for an espresso, near the fire-place. They seemed engaged in a lighthearted discussion which left me a bit sorry to interrupt. But business was my priority.

"I had a quick chat with Father," I began, abruptly silencing their words. "Yazeed arrives in a few days with his entourage of women and bodyguards. I suggest we all focus on sharpening our skills and getting to know Cuoco better."

"Good idea—let's ask Domenico to bring her to the guest house. It's really not that late and we can spend some time with her," Ziva suggested.

"OK—I'll call him," Benjamin responded, lifting his cell phone from the belt case.

"Cuoco has won the hearts of her teammates," I said. "Actually it's smart to get her accustomed to all of you."

"You won't get any resistance from me," Françoise added, grinning.

Within minutes, Domenico and Cuoco were in the garden: he smiling proudly, she, wagging her tail in quick broad sweeps. Spotting her friend, Ziva darted out the door. In recompense she received two licks and Cuoco's personally choreographed dance.

"Let me remind you," Domenico began, "Cuoco's language skills are in Italian. If you want her bi-lingual you will have to teach her English."

"That's funny," Benjamin said, chuckling. "But it does make sense."

We all enjoyed a hearty laugh—the first in a long time.

"I hope our four-pawed teammate is ready for her first mission. We'll be departing shortly," I said.

"Don't worry Antonio, she's as ready and eager to start the mission as we all are," Ziva responded.

"Cuoco will do just fine," Domenico added. "She's had pretty rigid training and did exceptionally well."

"Wonderful!" Benjamin said. "Do we have a definite departure date?"

"The day after tomorrow," I announced, watching amused as Ziva and Françoise exchanged concerned glances, perhaps pondering if they had sufficient time to prepare.

"I don't think that departure date is worrisome to anyone," I said teasingly.

Silence and smiles were the ladies responses.

# XXVII

The Lear Jet heading toward the French Riviera included a special four-pawed passenger who seemed to be enjoying the trip. My beautiful black and silver German Shepherd 'colleague' was clever enough to realize we were about to land. Standing in the aisle, she beamed her gaze, first on me then switched to Ziva, Françoise, and Benjamin wagging her tail as if impatient to be on *terra firma*.

"*Va bene Cuoco, siamo quasi la*, OK Cuoco we are almost there," Françoise reassured both in Italian and English. She certainly was a bright quick learning canine, and now bi-lingual!

Once the landing gear was released the jet touched ground on a small private air strip reserved for VIP pilots and passengers. We were just several meters distant from the recently leased villa that would be home base until the completion of our mission to eliminate Yazeed. Excitement was building.

We were met by a driver who quickly packed our luggage into the trunk, then made certain we, including Cuoco were comfortably seated in the limo for the ride along the breathtaking beautiful Corniche d'Or en route to our new residence.

No one spoke and I had to admit the silence seemed to intensify the panorama. When we arrived at the tall black gate to the villa, a well-dressed gentleman in a double breasted blue blazer and charcoal slacks greeted us.

"*Bienvenus*, welcome" he said smiling. *Je suis*—I am Jean-Pierre." I immediately recognized him as the broker in charge of the property.

He had come to show us around and answer any questions or concerns we might have regarding the appliances and house in general.

I'm Antonio," I responded before introducing Ziva, Benjamin, Françoise and Cuoco. After the presentations, he departed, leaving his business card with additional handwritten contact numbers.

"Françoise and I will settle the luggage," Benjamin said, "while you and Ziva relax and unwind."

"Sounds like a good plan," Ziva replied, "I think a nice shower would feel great right about now."

"I agree," I added, heading toward the bathroom in the master suite. "We'll meet in about an hour. That should allow us sufficient time to freshen up."

I headed directly for the bathroom, leaving a trail of garments as I stepped into the shower. The steady spray felt nurturing. Beads of water like agile fingertips, unwound the knots of tension in my neck and back. The sudden good feeling left me free from distractions, and able to organize my thoughts.

"How much longer will you be, Antonio?" Ziva shouted.

"I'm done—just have to slip into a pair of pants and a shirt and I'll be ready for the meeting. How about you?'

When I exited the shower I was greeted with a kiss and full body hug.

"I'll be ready in ten minutes."

She kept her promise, and as announced earlier, we reunited in the living room.

"I want to organize and structure a definite plan to reassure a successful mission,"

I said. "Our first priority is to localize Yazeed and discover his customary haunts. But we must exercise caution. I do not want to arouse any suspicion. Yazeed is shrewd and cunning and certainly no fool, therefore, we must be on our toes at all times."

Judging from the domino effect affirmative head nods, I had sufficient confirmation to believe we were all on the same page.

"Great—meeting adjourned." I said.

"I'd like to make a suggestion if I may."

"Certainly Françoise."

"You have the floor," Benjamin announced, smiling.

"How does a nice hot meal followed by a full 8 hours of peaceful sleep sound?"

"Idyllic," Ziva replied. "Can we entertain such delightful activities?"

"Just give me forty-five minutes in the kitchen. I promise you will sit at the table
delighted. As for the bedroom—you're on you own."

"Amen" Benjamin concluded. "Now let's prepare for a relaxing evening. I think we can all use it as a prelude for more serious things to come."

Cuoco barked her *don't forget me*, as we laughed.

"Don't worry Cuoco, there is a nice meal for you also," Françoise added, leaning over to pat her head.

As agreed we enjoyed a delicious meal followed by a hit the pillow and fall into an uninterrupted sleep, which I think we all felt, filled more of a need than a pleasure.

I was practically comatose when a slender ray of sun invading through a tiny opening in the drapes, settled on my face. The warmth and radiance, a silent alarm, awakened me to the new day. Startled by a pair of jet black eyes just inches from my face, I blinked several times, before Cuoco pounced on my stomach, gently swishing her tail across my face.

"OK Cuoco I understand: it was a long night and you're ready for the morning walk," I whispered gazing down at my beautiful sleeping beauty still lost in her dreams. "*Stai calma*, be calm Cuoco, you don't want to awaken Ziva. Let me slip into my robe, and I'll be all yours."

As expected Cuoco wiggled and poked her nose at my chin, spilling over on Ziva's side of the bed.

"Good morning," she greeted, stretching her long beautiful arms in my direction. Instead of hard muscle, she touched a vibrating ball of soft fur. "What's happening?"

"Cuoco and I are heading for the garden," I replied passing through the large double French doors in the entry of our bedroom. "Would you like to join us?"

"You won't be offended if I refuse," Ziva grinned. "Blame it on the aroma of Françoise's coffee. It's shower, dress and head to the table for me."

"OK—See you there."

Within a half hour, Cuoco had both exercised and satisfied her early morning hunger. I was united with Benjamin at a beautifully set table, complete with an eye pleasing centerpiece of multi-colored garden blooms. They were artistically placed between two white and blue platters filled with fluffy mounds of fresh scrambled eggs. Across the top, long slender slices of crispy bacon formed a crisscross design. Framing the *pièce de résistance* was a row of sliced roasted potatoes, generously bathed in butter. In several straw baskets lined with white linen napkins, hot biscuits sat cooling. To the right of each plate stood a tall crystal glass three-quarter filled with fresh squeezed orange juice.

"Who's ready for some hot coffee?" Françoise shouted. All hands reached for the ceiling.

"This looks absolutely delicious," I said taking the sizzling pot from her hand. "Please allow me."

"O no, Antonio, I will do the honors," she responded laughing.

"Where is Ziva?" Benjamin asked pointing to the empty seat beside me. A compelling presence, her absence produced an unmistakable void.

"Right here," a sing song voice chanted, as she entered the room. "You don't think I'd miss one of Françoise's sumptuous meals!"

"Now why would we even speculate on that absurd conjecture," I said, patting her equally sumptuous derrière, as she slid into the chair.

I had to admit the *scenario* was unique, especially to someone like Ziva. She found herself not only immersed in a rare microcosm for a young woman, but involved with three rather uncharacteristic individuals plus an out of the ordinary dog. To all appearances we seemed like a typical family. It's amazing what clever impersonators of normalcy we could be.

I was sipping the juice while Françoise pranced around humming a French song, filling coffee cups before seating herself. Had Ziva arrived fifteen minutes earlier she would have noticed Benjamin in the far corner, nonchalantly cleaning an assorted array of weapons we had taken along. Certainly this was not a common scene in the majority of homes.

"Good morning Ziva" I said with a vague hint of laughter in my tone.

"I am starving" she announced. Taking her cue, Françoise prepared a generously portioned plate, substantial enough to feed a 300 pound fullback.

"What's our plan for the day?" she asked, continuing to savor the delicious morsels on her quickly emptying dish.

Glancing at her, I couldn't believe how anyone could look so beautiful, stay so slim, and yet consume such massive quantities of food. It blew my mind at times.

Though she continued uninterruptedly to enjoy breakfast, Ziva's mind seemed to

Intercept my thoughts.

"I have a fast metabolism! Furthermore—you know how much I work out," she said between forkfuls. "This allows me to indulge, guilt and consequence free. Does that satisfy your curiosity?"

This produced a melodious chuckle around the table. Every woman would hate her after that comment, I thought. She's gorgeous, young, smart, and sexy and can eat like a football player, yet resemble a model. I guess it's true, life is not always fair.

After our appetites were gratified, and the weapons cleaned and put away, I asked Benjamin, Ziva and Françoise to remain for a briefing.

"I phoned my father last evening to inquire if there were any changes regarding Yazeed's Riviera visit. I was told he would contact me if anything new developed. I have not heard, therefore I assume all is *status quo*. Father is also setting up unlimited lines of credit for us at the three most popular casinos in the region."

"Since Yazeed traveled with a large entourage of women and body-guards, perhaps it would be smart for me to go with Benjamin to the local market place and try to find out if any large orders for food had been requested," Françoise, suggested, "especially since he opted to stay in a villa like ours."

"What a clever idea" Ziva said. "Meanwhile we will wait for Demetri's call."

Although Yazeed preferred to stay under the radar as much as possible, the nature of his business often made it quite impossible. I knew from past experiences, that timing and patience were required on our part if we wanted to be successful.

The sudden ring of the phone interrupted my thoughts. I grabbed my cell. Father was on the caller's side confirming the lines of credit had been opened.

"Antonio keep calm—all is moving according to plan."

Within the hour, we had the confirmation that Yazeed accompanied by three women and three bodyguards was scheduled to arrive tomorrow at noon. Through a local real estate agent with whom he had past residential dealings, he had leased a large villa. Moreover, it was revealed that his gaming pleasures would take place at the Casino Barriere De Cannes Crosiette in a private salon reserved exclusively for high stakes poker.

"That's very helpful info," Ziva said.

"Yes and no," I replied.

"I don't understand—why not?"

"Because the bad news is that the poker game is by invitation only, and Yazeed has to personally approve the roster of players."

"There must be a way to overcome this hurdle," Benjamin speculated.

"You will have to devise a plan to get me that list," I replied.

Benjamin nodded in agreement. "Then what happens once we get our hands on it?"

"One of the players must cancel his play date at the last moment, and I will slip in as an eleventh hour replacement, to save the game. Yazeed will be relieved to have the missing seat filled."

"And he will not have sufficient time to run a check on you. Great strategy Antonio."

"Thanks Benjamin—let's hope it works!"

"If possible I don't want him to be aware of my success at the tables during our last stay in Monte-Carlo. I'm afraid the unresolved incident of the two missing Turks could cause him to investigate a little deeper into my back ground."

"How will we get the list?" Ziva asked.

"Leave it to me," Françoise volunteered, grinning.

"Really?" Ziva said.

"Really! Don't be a doubting Thomas!"

"If you say so—I believe it."

Actually it was not surprising at all for Françoise to succeed in her mission. Her talents and love of the culinary arts together with her personal accolades for the head chef's preparation and presentations of sublime menu selections, earned her an invitation to meet him at the casino. In particular he enjoyed her praiseworthy words about the unusual spices he incorporates in his recipes.

Dressing hurriedly but elegantly, Françoise drove to the casino for her *rendezvous* with Jean-Jacques. Upon entering, it wasn't the aroma of sautéed garlic that grabbed her attention, but the pair of massive muscular arms that circled her waist, lifted her, and planted two kisses, one on each flushed cheek.

"Nice to see you also," Françoise said, once her feet were back on the food stained white tile floor.

"I bet you're kept running from skillet to oven with all the requests and different palates you have to please."

"*Si tu savais ma chérie* Françoise, if you only knew," he sighed, shaking his head. "Let's walk over to my work table and I'll show you the directory of special requests I just received from the casino manager.

"Any particular guests" Françoise asked?

"Yes—I'm told a group of international poker playing VIPs are in town for the big game. My assignment is to please them at all costs. You know—give them everything they want. Here take a look at these names and their requests!"

What a perfect moment, Françoise thought, taking the list from his extended hand. One quick glance and she had all the information she was seeking.

Proud of her accomplishment, Françoise was eager to spread the good news. Returning she quickly summoned the team for a meeting. I already recognized the energy of triumph, but waited for the confirmation.

"Jean-Jacques was absolutely darling," Françoise said glowing. "He literally played right into my hand and thanks to my keen eye, I was able to browse and remember not only the names, but the specific food preferences of each individual.

I glanced at the paper Françoise thrust in my hand. There were five names representing five men from different walks of life, yet each had a spot on the Forbes 400 wealthiest men in the world list. Although Yazeed had accumulated a great deal of money through his dealings with arms, he was not in the elevated category of the players summoned to the game.

Françoise did an excellent job. Her cleverly devised strategy to obtain the information needed for me to gain access to the game as a replacement was impressive: apparently she was an asset far greater than I had initially anticipated.

Placing the list on the table I wondered about the draw for these men. What could it possibly be? Money was not an issue to this group. Their five million dollar buy in was comparably to $5.00 for the average person. I had to have a seat secured at the table before the start of the game and realized there was one man I could depend on.

Reaching for my wallet, I pulled out a card given to me years earlier by a Texan with a noticeable limp. He had a huge warm heart and had offered me a new life in the USA.

Although Avi Levine had graciously accepted the card, Antonio Bastone would actually dial the number scribbled on the back in midnight blue ink. I smiled, wondering if the risk would be worth the info I was seeking. After all Avi Levine was dead and buried.

Drawing a deep breath I opted to trust my instincts and dialed the Las Vegas number. It rang twice before a husky voice with traces of a Texas drawl responded.

"Don't you know what time it is," he snarled. "Well you woke me up now speak—what can I do for you?"

"Hello Mr. Drunsen,"

"It's Boyle to anyone who calls this number. Who are you? Your voice is not familiar."

"Boyle, I'm Antonio Bastone. A friend of mine gave me your number before he passed away. He told me to speak with you if I ever needed advice on a special matter."

"Antonio before we begin let me assure you that I know who you are. The news of your success in Monaco spread quickly among the top pros. As a rule we prefer to know who we might be up against. We are not big on surprises—at least not if we can help it. When the word in your regard went from good to very good, I asked for your photo. Except for the beard and mustache I noted you bore a strong resemblance to a young soldier I met while vacationing in Israel.

"This boy had a gift at the table, something I had seen only once before in a player. His name was Chris Small and he passed away after suffering a massive coronary. I always thought it was a bit strange as he was a young man and in good health.

"Do you mind if I call you Tony? It's short for Anthony which is the American version of your name?"

"Sure Boyle—Tony is fine" I said laughing. I had to admit feeling somewhat startled a man like Boyle Drunsen had heard about my success in Monaco.

"So how can I help you Tony?"

"I need some information about a man named Yazeed. If I'm not mistaken he has a reputation as a top Texas Hold'em player?"

"Be very careful my young friend, Yazeed is not a man to mess with," he emphasized after an uncomfortable pause.

"I am well aware of his background. What I'd like to know is why people of great wealth and importance would be at his beck and call?"

"Pride—simple pride, Tony. Not one of them had the ability to take down Yazeed in any consistent manner. Some defeated him on rare occasions, but nine times out of ten they leave with empty pockets. In fact a number of top pros have tried with very little success, except for Chris Small. Regardless of the game, Chris always cleaned him out. In fact, I saw Yazeed flip into a rage the last time he lost to Chris, which was just before he died. Coincidence? Maybe, but I have had doubts for a long time.

The Israeli soldier I met, I think his name was Avi, had the skills to bring Yazeed to his knees. Too bad he died so young. Seems as if all the good ones meet untimely deaths.

It would give this old man a great deal of pleasure to hear that Yazeed was taken down. Good luck Avi... sorry I mean Tony. Be careful—remember Chris."

"Thanks Boyle," I whispered and returned the phone to my pocket just as Ziva and Françoise's animated chatter reached my ears. They were returning from their morning stroll.

"Antonio—Did you get the answers you were looking for?" Ziva asked.

"Yes, plus a bit more information than I had expected."

"What do you mean?"

"Boyle knows I'm Avi Levine, or at the very least he has strong suspicions. But for some strange reason this does not concern me, perhaps because there seems to be an honor code among professional gamblers. They tend to watch out for each other. Now we have to find out who would be the best player to eliminate, and how to go about doing it."

I once again pulled out the list Françoise had given me and scanned the names: Zarkose, Greek shipping magnet, Armando Ortega, clothing stores throughout Brazil, BatAvi'sta, mining and oil from Spain, Muskaw Melhi, Petrochemicals, oil and gas from India, Jeff Berzaros, Internet, from America, L. J. Lewis, finance and investments from the U.K. Pretty impressive I thought browsing over the food requirements listed to the right of each man's name. When I came to Berzaro's request for a tall glass of coke, lots of ice and two pieces of lemon with each meal and one at 8 P.M. to swallow some pills, I knew I had found my man.

"Jeff is our target," I announced to Benjamin, Ziva and Françoise. "If we could find that perfect something to slip into his 8:00 p.m. drink and knock him out, it would be ideal since the game starts at 9:00 pm sharp. I know for a fact that Yazeed is superstitious. The timing would be flawless. And Yazeed will never sit for a game with less than six players."

No one said a word. The only audible sounds were air leaving and entering our lungs. It was apparent from the silence that we were all racking our brains for the magic substance we could use to safely incapacitate the American. We each had an idea, the options, however would be too risky to his health.

"I think I have a full proof solution," Benjamin said, jumping to his feet. "There is an odorless, tasteless liquid that will purge the system for at least 12 uninterrupted hours. It is not harmful, but makes you beg for death."

"Of course—a liquid laxative. Clever, but where can we get it?" Françoise asked.

"Any pharmacy."

"And best of all," Françoise continued, "once poured into a glass of lemon coke he will never know what he is swallowing. Mr. Berzaros will not be harmed, unless he falls during one of his mad dash trips to the bathroom."

We all enjoyed a hearty laugh imagining the *scenario* Françoise had choreographed. I had to admit it was humorous to visualize a man of such great wealth and prestige seated on the john like every Tom, Dick and Harry worldwide. In that regard all men were truly created equal.

"OK enough laughter. We must plan for a successful mission. What seems rather trifle is in reality a delicate task, though vital to accomplish our goal. Too much is riding on this plan," I said.

"I shall go to the pharmacy" Françoise volunteered. "Ziva and I passed one during our walk this morning. I'll get the appropriate remedy for my ailing husband."

Françoise never ceased to amaze me. Bright, courageous, creative and ruthless in a certain sense, she was the all consummate team player.

Within twenty minutes she was back from the chemist, as the gentlemen at the pharmacy insisted he be called, with two small vials of clear liquid.

"He guarantied that one dose would be sufficient to purge a horse."

I'll admit I winced at the metaphor almost feeling sorry for our poor victim.

"Françoise, would you like to pay another visit to your new friend Jean-Jacques?" I asked. "This would grant you access to the kitchen and reassure us the plan will come to fruition."

"I'm not all that happy with this plan," Benjamin confessed, recognizing the risk his beloved was taking. But I do understand this is the only way it will work. I want to go with her."

"No"—I said vetoing the idea. "However Ziva could perhaps distract Jean-Jacques and provide some protection for Françoise." I had witnessed my lover's defense strategies in action and felt certain she could handle any situation in the kitchen.

"This is reassuring," Benjamin said.

"OK—here's the plan. At 7:45 Ziva and Françoise will go to the kitchen in the casino to complete the task."

Ziva hesitated a few seconds. "Antonio, I think that's cutting it too close. We should present ourselves around 7:15. This will allow some time to exchange a few words with Jean-Jacques, and make certain we put the liquid in the right glass.

"OK—now get some rest. We have a long night ahead. Also I want to phone Prince Robert to clear the way in case any unforeseen problems arise."

Reaching for the phone, I dialed the Palace. It rang four times before a voice responded.

I presented myself and requested His Highness.

"Monsieur *Son Altesse Sérénissime* is on the other line. Please hold for a moment and he will be with you.

"*Merci.*"

"Within a minute the Prince was on the line.

"Hello my friend," he responded in a soft voice with just a slight accent. "How are you and your beautiful Ziva?"

"All is well" I replied. We chatted for several minutes exchanging pleasantries and family information, before I up-dated him regarding our whereabouts and the reason for my call.

"*Son Altesse* may I ask a courtesy of you?"

"Certainly Antonio—how may I be of assistance?"

"If I may I'd like to have your good word on my behalf at Casino Barriere De Cannes to assure no one will question my presence or seek information about me. I prefer not to have my family name known at the present time. Please if you are in agreement, just refer to me as Antonio or Tony."

"No problem. I will be happy to speak on your behalf. Since I'm heavily invested in the establishment you mentioned, I doubt granting your requests would be a problem." Graciously, he reassured with more than a hint of laughter in his voice. I couldn't help thinking that his name alone would move mountains in this part of the world.

"I will make the call as soon as we hang up."

"Thanks for not asking any questions," I responded. "I will explain all when the time is right."

I bid the Prince goodbye and went to join Ziva. The air was filled with excitement. My pulse raced as I whispered; "today is the beginning of the demise of Yazeed.

# XXVIII

I opened my eyes at 7:03 AM still basking in the aftermath of my torrid night of love with Ziva. Turning to savor her beautiful face, I brushed my lips teasingly over hers, ever so gently fearful of disturbing her peaceful sleep. Perhaps she was still dreaming of our passionate antics, hours earlier. Nevertheless it was now time to put aside the love making reveries, and focus on the business of our mission.

In my mind I reviewed the essential steps of the plan, searching for even the slightest flaws that could potentially impede the outcome we expected. Basically, the strategy involved the united and precise efforts of Ziva and Françoise to make certain Berzaros' drink contained the appropriate ingredient—aka the laxative. Once this was accomplished it was up to my savvy not only to get invited to the table, but to execute the plan to eliminate Yazeed without breeding the suspicion that his misfortunate health episode was the result of a homicide in lieu of natural causes.

Ziva and Françoise had the prefect pill. Once ingested with a swallow or two of liquid it would in a brief span of time cause death by cardiac arrest. Any autopsy performed, thereafter, would confirm the cause of death. It was fool-proof.

How funny I mused reflecting on Boyle Drunsen's comment about the untimely demise of Chris Small. Who knows if Yazeed had been instrumental in his passing, using the same method to abolish a man he could not beat?

"Antonio, what time is it?" Ziva said, yawning.

"7:35—aren't the numbers on that clock big enough for you to read," I teased.

She laughed, hurling her pillow at me. I ducked and ran for the shower, knowing with certainty I'd have company under the hot pelting spray in just a few seconds. Though I make no pretense to papal infallibility, when it came to Ziva I was pretty accurate. Thus, we enjoyed a lengthy and tantalizing morning moment.

Two hours later following a sumptuous breakfast compliments of Françoise, we took Cuoco for a morning stroll. Returning, we were greeted with another cup of fresh pressed coffee. When the satellite phone rang, Benjamin walked over to the table to respond.

With his nod, I understood the caller was the Prime Minister of Israel.

"Yes" Benjamin said in Hebrew, a language foreign exclusively to Françoise. "Whatever you feel is best for our country shall be done."

Putting the phone back on the table, Benjamin turned to face us.

"Plans have changed. There is no longer a wish for Yazeed to be eliminated. Apparently he has a great deal of valuable information regarding Iran's nuclear locations. Antonio when you devise a plan, the Prime Minister will put all Mossad's resources at our disposal."

"That new order does change things," Ziva said, speaking first. "It's so much easier to kill than to disable someone like Yazeed. And how do we get him out of the casino with a room full of people and all his body guards?"

"I have an idea," I said, breaking my pause of silence; "and with the Mossad's intervention it will work. Since the game is tomorrow night, we must work heard to put our plan together."

"We're ready," Ziva said, speaking on behalf of the team.

"Benjamin, contact General Levy. Tell him we will need an ambulance on standby all night if necessary, not more than five minutes distant from the casino. Be sure it's manned by a male driver and an agent dressed as a nurse. Also please get precise information on the pill we have. Find out if cutting it in half will give the impression of a heart attack without killing him. Furthermore make certain the ambulance personnel are connected to our phone set up. When summoned, they must arrive within the time frame I have indicated.

"Ziva, you and Françoise will leave for the casino around 6:30. Benjamin will drive you and be there as your backup in case something goes wrong. I will be at the high stakes black jack table around 8:15 to meet you all. Is that clear?"

"Yes-Antonio," Benjamin responded while Ziva and Françoise nodded their agreement.

"OK-now we must wait for General Levy's call."

As if on cue, the phone rang. Within seconds the General and I were connected. We spoke for several minutes.

"Antonio looks concerned," Ziva whispered to Benjamin. "I hope it's nothing serious."

"Let's wait before pushing the panic button!"

"It seems the genius who made the kill pill is on holiday with his girlfriend," I said. For obvious reasons he did not leave a forwarding address to secure his wife would not get wind of his *scappetella* as the Italians define a frivolous adulterous escapade. However, resorting to some unusual strategy, they were able to locate him."

"Do we have an answer to the pill question?"

"Yes Ziva. The pill can be cut in half and still be effective to simulate a heart episode without actually killing Yazeed."

"I don't feel comfortable with any risk, but I do realize this is the only possibility to complete our mission," I said.

"Then we shall cut the pill and proceed as planned," Benjamin added.

The instructions were carefully followed and the half pill was slipped into a small compartment under the sparkling diamond ring Ziva would wear to the card game.

"Let's all get some rest," I suggested. This is an important game; the last Yazeed will play in a long time, assuming all goes well."

We ate a light but nourishing lunch and each indulged in an hours nap. It's amazing how curative and energizing a nice meal, followed by a bit of relaxation can be. Recharged we faced the evening eager to set our plan in action.

A floor length black beaded cape draped across her shoulders gave Ziva a dramatic stately appearance. She looked absolutely ravishing. Undoubtedly she was a show stopper.

Françoise on the other hand chose a chic black Ralph Lauren tuxedo with a form fitting mid-calf skirt slit enticingly just several inches below her left hip. Her tiny waist was accentuated behind the slender jacket.

Unfortunately Benjamin's tuxedo did not conceal the muscle mass he carried on a short frame, though the overall look was decidedly more elegant than his standard daily garb. I selected a single breasted, two button silk mohair tuxedo, which I paired with a less fancy shirt. Instead of the characteristic *papillon*, bow tie, I chose a long black satin Hermes *cravat*.

"Don't you look princely, and I might add, so sexy," Ziva whispered, nibbling my ear. "You'll have most of the women in the casino wishing to share you bed."

"Ziva—you are priceless and precious. The truth is—every man will want to crawl under your covers."

We enjoyed a quick kiss and an even quicker chuckle.

"The game starts at 9:00 PM," I reminded her. "As agreed we should arrive at 7:15 to allow Françoise sufficient time to spike the American's orange juice and have him start his course to the men's room. I want you to accompany her. You'll serve as a distraction. Of course Benjamin will be nearby as a security measure, in case something goes awry. Meanwhile I will make certain Prince Robert spoke with the casino manager. Just want to have the reassurance all the bases are covered. Every part is detrimental to the success of our mission."

"Antonio is right," Benjamin said. We can never be either too sure or too confident. Anything can happen at the last minute."

"Are we all ready?" I called, elevating my voice several decibels.

Three well coiffed heads nodded in agreement. "We'll meet at the high stakes Black Jack table when part one of the mission is accomplished.

"Let the games begin."

"I'll drink to that," Benjamin said raising his arm in a sweeping gesture.

We slithered into two cars to alleviate any suspicion, and drove to the casino.

Françoise and Ziva worked their way into the buzzing kitchen. Upon spotting her familiar face, Chef Jean-Jacques greeted Benjamin's love, as if she were a long time friend in lieu of a recent acquaintance. Smiling he savored every inch of her sexy body comparing her delicacies to one of his masterpiece dishes. When his glance met Ziva's he was rendered speechless by her extraordinary beauty. However, it was Françoise with her alluring aura, the woman who made his pulse race. Sweating and somewhat embarrassed by his obvious reaction he shuffled his feet several times before speaking.

"You ladies are far too lovely for my chaotic kitchen," he said trying in vain to justify the beads of perspiration forming along his forehead.

In French Françoise introduced Ziva as her employer's girlfriend who had been impressed with the culinary delights served at the hotel and had requested to meet the Chef. Turning to Ziva, Jean-Jacques thanked her in heavily accent English.

"*Madame* I can only hope my meals are half as appetizing and sumptuous as you are."

"Thank you" she whispered. "Your gallantry is equal to your *bravura*."

While the two exchanged compliments, Françoise quickly scanned the kitchen searching for the tray destined for delivery to the Berzaro suite. Persistence brought fruition. On the side of the back counter she noticed two glasses filled with soda toped with two lemon wedges. Beside the drinks she glimpsed a five by five square card. Scribbled in black ink was Mr. Bezaro's name and suite number.

Strolling toward the tray Françoise carefully removed the caps from the two bottles of liquid laxative. For a brief second she felt a pang of guilt for the fate of the innocent American and his unlucky guest with whom he would be in competition for the race to the bathroom.

# XXIX

Five men were seated around the table, awaiting the arrival of the final player. Patience was wearing thin as the stakes were high. Every second of lingering anticipation played havoc with their nerves. What or who was keeping Mr. Berzaro from such an important appointment?

A tall lanky gentleman, with dark wavy hair and a thick mustache, approached the table. Leaning over he whispered a message in Yazeed's ear.

'Thank you Paul," Yazeed said, scowling. I'm sorry to hear that Mr. Berzaro and his wife have suddenly become ill." He was about as convincing as a mass murderer repenting.

"He is upset," Mr. Lamont continued, "and sends his apologies."

'They probably ate something that didn't agree with them" one of the other men added. "We have all been there before."

"Yes and they feel uncomfortable and at a disadvantage to be sick in a foreign country, so they decided to fly home to consult their physician," Paul said.

Yazeed's face turned ugly. His jaw tightened. Among his fellow players it was well known that he was reluctant to start a game with less than six players. Pulling away from the table, he rose to his feet. Paul Lamont turned in his direction.

"Yazeed, if you're interested I know a man who is willing to meet the buy in and would love to join the game."

Although Yazeed was fearless in the Texas Hold'em world, he was somewhat apprehensive of people he did not know.

179

"Who is this man? What do you know about him?"

"He's a very close friend of Prince Robert. In fact His Highness phoned me yesterday and specifically requested I fulfill all his needs. Besides he was spotted playing four hands of Black Jack five thousand per hand.

"Call him and ask him to come here. I will decide when I meet him," Yazeed blurted between clenched teeth.

Lamont left, phoned and asked if I was interested in joining the game. Several minutes later Paul walked over to the table. I stood at his right—Ziva his left. Trailing a number of paces behind were Benjamin and Françoise.

"Yazeed—May I present..."

"My friends call me Tony," I said interrupting Paul. "And I hope I can join your table. When I extended my hand toward Paul, I tried my best to soften my often intimidating handshake. I was playing it cool and didn't want to risk my chance to play. I was hopeful he had not heard about my success during his visit to Monte-Carlo.

My fears and concerns were unwarranted. Yazeed hardly listened or paid much heed to my actions. His eyes remained fixed on Ziva.

"And who may I ask is this gorgeous creature?" he inquired, loosening his jaw for a brief moment.

"She's Ziva, my travel companion," I replied, inwardly proud. I knew her beauty was causing him to squirm, and I knew he could ogle and covet to his heart's content, but she'd never be his.

Of course Yazeed entertained different thoughts, believing my gorgeous love would be a fantastic addition to the three beauties currently in his collection. Once again I extended my hand in a courteous gesture of presentation, never certain how he would react. The answer came soon enough as he failed to accept my handshake invitation.

"Tony" he said, clearing his throat, "Mr. Lamont assured me you have the funds to play. Since we are missing a hand, have a seat. It will be my great joy to empty your pockets."

Laced with subtle echoes of arrogance, his tone betrayed every thought passing through his mind. I could read him like a book.

Hesitant to wait for a reply, he continued to undress Ziva with his eyes. The room was swaddled in silence. Three of the other four players also sat mesmerized, not daring to blink as they followed her every move. Meanwhile I seemed to have caught the fantasy of the fourth player whose eyes bore right through me.

Distracted by Benjamin's sudden sneeze and whispered apology, Yazeed turned to check out the duo just arriving. Hastily he sized up the petite but attractive older women as Ziva's maid and the short stocky man in the ill-fitting tuxedo as my body guard.

A shrewd and sinister man, Yazeed paid attention to his gut feelings, a strong inclination cautioning him against underestimating Benjamin. Guarded, he arrived with three of his toughest men who offered the reassurance he would be protected in the event an unlikely situation should arise.

I took my seat around the table just as the dealer arrived carrying a carton of new cards. As is customary he broke the seal on the first deck, turned them face up for all the players to view, and started shuffling prior to the start of the game. Yazeed seized the moment to introduce the other players: "This is Zarkose" he said pointing in the man's direction, "he is in shipping. Next we have BatAvi'sta from the Mining and Oil world, then we have Melhi, the Petrochemical King, Dang from Commodities, Al Saied, Construction, Lewis Investments, and I am in Marketing."

"Nice to meet you all," I said smiling.

"What's your profession Tony?" Yazeed asked.

"I spend the family fortune wherever and whenever I feel the urge!"

Caught off guard by my unexpected wise-guy response I was certain he believed he would have an easy time releasing me from my money, and win Ziva as the crown jewel of his female collection. My reluctance to give a serious reply left him even more determined to take me down. He had worked hard to build his Empire, risking his life more times than he cared to admit. Presently, with his involvement in Iran assisting the Iranian leader in his bid to become the most powerful man in the Middle East, he could not digest the newcomer seated across the table who apparently had the good fortune to be born into great wealth.

Not on my watch, Yazeed thought! The dealer had finished mixing the cards.

"The rules are as follows," he began once the cards had been shuffled; "there will be a thirty minute break every three hours. Any player who for whatever reason is forced to leave the game, will forfeit his residual money. These funds will be divided among the remaining players. Let me be clear—absolutely no exceptions will be tolerated. Blinds will start at five and ten thousand and escalate every half hour. Are there any questions"?

Since the men were seasoned players at Yazeed's table, all heads turned in my direction, awaiting my response.

"I hope Lady Luck is with me this evening," I said, slamming my hands together in self-applause. Undoubtedly I was doing a great job of antagonizing my fellow players. In fact, the looks of disdain and sneering grins shot in my direction confirmed my feelings.

"With that said, let's begin the game," Yazeed shouted.

With nimble fingers, the dealer quickly released the cards. We played a number of hands before the first scheduled break was called. I guess my comment about Lady Luck was a bit more realistic than most imagined. My hands were favorable and I was up a large sum of money. However, despite the good fortune, I was unable to get a handle on Yazeed. He revealed not even the slightest hint of any tells. I'd just have to be a bit more patient. When the dealer signaled that it was time to break and get a bite to eat, the Arab took over as money leader.

After freshening up we met at the bar for a drink and quick snack. Since I had skipped dinner, I was famished and feeling a bit light headed. This was a poor tactic and I vowed never to sit for a game on an empty stomach. Proper nutrition was essential to keep my attention focused and my mind sharp.

"Well Antonio what have you learned about Yazeed?" Ziva asked.

"Absolutely nothing!"

"Nothing?"

"Nothing except that he is every bit as good as Drunsen said he would be. Besides, I don't like leaving our fate to chance!"

"I'll admit I'm surprised," Benjamin said. "This is the first time your skills have failed to reap an abundant harvest."

"What's next?" Ziva inquired, "What do we do now? To my knowledge we do not have a backup plan, and time won't permit us to create one. The game resumes in less than three minutes."

"The game is not over. Start using your combined brain power to come up with a winning strategy. The three of you together should be able to do it," I said, putting the onus on Benjamin, Ziva and Françoise. Now if you'll excuse me I have to return to the game."

Ziva gave me a kiss as I rose from the bar and turned on my heels to head back to the table.

"And where is your beautiful companion?" Yazeed inquired as I slid into my seat.

"Sipping her preferred champagne at the bar," I replied shrugging my shoulders.

As the dealing began my mind brought me back to the plan I had devised just the day before. It was relatively effortless, though it required precision timing and amicable circumstances. Ziva had to catch Yazeed's attention and slip the pill concealed in her ring into his drink. Once accomplished, the segue would be easy. The paramedics would be summoned, and the waiting ambulance would rush him to a plane parked in the apron of a small airport. From there he would be flown to Israel.

It would have been a lot easier just to assassinate him I thought, reviewing the steps of the plan yet to be set in motion.

I could not permit myself to be distracted or loose focus. There was too much riding on this game. Quickly I gazed down at my cards, folded the hand and centered my eyes on Yazeed to try and discover a flaw in his game. If Chris Small could succeed there was no way I'd accept failure.

I noticed Zarkose's jaw tighten once Yazeed had trapped him. He slow played three tens and when the shipping magnate went "all in" with two high pair, Yazeed took him down, giving him a huge money lead. One down and five to go, I thought.

An odor began to permeate around the table, a scent I had noticed earlier though I paid no heed. Mysteriously, it seemed to surface then fade when the dealer shuffled and dealt to the remaining five players.

From the corner of my eye I caught a glimpse of Ziva approaching with a Champaign flute. What a vision. Removing her cape, she left her bare shoulders exposed to several sets of ogling glances. The body hugging white gown, announced she was braless. Despite his track record for bedding endless international beauties, Yazeed was unable or unwilling to conceal his arousal. His quickened breathing left me silently delirious. He would never feast on what I was blessed to enjoy.

Arriving from behind, Ziva bent over lowering her mouth directly opposite my right ear.

"We still don't have a plan," she whispered.

"That's funny," I said chuckling. I had to give the impression she had made a humorous comment, though the moment was far from amusing.

The next two hours seemed to fly by. L. J. Lewis, Ortega, and Melhi succumbed both to Yazeed, and my skilful maneuvers. Yazeed ended Melhi's game. At that point I detected a return of the baffling odor. What was it? I had to decipher this phenomenon; it would help me achieve my goal. My memory kicked in as if for emergency first aid and I recalled Yazeed's tell and why Chris had been eliminated. Short had solved the mystery.

I had a moment of enlightenment. I realized Yazeed's arrogance emitted a pungent scent when he had someone trapped. Apparently, none of the other top poker players was onboard except for the late Small, and now me. The realization enticed my lips into a smile, which immediately caught Yazeed's attention.

"What may I ask is so funny Tony?" he asked. "Please share the joke with us. We all enjoy a good laugh."

"I am going to win all the money piled in front of you and buy Ziva whatever she wants," I boasted.

Rage crossed Yazeed's face for a brief second. No one seemed to notice the fleeting grimace concealed behind a laugh.

"Perhaps you would like to include your beautiful Ziva as part of the winner takes all prizes"?

"And what may I ask would you contribute to the pot?"

Yazeed nodded toward the three women behind him.

"As much as it is a very tempting offer, Ziva is her own woman. In other words she is free to choose with whom she wishes to spend her time."

With that said, Ziva was right on cue. Raising her glass she formed a silent "good luck" with her full carnal lips, openly flirting with Yazeed.

I knew he desired two things: to possess Ziva, and to destroy the young man in front of him who dared believe he could defeat him. Only one man had succeeded and he is no longer alive to brag about his triumph. The poor fellow was struck by a coronary and succumbed, or so everyone was led to believe.

I caught Yazeed's smirk just as quickly as I caught his bogus cough. How transparent he is, I thought.

"What are you waiting for—deal, he snarled, turning to the dealer.

Great—he's upset and nervous. I rejoiced, unbeknown to the other players. My opponent was beginning to break. I still had half the table money and Yazeed had the rest. This meant we were on equal turf, a circumstance that seemed to surprise those who had previously fallen, since his reputation identified him as one of the best if not the best Texas Hold'em champ in the world. I on the other hand was a big question mark—a universal unknown.

The dealer kept shuffling and dealing, hand after hand. First Yazeed had the edge, and then the tide shifted in my favor. My opponent was beginning to realize I was much more than an ordinary player. Each time he tasted the sweetness of triumph, I would fold. Frustrated, he was unsuccessful dually in trapping me, and in discovering my tell. If he wasn't so nervous, he'd be amazed or maybe even impressed.

Certainly he bore no resemblance to the man who imposingly took his seat at the start of the game.

The ambiance around the table changed. Yazeed relaxed, glanced down at his cards—pocket aces. Meanwhile my eyes settled on a pair of deuces. Though it was not a great hand, it actually wasn't bad for a head to head. Drawing a deep breath, I opened with a $250,000 bet. My opponent slowed, played his hand and just called. Then came the flop—two deuces and an ace. How ironic—this was the same hand he had played against the Turks and folded his aces full against the four of a kind.

I raised my bet to $500,000. Once again Yazeed just called, reading me for two pair. Like a sudden skunk spray, the odor he emitted grew stronger and stronger. I was afraid I'd gag. Certain Yazeed had aces full and was waiting to take me out, I called his play.

He was ready to take me down and walk off with his prize—the money and Ziva. The turn and river cards would not encourage any change. He was ripe for the kill.

I opened with $2,000,000. Yazeed looked across the table and raised his bet to $3,000,000. I focused on my cards, and paused for a moment. If nothing else, my hesitancy created a mystery bred concern.

"All in" I called leisurely pushing the rest of the money in front of me into the center of the table.

Yazeed removed his black glasses, jumped from the chair and straightened to his full six foot five inch height. His tightly sealed lips parted just wide enough to flash a smile, first at Ziva and then in my direction. The stench intensified; spasms were coming like labor pains, seconds before giving birth. I hoped the game would end before my stomach betrayed me.

Then in slow motion, Yazeed imitated my previous move, sliding all his money into the center of the table. Without saying a word, he threw down a pair of aces, revealing a full house. A smile crossed his pock marked face as he reached over to rake in the pot, but not before I threw down two duces, one at a time. Undeniably my four of a kind was the winning hand! Suddenly the foul aroma deserted my nostrils like air from a balloon pricked by a pin. Icy, stoic, detached and unaffected, Yazeed was visibly unfazed by his $30,000,000 loss; perhaps certain he would settle the score in the near future.

Bystanders who had surrounded the table while millions of dollars began to pile up for a lucky player to claim, broke out in shouts of *bravo*. Yazeed headed for Ziva, lifted her free hand and planted a kiss across her knuckles. Reaching for her half-filled flute, he stole a sip of Champaign, unaware she had anticipated his arrogant gesture and slipped the pill in just seconds prior.

"Congratulations Tony—We will meet again," he said extending his hand. Grabbing mine, he applied a power grip, believing he'd bring me to my knees. What he failed to foresee despite the hours at the table, was the large dimension of my hands: until it was too late.

I tightened my grip leaving him feeling as if his hand and fingers were crushed in a vise. Witnessing his face contorted in pain, I extended a bit of empathy, loosening the pressure, just in time to offer respite to a man who would soon be the victim of a harrowing experience.

Head lowered Yazeed turned to walk away. It was obvious defeat was neither his habitual experience nor harmonious with his haughty, overconfident personality. Taking several steps, he slowed his stride to catch his breath. He seemed to be in respiratory distress. Pausing, he clutched his chest apparently overpowered by a sudden jabbing pain. I noticed his complexion pale as fear mounted in his eyes.

I hoped the pill would not result in a fatality, and send the plan in tilt.

"He's having a heart attack," Françoise shouted. "Call for an ambulance."

"We have a physician on staff," Paul Lamont reassured, dialing an extension on his cell phone.

"We can't waste any time," she yelled excited. We must get him to the hospital at once. I am a registered nurse and recognize the symptoms of a serious situation. This man needs immediate emergency attention. The hotel physician can do nothing for him."

Françoise summoned the ambulance as agreed earlier. The increasing volume of the sirens, guaranteed help was soon arriving.

"Thank God" Lamont whispered relieved the problem would be out of his hands and no longer a potential liability for the hotel.

Within minutes a tall athletic man dressed in a navy uniform arrived followed by a heavy set woman pushing a gurney on top of which sat a large dark metal box holding a heart monitor and resuscitating equipment. Around her neck she carried a mask connected to an oxygen tank anchored over her right shoulder. As she hurried to the patient, she cleared her way through the throng of curious onlookers who had gathered to find out what had occurred.

Confused and stunned by the unexpected turn of events Yazeed's bodyguards quickly regrouped.

"I'll need one of you to come with me, the other can stay behind with the women," the head guard ordered.

Two well-muscled men rushed to Yazeed's side, standing at attention while the paramedic worked on their boss, defenseless and inanimate on the gurney. An oxygen mask was strapped around his head to facilitate his breathing.

"Hurry-take him outside and load him into the ambulance," the paramedic shouted, "this guy needs immediate emergency care—he's crashing!"

Yazeed's bodyguards rushed into the ambulance alongside him as his heart was being resuscitated in a desperate attempt to save his life. Meanwhile I collected my winnings and departed with my beautiful Ziva snugly attached to my right arm. What a reward for having defeated the world's premier arms dealer.

Ever vigilant Benjamin and Françoise walked several paces behind, covering our backs. Thirty million dollars was no small pot of gold. Together as planned we headed to the bar to relax, celebrate and await confirmation the mission had been accomplished.

The ambulance sirens blasted through the night, forcing cars and pedestrians away from the main thoroughfare. However, amid the evening ruckus, the two bodyguards failed to notice the nurse strap on an oxygen mask over her face seconds before a muffled hissing sound invaded the rear of the ambulance. Both men grew drowsy, collapsing into a deep narcotic induced sleep. What they failed to realize was that upon awakening they would find themselves in another country; a destination destined to alter their lives and Yazeed's.

The ambulance continued its hurried pursuit, making a sharp right onto a dimly lit side street leading away from the Hospital. Immediately the sirens were silenced. In the distance a jet sat ready to transport the trio to their new home.

When the vehicle pulled up beside the aircraft the pilot deplaned. A young blonde steward ran to the back of the ambulance to meet the gurneys. The paramedic helped unload his precious cargo and transferred the sleeping beauties to the jet. Bound and disarmed they were taken prisoners.

Quickly all evidence was removed from the ambulance, discarded on the runway and set a fire. No one could ever depend on a mound of ashes to prove any wrongdoing. It was perfectly orchestrated and all clues covered.

When the jet took off I received a call that eased the tension in my neck and shoulders and put a smile on my face. Witnessing my transformation, Benjamin, Ziva and Françoise applauded. The mission was accomplished.

"In just a few hours, our friend Yazeed will have a new home," I announced. "We must now tie up loose ends.

Paul Lamont, Yazeed's three young ladies, and the remaining bodyguard must be convinced they are in grave danger unless they immediately flee to a distant destination. They will be informed that his organization will seek a culprit to blame for the mysterious disappearance."

"I think money will take care of Mr. Lamont," Ziva said. "It will silence him. As for the rest, I think it best to spread the word that the irate Iranian leader lost his patience with Yazeed and upon hearing of his trip to the French Riviera decided to set him up as an example of the consequences befalling those who procrastinate in complying with his wishes."

"*Brava* Ziva—excellent reasoning: Brains and beauty, what more could a man ask for?"

"And don't forget brawn," she replied punching me on the arm.

"It's been a long stressful day. Poor Cuoco, she is probably feeling lonely and abandoned. Let's dedicate some love and attention to her. We can continue where we left off tomorrow," Benjamin suggested. "I hope everyone agrees our way was best. I'd hate to have to resort to more drastic measures."

# XXX

Our mission with Yazeed was unanimously termed successful. We had eliminated a global threat without actually taking his life. However, we had some unfinished business to tend to. Moreover, I had to pay Mr. Lamont a visit. Visibly shaken by the previous evening's events, I could only begin to imagine his thoughts.

"I'm off to see Lamont," I said, walking out the door.

"I'll follow just in case a situation may arise," the ever faithful Benjamin added.

"No need Ben, why don't you remain with the girls. I'd rather you keep an eye on them. I'll call as soon as business is finished."

Much as he neither agreed with nor liked my suggestion, he complied with my wishes.

"I'll be back shortly and we'll celebrate the outcome of the mission with another wonderful dinner signed Françoise."

I turned and departed without giving anyone the opportunity to even leak a comment. En route to Mr. Lamont's I reviewed the *scenario* in my mind. Within minutes I pulled into the dimly lit driveway. Entering I was escorted to his office by a short slender, well dressed middle-aged gentleman in dark rimed glasses.

"Mr. Lamont, Tony is here to see you."

I walked in just as Paul was turning in his swivel chair to greet me. Rising to his feet, I noticed his complexion pale.

"Good evening Tony, how may I be of assistance? Have you heard any news about Mr. Yazeed?"

"That's why I am here," I responded feigning concern. "The word is he was abducted by some powerful individuals who are not in agreement with the Western World's way of life, and transported to their country along with his two bodyguards. For some reason you are being named as a catalyst for his fall from the Muslim faith."

"But I had nothing to do with any of it," Lamont stammered, clenching his fist. "I merely took care of his casino needs. What could anyone possibly want from me?"

"I really can't answer that" I replied, "but I am sure you're aware these people do not think like we do. My advice to you would be to get as far away from here as possible and the sooner the better."

"Tony—I don't have the resources to do what you are suggesting," he said. I noticed a row of glistening sweat beads roll from across his brow down the side of his hollow cheeks. All color had drained from his complexion.

"Perhaps I can help you. As you know, I won a great deal of money last night and I do feel some responsibility for your situation. Would two million provide a comfortable life style in the Cambrian?"

His eyes grew wide with surprise and relief.

"I can give notice today and be on my way with my companion tonight," he replied. "But, I'll have to give my employers a reason."

"That's the easy part. Tell them your aunt passed away and left you a great deal of money and your presence in the United States is required to handle the bureaucratic paper work for the inheritance. Once there you can deliver your resignation; then disappear without any traces."

"Great plan Tony! If you'll excuse me I'll start packing immediately. Thank you, I will be indebted to you forever." He grabbed my hand in a gesture of gratitude and appreciation.

One down and four to go, I thought as I drove back to meet Ziva, Benjamin and Françoise. Now Yazeed's three women and his remaining bodyguard had to be dealt with.

Pulling up to the villa I spotted Benjamin taking Cuoco for a walk.

"Perfect," I whispered, "just the man I need."

"How did it go Antonio?" he asked, opening the car door. In a split second Cuoco was on my lap, brushing the tip of my nose with her warm moist tongue.

"*Stai calma*—calm down Cuoco," I said patting her head. "Will you let me get out of the car?"

Benjamin reached in and lifted her off my lap, leaving me free to turn and exit the vehicle.

"The first part went well," I confirmed, "but I'll need your help to settle the rest of the situation. Let's continue the discussion inside; I want Ziva and Françoise to be involved."

"Involved in what," my love asked, catching my final words. How astute she was—nothing would ever slip by her.

"In dealing with Yazeed's three women and the bodyguard. Lamont will be gone in the morning."

"I think it would be a good idea if we all went to see the girls, to calm them down. I'm certain they are scared and questioning what happened to Yazeed. Besides, we don't know what languages they understand."

"Good idea Ziva," I complimented. Let's go find them."

"Did you ask Lamont if he had any idea where the three girls and their bodyguard might be?"

"No my love, I didn't. "Be patient a moment while I ring his office before he goes out on the run."

I obtained Lamont's extension number from the receptionist. Grabbing the lobby phone I hit the right numerals to make the connection. Careful to thwart eavesdroppers, I whispered several words before returning the receiver to the cradle.

"We're in luck," I said, turning to Ziva, Benjamin and Françoise. "Apparently the three women and the bodyguard are in the hotel awaiting news about Yazeed's condition. Let's pay them a visit."

"I'm ready," Ziva said.

"Please notify them of our arrival," I instructed. The concierge lifted the receiver to comply with my wishes.

I led the way directly to the elevator with a quick almost impatient pace. My team followed, hardly daring to lag behind. Once inside, while the ladies checked their hair in the grey fume' mirror, Benjamin tapped the top number. When the door opened, we headed to the end of the corridor.

Without pausing I knocked twice.

*"Entrez*—come in," a husky male voice ordered. Judging from the emphatic tone I was certain our visit was not viewed as a friendly encounter. Ice cold eyes met mine the moment I pulled open the door. He's not exactly thrilled I thought, chuckling inwardly. Actually he agreed to allow us entry, thanks exclusively to Lamont's reassurance.

When I surveyed the surroundings I was shocked to gaze upon three scrubbed faced teenagers dressed in casual every-day clothing— a far cry from the exotic, heavily made up ladies of the evening spotted at the casino during the card game. My guess was they were 18 or at maximum 20 years old.

"Why are you here?" the steel faced bodyguard growled in heavily accented

English while sliding a hand over his weapon. Do you have any information about my employer?"

Walking over to him, I repeated the words I had spoken earlier to Lamont. I emphasized the sinister role of the other two bodyguards in Yazeed's employ and their intentions to take over his business.

"It was all a plot," I said firmly.

"That's a lie! We did no such thing," he shot back, reaching for his gun. Caught off guard by the sudden cold hard metal pressed against his spine, and my arctic gaze, fixed on his, he realized he failed to notice the short stocky man approach from behind.

"We all know it's not the truth. It is a story, Yazeed's second in command concocted so he could take over and push the blame on others," I said. "What is your name?"

"Ashmed," he responded. I observed as his shoulders curved forward then sagged. Leaning over, I removed the weapon from his waist band.

"Your English is not bad," Ziva said.

"Yazeed requires all his employees to be fluent in at least three languages."

"Do any of you speak English?" I asked, turning toward the three young girls. No one responded.

"One girl is from Turkey," Ashmed volunteered and the other two are from Iran. They all speak Arabic."

"Good" Ziva replied in Arabic. "I assume you all have passports."

Immediately all three nodded affirmatively, a gesture quickly mirrored by the bodyguard.

"If we arrange to have you fly to Italy, and provide you with sufficient funds to take care of your needs, would there be a safe place you can go to?

The young lady from Turkey raised her hand as if she were still in school: "My name is…"

"Stop!" Ziva interrupted; "it will be safer to keep your identities secret. We just want to be certain you have a safe haven for refuge, because you cannot return to your homes."

"We have often discussed how we would live if we ever gained our freedom," the young Turkish woman said, assuming the spokesperson role for the group. "We were sold to Yazeed by men who snatched us from the safety of our families in the darkness of night. I know we cannot return to the land of our birth, but I do have relatives in Canada who would be eager to offer refuge. Once there we can send for our loved ones."

Within minutes my cell phone buzzed. Lowering my eyes, I noticed the call was from Benjamin.

"Antonio, as usual your name worked like a charm. It's all set up. Françoise and I are ready to take the girls to the jet. The pilot has been advised of the journey and will file the proper flight plan. Françoise and I feel we should accompany them to Naples, and remain in their company until they board their flights. You and Ziva can go home. We will contact you as soon as they are safely on their way."

"Sounds like a good plan—I should have thought of it myself," I said.

"It's been an endless and exhausting two days, consequently, four heads are better than one," Benjamin chuckled.

"This is one of those few rare times during which I see Benjamin so relaxed and laughing," I commented to Ziva. My gut feeling is that everything is going to turn out right.

"Let's get moving or nothing will happen," I said. Ziva jumped to her feet. I motioned the group to follow me to the elevator. Two minutes thereafter, we exited through the back entrance of the hotel, unobserved. As planned, Benjamin and Françoise where waiting to escort the girls to the limo and bid each a safe journey.

Shortly before dawn the following morning, an unmarked plane landed on a secret runway, known to just a handful in the upper ranks of the Mossad. Upon touching ground the three narcotized passengers were quickly whisked off to an unassuming white building where the target man, Yazeed was transferred to a private room. Less fortunate, his two bodyguards were taken to another area and secured in a locked cell.

Meanwhile Yazeed woke with what seemed like a serious hang-over accompanied by concussion like confusion. Trying to collect his thoughts and focus on his last conscious memory, he recalled the sudden onset of a sharp chest pain with gradually worsening pulmonary congestion. Looking around the room he tried to get his bearings. It all seemed so sterile, so unfamiliar. Suddenly his eyes focused on a diminutive man who seemed lost in the huge chair he was occupying. On his face he wore a huge smile.

"It's good to see you awake," former General Levy greeted; "are you hungry? Would you like something to eat or perhaps you'd prefer a refreshing drink?"

Yazeed shook his head as if trying to flush out the cobwebs. He gazed at the vaguely familiar face trying to recall his identity and where they had met. And then like a bolt of lightning he suddenly remembered who and where he was. With the flash recognition a rush of fear spread within, leaving him overwhelmed for the first time.

Meanwhile, Ziva and I returned to the villa somewhat anxious. We had agreed to wait for Benjamin's call announcing the success of our mission. To keep her nerves from fraying my lover drew a warm aromatic bubble bath before indulging in full immersion. I on the other hand, sought a functional diversion attending to Cuoco's somatic and natural needs. If nothing else, a walk would perhaps help me consume some of the nervous energy fueling my restless dearth of patience. Thirty minutes thereafter, I was in the shower, purifying mind and body.

In the interim, Ziva slipped between the sheets dressed in a shear red silk teddy top with nothing underneath. Swishing the soft plush towel against my shoulders I paused a moment to glimpse the delicacies soon to be mine. Like a bolt of lightening igniting the sky, I was fired up to claim my treat. With the graceful pounce of a mountain lion I took my reward. The pleasure was all consuming. From nowhere specific a deep growl arose in Cuoco's throat. I turned just in time to catch the short thick hairs on her neck rise. With the swiftness of a gazelle, she walked toward the bedroom door.

Who or whatever is at the door risks strangulation, I thought jumping into the pair of pants I had dropped beside the bed moments earlier. Snatching my gun from the nightstand I left the room and headed toward the stairs. Cuoco, my vigilant bodyguard kept pace with my footsteps, certainly questioning as I did if the alleged prowler was friend or foe.

When the door bell echoed, I quickened my stride as did my faithful companion. Nearing the entry I noticed through the glass pane, two uniformed men from the local *Police Municipale.* Quickly I tucked my gun behind a large bronze statue in the foyer and gave Cuoco the command to sit just as I pulled open the door.

"*S'il vous plaît pardonnez-nous,* please forgive us," a middle-aged officer of medium stature greeted. I could see his jaw tighten betraying his anxiety.

"*Monsieur* may we speak with you a moment?"

"Certainly how can I help you?"

"We are investigating a missing person alarm, a man known as

Yazeed, and were sent to ask you a few questions about him and the rest of his entourage.

"We questioned all who participated in the card game. You *Monsieur* are the only player we were unable to contact until now."

"Come in I will be happy to answer any questions I can. But be advised that my friends and I probably cannot supply any information you don't already know."

"*Merci Monsieur.*"

"I first met Yazeed at the casino the night of the big game. Initially I was unaware of his identity or professional aspirations until one of the other players told me how he earned his livelihood. Quite frankly if I had this information previously, I doubt I would have sat in the game. I don't like being involved with people like him: they scare me."

"Yes, you are correct, *Monsieur*," the officer said; this man is definitely not someone you would want as an enemy."

"Exactly—anyway my friends and I are leaving as soon as we take care of our own affairs. It's too bad things turned out as they did. We were looking forward to enjoying a relaxing and fun vacation in your beautiful city."

"We are sorry you are leaving. This is usually a peaceful city loved by tourists and natives. There are no more questions. We await the return of *Monsieur* Lamont so we can put an end to this matter."

You will wait forever, I thought, knowing full well the man in question was long gone.

"*Encore un fois*—once again, kindly accept our apologies for the disturbance. Please do return to our lovely city again."

"*Merci*—we certainly will."

From the corner of my eye I noticed Cuoco had assumed a standing position. She was even more intelligent than I had thought. Dark olive eyes darted from me to the men in uniform as she followed every word of the conversation.

After the police left I gave my canine companion a pat on the head.

"*Brava* Cuoco," I whispered. "Now I need a good stiff *espresso*."

Once the thick dark brew touched my lips, I sat quietly reviewing how efficiently Yazeed's girls and Ashmed at been dispensed with. Ziva was definitely on top of the situation, arranging a series of checks each in the amount of $50,000 dated at one year intervals for a twenty year period, plus an additional $20,000 for their personal expenses. All three received the same "stimulus package." This would take care of their needs for quiet a lengthy period of time.

I smiled, imagining the surprised expressions on their faces, once they emptied the envelopes. Ziva was undoubtedly a jewel. Consequently, it was now time for her recompense, a payment I too would enjoy.

# XXXI

It was time to proceed to the next step. Seated with my ever faithful Cuoco beside me I awaited Benjamin's call announcing the resolution of our last issue. Meanwhile not one to squander time in idle reveries, I reviewed the file on Zarin Doust. In all honesty the Mossad had not put together a detailed dossier. With the exception of his role as a key source of funding for many terrorist operations around the world through his vast drug operation, not much else was revealed in the few pages of the file.

Details about his private life were non-existent. It was not easy to design a mental picture of a man when so little facts were available.

"Antonio have you found any kinks in Doust's armor?" Ziva asked, strolling across the sun-lit patio carrying in each hand a steamy cappuccino. When the aroma of the freshly brewed beans teased my nostrils, I reached for the cup without taking my eye off the page I was reading. Guiding my reach she placed the cappuccino directly in the palm of my hand just as I shook my head in answer to her question.

"Be careful—it's scorching," she admonished.

I took a cautious sip, wary not to burn my tongue, and placed the sizzling brew on the table.

"I know this may sound strange, but except for his drug and money funding dealings, he lives somewhat of a monastic life."

"What do you mean by 'somewhat of a monastic life?'?"

"Well he has no apparent vices, no affairs or sexual escapades with women, men or children, and he's not a known gambler."

"Sounds as if he will be harder to bring down than the other two—that is without making it seem like a Mossad intervention." Ziva said.

Before I could respond, the phone rang, momentarily interrupting our discussion about Zarin Doust.

Glancing at my beautiful love, I reached for the phone, hoping for the best.

"Antonio—we're on our way home." Benjamin's voice was loud and up-beat. "Everything has been accomplished. Françoise reassured our four friends that the money would be there for them as long as they maintained their part of the agreement to keep a low profile, and stay clear of the radar so that Yazeed's men would not be able to find them."

At what point are they now?" I asked.

"The three girls are flying to Canada, while Ashmed is en route to enjoy freedom in the USA."

"*Bravo* my friend and give a kiss to Françoise. We need you—come back as soon as possible. This last guy will prove to be the most difficult to take down. As soon as you and Françoise get here, we will return to Italy and start devising a plan of action."

"We should be landing in about two hours, assuming there are no unexpected delays," Benjamin said.

"I don't want to waste any time. Ziva and I will start packing. Tell the pilot to refuel if necessary. *Ciao* for now. Have a safe flight. When you land I'll up-date my father."

"Do you think taking Doust down will be more complicated than the others?" my love asked, as soon as I ended the conversation with Benjamin.

"Only because the information we have is not very detailed. Apparently he has no known vices unless he is a master at camouflage, which is doubtful. Also, he has a very plain and simple lifestyle, is an impassioned believer in the Muslim cause, and uses all the money from his drug dealings to fund the destruction of Israel and the Western world."

"There has to be a crack in all this," Ziva sighed. We'll wait for the others to get here. They are on their way."

"You are right, love, we should head to the airport."

When Benjamin and Françoise deplaned, we exchanged kisses and greetings, and immediately departed for Italy. Time was of the utmost importance. Moreover, I was eager to see my father and listen to any advice he was willing to impart.

The flight to Italy was quick, smooth and relaxing. I spoke with Benjamin while the girls exchanged light hearted banter, until we landed. Once at home, I quickly freshened up and approached Father.

"Antonio you have a tough job," Demetri said after I filled him in, "but I am confident you will succeed once again. We'll discuss more in the morning. Come let us join the others before your mother becomes irate."

Of course my meeting with my mother was sweet and emotional as always. She treated me upon every return as the prodigal son returning to the fold after an endless absence. I had to admit, though certainly not to her, that it was somewhat endearing.

When I returned to my room I summoned Ziva, Benjamin and Françoise. It was time to draw up a plan and plot a strategy.

"Let's meet in the dinning room," I said to Benjamin. How about in thirty minutes?

"We'll be there."

Prompt as always we reunited. We sat huddled together, surrounded by endless sheets of note paper decorated with line after line of hand scribbled information.

"This is frustrating," I said, jumping to my feet. "There has to be more than what meets the eye. Obviously we are missing something—but what?"

"Calm down—we'll find it, my love" Ziva said, extending her hand in a gesture inviting me to return to my seat. "Time is still on our side. Furthermore, Doust is unaware we are after him."

"True—but the longer we procrastinate, the more money he will raise giving him the power to destroy our people and create a climate of war," I responded.

Perhaps you can fall back on your expertise with the long rang weapon you used so successfully in your other life," Benjamin suggested.

"Wouldn't that point the blame directly to Israel" Ziva asked. "That's the one thing we must try to avoid at all cost."

Just then Demetri Bastone walked into the room, pulled out a chair from the table and slid in.

"I have been giving considerable thought to your project, and have come up with an idea," he announced. "I'd like to get your opinions."

"Father, we are all ears. At the moment we trapped in a frustrating impasse."

"Son, you have won a great deal of money. Why not let it work for you?"

"What do you mean? Can you be more specific—do you have something concrete in mind?"

"Who among the people we know might have more information about this man and his organization than your friends from Israel"?

"I know Frank Aiello does not deal in drugs. Perhaps one of the other Dons views things differently from Frank," I said. "To tell you the truth, Father, he is the only one I trust."

"As do I—especially with money matters. There is no predicting what people will do for dollars. I have known for years that the Turks and Pakistanis have no great love for the Iranians, although they do business together. Perhaps the same holds true for those who deal in the poppy fields."

Demetri rose from the table. "I'll make a few phone calls and find out if my suspicions are correct. In the meantime I'll leave the four of you free to put your heads together and devise a plan."

"Thanks Father we always appreciate your intervention."

"You'll get him Antonio—I have no doubts."

"Sure appreciate your optimism."

"Remember—We are not defeatists!"

As soon as he departed I considered Benjamin's comment about my expertise with long range weapons.

"You gave me an idea Benjamin," I said, "suppose we applied our skills to take out some of the lower echelon of Zarin Doust and his suppliers' organization. This could trigger a war among them, maybe even rendering Zarin a battle causality."

"I like it Antonio—you're a genius," Ziva shouted. "Moreover, it's about time we start fighting the way we know best."

"I agree with Ziva," Françoise said. "Actually I'm pretty sure we are all in agreement."

Heads nodded affirmatively as Demetri re-entered.

"Do I see a unanimous agreement here," he said smiling. "Well while you were discussing, I was on the phone for over an hour with some rather influential friends. My suspicions are correct. The Turks are one of Zarin Doust's biggest suppliers, and although he has not created any problems, his constant haggling over price has caused a rift among the growers. They feel he is taking too big a profit from their labor."

"Do I see a ray of light here?" I asked. "If I am not mistaken, our man Doust may actually have a flaw. This is perfect—just what we need to seed a battle between the two groups."

"What are you thinking Antonio?" Benjamin jumped in.

"We have approximately $19,000,000 remaining from the game, plus the $5,000,000 I started with. This gives us a total of $24,000,000 to invest."

"Invest?—what do you mean." I could see Benjamin was intrigued.

"$24,000,000 is sufficient to start our new business."

I noticed my father straighten in his seat. He was clearly interested in hearing my plan. "Father is there a way we can contact the Turks to buy drugs without your personal involvement?"

"Do you think I would have returned unless I had the information you need?" Demetri said laughing. "I knew you would use the money to finish Doust. However, I must caution you. This is not an easy task. You are dealing with ruthless individuals, and if any of you were harmed, I'd never forgive myself—plus your mother would kill me."

"We will be careful," I promised, hoping I could be true to my word.

"Antonio, their lives are in your hands," he said, handing me a sheet of paper. Of course Father knew I would die protecting my faithful teammates.

Within seconds he gave me a paternal hug and departed.

Curious, I glanced at the names and telephone numbers scribbled in my father's hand writing. As my eyes darted down the page I realized they were a blur of unknowns, until one name grabbed my attention: President Bellini of Italy who, rumor had it not only enjoyed the white powder, but sold it to his wealthy friends.

Next to the President's contact info was a note advising I could use his name when dealing with the Turkish growers. Thankfully Ziva spoke Turkish and would fill the role of interpreter whenever necessary. The unfamiliar identities on the list were growers. Two were signaled out with asterisks, and classified as *unhappy* with Zarin.

"I think the best way to attack Zarin is to use his frugalness," I said. "Ziva I'd like you to call the two men whose names are starred since they seem to have points of contention with Zarin. Advise them you are speaking on behalf of a very wealthy group of men who are interested in purchasing large amounts of cocaine. Given that no middle men are involved, the group will pay top dollar for their efforts."

Ziva reached for the list and immediately dialed the first starred number. After three rings a hello echoed through the receiver. Several minutes into the conversation I noticed her voice took on an aggressive tone, which led me to believe she was getting flak for being a woman. My gut told me this was a situation they were unaccustomed to and certainly uncomfortable with.

"The boss speaks English," she whispered, handing me the phone, and will speak only with the man in charge." Her flushed complexion and quickened breaths hinted she was angry and upset. When she gave him the finger I had the confirmation. Smiling, though careful not to let her see my parted lips, I took the phone.

"Hello—my name is Tony. With whom am I speaking?"

"Tito! Tony will do for now until we get to know each other a little better."

"Agreed. Let's get down to business and the reason for my call. First of all, do you want my action—yes or no? If yes, are you capable of handling an opening order for 300 Kilos?"

There was an almost uncomfortable pause at the other end of the phone. "Do you know how much money is involved?" I said interrupting the silence.

"For all I know you could be Interpol or some other law enforcement agency or even some organization trying to rip me off," Tito said indignantly.

"Would a call from President Bellini of Italy offer reassurance?"

"You are close to the President!"

From the surprise in his voice I knew I had pushed the right button, especially since it was well known in certain environments that the President was closed and private, allowing few people into the inner circle of his *side* business.

"I can give you his private number," I said. "Verify my reputation whenever you wish. You still haven't answered my question. Can you supply my needs or should I look elsewhere?"

"I can fill half your order—another customer needs the remaining."

I knew he was referring to Doust.

"Listen Tito, I'm not interested in someone else's needs. I'm willing to up the ante. How does $15,000 more a kilo sound?" I was certain he was stunned by my offer to increase the price by four and a half million, pushing Doust into a bad light. He would surely enjoy hearing the rage in the cheapskate's voice when informed of the sudden inflation and the new price he would have to pay if he wanted the merchandise.

"Let me get back to you, Tony, I have to make some calls."

Once again I could read him like a book. Blinded by the profit surplus, Tito's first and only call went to Zarin Doust to inform him a new player who was willing to pay far more had entered the game. True to expectations, the Iranian was enraged, deviating from his cool, calm and collected demeanor.

In the meantime I asked Ziva to phone other growers, mention Tito's name and make similar offers. Obviously all were eager to do business as there was no love lost in their relationship with the Iranian. This created the much desired domino effect as Doust started to receive several calls regarding the sudden inflation hitting the market. All he knew about the new organization was the name Tony. When he had calmed down sufficiently, he demanded information about these individuals—who they were and where they came from. He was coerced into offering something concrete to the questions he was bombarded with.

"Doust—their head is Tony," Tito said nervously, "and I must give him my answer."

"Call and tell him you are willing to accept his offer. Set up a time and place, and inform him there is a $2,000,000 good faith deposit."

"What's in it for me," Tito growled, feeling uneasy.

"I'll raise your share in my business 50% and give you $5,000 more per kilo—how does that sound?"

"I'm in."

"Contact me as soon as all the arrangements are finalized. I want more information…like who these people are and who their boss is."

Nodding his head as he spoke into the phone, Tito agreed. "This is great," he whispered after hanging up. "I win either way. More profit and more business: but first I have to make the call that will change my life forever."

Meanwhile Ziva and I awaited the much anticipated ring of the phone.

"Calm down," I said, he'll call. And before I finished the sentence the phone was buzzing.

My beautiful love responded on the fourth ring, not to appear exceedingly anxious. "It's him," she mimed, covering the speaker with her hand. She is clever, I thought smiling as I reached for the phone. .

"Hello" I said, following an almost half-minute pause. I listened as Tito spoke briefly.

"I have no problem as far as the money is concerned," I responded, "but I will tell you where and when we will meet. If this arrangement is not possible, just say the word, and I will take my business elsewhere."

A sigh shattered the silence. Tito's greed trumped all, even suspicion and caution! My guess was that he would inform Zarin regarding his unavailability to pursue further, unless he agreed to my terms.

Additionally, I had approved the $2,000,000 good faith deposit, which he felt he deserved for his part in the deal.

Satisfied to have once again received confirmation that greed always triumphs with individuals like Tito, I drew a deep breath. The bait was dangling in the water. Now I had to find a location that would reassure them, yet provide me a clear, precise shot from my deadly long range weapon. As always there was no room for error.

After discussing with Benjamin, Ziva and Francoise, we chose a small airport in Turkey since it was Zarin's homeland. The familiar territory would calm any fears Tito might be entertaining. Additionally, the wide open space would make it difficult for them to orchestrate any traps. The plan seemed air tight. Confident, I phoned Tito to lay out the time and place. Given that the airport was just a 45 minute drive from his house, he was agreeable. Shortly thereafter, Zarin was notified of the details.

I uncovered the sniper's weapon that had served me so well over the years, and earned me the Silent Assassin title during my years of service with Israel's Special Forces. I had to make certain it was in pristine condition.

Benjamin cleaned his Glock scrupulously, Ziva busied herself with her knifes, and a small but powerful 38 caliber pistol, and Francoise sharpened a tiny razor she believed might come in handy in close contact. The energy was vigorous; the silence thick like a slab of cement, until Demetri entered accompanied by a man we all loved, Domenico: Hat in hand and a sawed off double barrel gun tucked under his arm.

"My son this man has saved my life more times than I care to remember. It would reassure me and your mother if he would be part of your team for just this one mission."

I walked over to Domenico and with a simple hug demonstrated my consent.

"He is more than welcome to join us; thank you Father. I know how much Domenico means to you; therefore I will make certain he returns safely.

Tito may not be aware the airport we selected for our meeting has been closed for about two years, but I am sure Zarin will be well informed and have extra men on standby. There are three small hangers plus a deserted tower. All can be used to set a trap. Ziva and I will arrive there two hours earlier than the scheduled meeting.

The tower is perfect for me to assemble my equipment. Ziva will be my back-up."

"Son, I see you are well organized as always."

"These are missions with great potential danger, and I want to be sure we will be successful without incurring any casualty or catastrophe."

"That's the only way," Father said, rising to his feet. "I'll leave you with your team to finalize plans."

"Thanks Father, you will be fully briefed," I promised. "But now we must get down to business.

Benjamin, you, Domenico and Françoise will meet Tito. You will have the money he requested. If he asks for me, just tell him I am nearby waiting for your call confirming everything is proceeding according to plan."

"Hopefully it will all run smoothly," Ziva added.

"Well—I wouldn't bet on smooth. I expect Zarin and company to make some kind of move on the three of you. But rest assured—at the first inkling of trouble I will take them out from the tower."

"Benjamin, don't kill Tito. I need him to up-date Zarin on all that has occurred. He must understand that we intend to work with the other suppliers to satisfy our needs."

"Don't worry Antonio, I'll be sure Tito sees the money in the duffel bag. By the way I checked with the Bastone jet pilot. Flying time to the closed airstrip is between two and two and a half hours depending on weather conditions. Since the meeting is scheduled for 1:00 PM, take off should be at 5:00 AM to allow sufficient time to get everyone there."

After the plan was carefully reviewed with Benjamin and the ladies, I began packing the items Ziva and I would need for the mission, including an Uzi and enough ammunition to handle any and all unexpected problems. I suggested to my team mates that relaxation and an early to bed ritual was my advice considering the day ahead. There was no opposition.

Though not required, Françoise had fresh brewed coffee and a handful of biscotti on the table at 5:10 AM the following morning. She was truly a jewel. In silence we took full advantage of her offerings, before departing for the airport.

# XXXII

The take off was seamless, and within a little more than two hours we were in the midst of a rather bumpy ride along the abandoned airstrip of an airport which had been shut down over two years prior. As instructed, the pilot taxied to the old dilapidated tower. Though badly in need of repair, it was perfect for our needs. So far everything was perfect.

The jet came to an abrupt halt. We exited. Ziva and I unloaded the gear, headed up the tower stairs and turned to wave to the pilot. I glanced at my watch calculating the trip and unloading took all of two hours and twenty minutes. We were right on schedule.

The odor of humidity and mold was pungent and penetrating. Quickly I surveyed the surroundings in search of the best window to offer protection from any eventual enemy fire. Simultaneously I located a successful spot to set up my weapon. The small window adjacent to the main viewing area seemed appropriate.

"Ziva this is perfect," I said pointing toward the window I had selected. Walking over she gave a quick browse.

"From here you have a full view of the landing strip, and a clear shot at anyone exiting the car—Tito and his bodyguards."

"Yes—it looks like everything is going according to plan," I said, drawing a deep breath. "But we are just at the preliminaries."

"Let's sit a moment and unwrap the box your mother prepared for us."

"You do the honors, my love," I said, watching her eye the package with curiosity.

"I'm starved—I hope it is food."

"You continue to eat like a linebacker and look like a model. I'll never understand it. I guess life is not fair at all," I teased laughing.

Once unwrapped, we enjoyed a much coveted cappuccino and delicious cold chicken, arugula and sliced tomatoes, resting between two slices of crusty Italian bread. We consumed the "box breakfast" enjoying every mouthful as if each was a morsel of a finely prepared gourmet meal.

As usual Mother was right—Ziva and I were starved.

"Antonio—your Mother is precious—look at the wet wipes she included so we wouldn't soil ourselves like children.

We enjoyed a hearty chuckle, cut short by the echo of tires crunching the gravel along the pock marked runway. Quickly we assumed our pre-designated positions in front of the window we had designated as the kill zone.

My heart raced! Three men of stocky stature exited the car in front of one of the vacant hangers. Over their shoulders high powered rifles were slung. Belts crammed with extra ammunition, circled their thick waists.

"I tip my hat to Zarin," I whispered; he had the same idea or call it premonition I did. Thankfully time was on our side."

The men opened the old hanger and drove the car out of sight. As I had predicted, they were components of plan B, devised as a security measure in case something went awry during my meeting with Tito.

I gazed at my watch. I had just several hours to resolve this unexpected development.

"We have to get rid of them as fast as we can," I said. "If they step outside I could take them down from here, but I'm not sure I could do it before one of them gets word to Zarin."

Just then the side door to the hanger opened and one of the men walked into the humid morning air, slapped a pack of cigarettes across his knuckles, pulled up the sprouting butt, lit up, inhaled and slowly exhaled the toxic poison from his lungs.

"This guy is addicted to that junk. I bet he is back outside in less than fifteen minutes. If I'm right I can take him out with this," Ziva said extracting the stiletto from the leather case strapped to her side. It will be quick and quiet and when the other two come looking for him it will be your turn, Antonio."

Ziva was right on the money. In approximately thirteen minutes the same man emerged from the side door of the hanger to enjoy a smoke.

Lochman as he was named drew the last bit of smoke from the strong Turkish cigarette he was hooked on: "One day these things are going to kill me" he said, tossing the still smoldering butt, unaware someone was listening. Little did he know his prediction would ring true sooner than anticipated.

"Time for me to go," Ziva announced; "I can work my way around the side of the hanger where there are no windows and come up behind the back of the door. The next time he steps out for a light up, I'll slit his throat, and he will smoke no more."

"Hurry—go now the sun will rise shortly and I don't want you to be seen. It's too dangerous. If anything happened to you my life would be meaningless," I said, giving her a quick kiss on the lips.

"I'll be back soon. No need to worry."

In the blink of an eye, Ziva was gone. As planned she worked her way to the far side of the hanger ready to insure Lochman's destiny with death would be on time. Almost to the second the tall Iranian stepped out for his last cigarette. What precision!

Lochman reached toward the pocket of his shirt eager to gratify one of his pleasures. Flicking his lighter brought immediate satisfaction. However, cutting the pleasure short, a long slender arm yanked his chin up causing him to drop both the unlit cigarette and the lighter. With a quick clean swipe and agile hand Ziva severed all sound and feeling except for a muffled gurgle—Lochman's final word. In less than ten seconds he was on his way to *rigor mortis*. Stained to the waist with blood, his lifeless body lay on the cement floor.

Immediately Ziva dragged the deceased Iranian away from the open door. Hurriedly she placed him alongside the hanger, making certain he was out of sight to prevent his colleagues from discovering he had been eliminated. Crouched beside the corpse she waited, not daring to take a breath, hopeful the others would come out together, allowing me to successfully complete my part of the mission.

"Lochman! Lochman! Where the hell are you?" a deep voice bellowed. "You and your stupid habit—it will be the end of you one day! You know how important this job is to Zarin." The words grew louder as the man approached the door. Within minutes, the mysterious voice had a face. Stepping outside a muscular guy in dark rimmed glasses, gave several glances to his surroundings, expecting to catch sight of his friend. Had he glanced down and to his left he would have noticed a trail of blood originating from behind the hangar door, meander toward his scuffed boots.

"Ishmael—get out here—hurry! Something is wrong and I may need your help."

He had an eerie premonition things were not as they should be. Ziva heard the thumping echo of Ismail's booted feet pounding the cement as he ran toward the open doorway. Suddenly he appeared; his automatic rifle at the ready.

Ishmael reached the man who so animatedly beckoned him just in time to see a bullet bore a hole the size of an orange, in his head. In a heart beat he was prostrate. Like camouflage paint, a spray of blood covered his face, masquerading his broad distinctive feathers. A trained fighter, Ismail dropped to one knee weapon at the ready, peering through the pre-dawn darkness trying to pin point the exact location of the sniper's attack.

He never knew what hit him. Perhaps he saw the flash of light that announced the fatal shot aimed at his cardiac region—perhaps not! But in an instant he was gone. Tumbling face forward, he landed parallel to his fallen comrade.

Ziva signaled me with her right hand: I had the confirmation that the first step of the mission was completed. It was also my cue to leave the tower and help her dispose of Zarin's disabled plan B puppets. Together we dragged the bloodied corpses into the very hanger they chose as a safe haven, and shoved them one by one into the car that carried them to their death.

"What about all this blood?" Ziva asked.

"There's a pail and shovel in the tower. We'll bury the stains under dirt and rocks. I doubt anyone will notice the cover-up."

"That went pretty smoothly!" she said smiling.

"Yes—thankfully. Now we have a few hours to regroup and recoup before phase two begins.

"I noticed a dripping fountain. Let's wash up and get ready."

"Good idea," I said, extending my arm in a chivalrous gesture to invite her to the water source.

The splash of cool liquid felt revitalizing on our tired faces. It was amazing how restorative water could be. Refreshed, we sat side by side on the hard floor. Ziva rested her head on my shoulder.

"It feels safe," she whispered. I smiled, caressing her cheek.

"My love, we're ready for the next act to unfold."

"It's almost time," Ziva responded, gazing at my watch. They should be arriving at any minute now."

I nodded in agreement, gently lifted her head, planted a reassuring forehead kiss, stood, and elevated my eyes skyward to check for any signs of an approaching jet. On board would be the rest of the crew arriving to help with the next phase of Zarin Doust's elimination.

"Did you hear that Ziva" I whispered. "Sounds like a plane coming in for landing."

Just then a large black van headed toward the hanger raising a mound of dust, unaware it was now a mausoleum housing the remnants of the ill-fated plan B participants.

The landing was bumpy. The wheels screeched as the unmarked plane came to an abrupt halt. On its heels a black truck with a heavily smudged windshield pulled up not more than 30 yards distant from the aircraft's tail. The rest of the team was here.

When the door of the jet opened a short stocky man carrying a large duffel bag exited. Following close by, a petite women and massive burly man stepped forward. Though older, his presence was intimidating. Benjamin, Françoise and Domenico were here to complete the team. Receiving the confirmation I desired, I breathed a sigh of relief.

Meanwhile the van doors slid open revealing six heavily armed men. One by one they emerged, forming a straight line in front of the open doors. The silence was interrupted exclusively by the echo of mincing soot and gravel, underfoot.

"All's clear," a voice shouted in Farsi. "It's safe to come out!"

A short man standing not more than 5'3," Tito had an oversized head, noticeably cropped arms, and a pair of stunted hands resembling those belonging to an adolescent.

"Are you Tony?" he chirped in a high pitched voice befitting his diminutive stature. Nervously he fixed his gaze on Benjamin. Domenico stood in silence several paces behind.

"Tony will be here shortly," he responded, hurling his duffle bag at Tito's feet.

Gazing down at the tightly fastened bag, Tito summoned one of his men with a brisk hand gesture.

"Look inside" he bellowed, in his native language.

Approaching the sac, the tall muscular man dropped to one knee and pulled the long curved knife hanging from a belt partially hidden under his long navy pullover. With a wide sweep of his arm, he sliced through the rope securing what was supposed to be Tito's reward for setting up these infidels for Zarin.

The scene was *manna* to the eyes of a starving man. Tightly fastened packets of money trickled through the large gash in the fabric. Judging from the satisfied look swiping across his face I was certain, even from afar, he took pride for his part in the deal with Doust. A fleeting glance at Ziva told me she was in full agreement. Tito had no idea we witnessed his meeting with Benjamin, undercover.

"When do you expect this Tony character?" Tito asked feeling cocky. He now had the cash and likewise the advantage. Money was irrefutably a power tool.

"Tony should be here any minute" Benjamin replied. "In the

meantime I'd like to see some of the coke his money bought him," he continued, waving his hand toward the exposed cash.

Again Tito addressed one of his men who quickly turned toward the van as if preparing to get the requested merchandise. Instead, he wheeled around pointing his weapon at Domenico. Stymied in his tracks by a sudden blast from the double barrel shotgun his designated victim had hidden behind his back, he never knew what hit him.

Three shots rang out in quick succession. Each bought down one of Tito's bodyguards, all with parts of their brains oozing through their bloodied hair. Benjamin whipped out his Glock with incredible speed, immediately eliminating the last player. Standing alone with an icy razor pressed against his skinny neck, Tito babbled for mercy. At least he had the smarts not to underestimate Françoise's ruthless commitment as she held the weapon steady against his pulsating jugular.

While Tito begged for his life, he spotted a tall bearded man accompanied by a beautiful woman with the height and demeanor of a runway model. Desperate but not irrational, he realized the mysterious Tony was approaching with the woman he had spoken with on the phone.

I elongated my gait, impatient to reach my destination. Ziva followed.

"Françoise I have it now. You can step away and remove the razor," I said.

"Tito—This is how you deal with a man who is willing to give you a $2,000,000 good faith deposit and place an order costing an additional twenty million"?

"You don't understand, Tony, this was not my idea."

I could see he was trembling.

"I'm just following Doust's orders. He told me to do this and to find out who you are and who you are connected to."

"Who is Zarin Doust?" I shouted, leaning toward his sweaty face, "and what business is it of his who I buy from—whether it's you or another supplier?"

"Zarin is the biggest dealer in the Middle East. He was upset that you offered more money than he had been paying. Let's say he is not someone who likes to part with money. In fact for a man who handles hundreds of millions in drugs each year, he lives a very Spartan life, comparable to a religious leader."

Tito's word confirmed all the information I had received from Mossad.

"Listen Tito—I suggest you go back to Zarin and inform him that we are not to be messed with. My people control most of the docks around the world; therefore if he wants a fight, he will get more than he bargained for. Furthermore, we will no longer consider you in any future dealings. The loss of many millions will be the price you pay for not informing us of Doust's double crossing plans. Is that clear?"

"Ye…yes Tony—but it is not m m my fau…"

"I don't care whose fault it is. I'm not interested in excuses. It should not have played out in this manner. Besides, you can take back the three men Doust sent to eliminate you if anything went wrong. They are in the hanger next to your van."

Tito turned his gaze toward the last resting place of Zarin's backup plan and shook his head no. His strategy was to negate he ever knew anything about the surplus men or the arrangement.

"You can also inform your monk boss that we anticipated his intentions from the start: for that reason no one is alive except you."

I knew the seeds I was planting would eventually drive Zarin crazy. He would no longer have a responsible trustworthy man.

"Go—you're free to go Tito. Just get lost," I said. Still trembling he staggered toward the van, breathing heavily.

"Now we can sit back and watch Zarin destroy himself without lifting a finger," Ziva said.

I had to admit it was satisfying to watch Tito drive off in the van, a tiger with neither claws nor teeth, a scared and broken man without a tomorrow.

"Back to work," I announced as we walked toward the unmarked jet en route to the next phase of our mission.

Meanwhile Tito drove to meet Zarin, his heart pounding like a jack hammer. Overcome with a sudden paroxysm of coughing, he was powerless to loosen the knots of panic forming in his throat. Considering the news he was carrying, he fully anticipated the rage of his boss once up-dated about the events occurring at the air-strip.

However, the scene took a different turn. When informed, Zarin remained silent. Only a throbbing vein on his right temple betrayed his anger.

"You didn't have any additional assistance?"

"Nothing at all—I swear on the life of my family. We were unexpectedly ambushed by a large group of well-trained, armed men. All your guys were killed. It was a trap. And they never brought the good faith money as promised."

Sure it was a blatant lie, but Tito knew if he told the truth he would be dead on the spot. This was a life or death situation and he wasn't a gambling man especially with such high odds stacked against him.

"It sounds like this man Tony is part of the Mafia. What does he hope to gain by cutting into my territory and resources?" Doust questioned.

"Perhaps it has something to do with the 9/11 attacks. They might have lost family and for those people family is everything," Tito responded.

"You may have a valid point; I will start looking into it at once. Keep your mouth shut on this. Do you understand?"

Nodding affirmatively, Tito turned and departed from his boss' Turkish office. As soon as he was out the door, Zarin buzzed for his number two in command.

"Hassan I want you to contact some of our Italian friends and find out if there is a new player from their organization cutting into our line of work. I don't have too much information except that he answers to the name of Tony, and works with a beautiful woman who speaks Turkish and Arabic."

Leaving Zarin still fuming over the loss of nine of his best men,

Hassan nodded and left the room, ready to start his fact finding mission. In his mind churned possibilities pointing to the traitor who divulged the secret concerning the trap he had set up.

Much as he despised Tito, he knew he was not the culprit since he was uninformed about the three extra men sent as backup in case anything unexpectedly twisted out of kilter. Moreover, Zarin neither welcomed nor relished gaining full control of any situation, and the more he lingered on the thought the more enraged he grew.

"Hassan, as a first order of business we must find out all we can from his American partners who earn big in the white powder business."

"I'll get on it, and alert you as soon as I find anything relevant."

"I await your call," Zarin replied spinning in his mind, the names and interactions of his loyal team in a desperate attempt to find a word, gesture, action, anything that might provide a clue to the betrayer of the cause. Sadly he found no one who presented even the slightest hint of suspicion or concern.

Something was slipping past his attention. He was a bright man, some even considered him brilliant, yet he could not find the slightest evidence of a blatant betrayal that had cost heavily. He believed his steadfast confidants would sacrifice their lives for him, and remain deeply committed to the pact they had made to rid the world of all disbelievers in Allah.

Resting his aching head on the desk, Zarin suddenly sat up-right when Hassan knocked.

"*Gelir*! Come in! Any news?" he asked. Hassan shook his head no.

"It seems no one has any idea about what we are talking about and I must admit as much as I dislike them, I do believe they are telling the truth."

Not happy with the response, Zarin waved him away without making eye contact and returned to his thoughts. From a side glance he noticed Hassan's lingering presence.

"Is there something you failed to tell me?" he asked, gruffly.

"Well—once I ruled out the Americans, I questioned who would benefit most from this situation."

"Of course" Zarin shouted. "It is so simple. I overlooked the obvious even though it was right in front of my face. It has to be the Turkish connection. Apparently they have become discontent with the vast amount of money we made for them over the years."

Hassan smiled, satisfied he was able to help resolve a pressing situation.

"What now? What's next?"

"Bring Tito to me at once. If that piece of camel dung is not directly involved, he will certainly know who is. There is a reason for the sudden stand they have taken regarding their demand for an increase in price. No one takes money meant to provide us the possibility to keep our pledge to Allah to return the world to its rightful faith!"

"Exactly" Hassan responded bowing his head. Turning on his heels he headed for the door.

"Thank you my friend. Thank you for showing me the light in my tunnel of darkness."

Zarin took a deep breath, rose to his feet and stretched like an alley cat awaking to a sunny day after a tempestuous evening of icy winds and deluging rains. Convinced he was on the right track he relaxed. Apparently the newfound certainty was the perfect remedy for his excruciating migraine. As it arrived like a ton of bricks, it suddenly dissipated into thin air.

# XXXIII

It was always exhilarating to be back in Italy. Benjamin and Françoise decanted a bottle of Amarone della Valpolicella from Father's prestigious collection. Ziva selected the appropriate crystal glasses to best savor the delicious nectar. Seated in the garden at the Bastone Estate, I felt relaxed and empowered to take on the next part of our mission.

This stately villa was now home to all of us. We loved to unwind and gaze up at the starry sky. Regardless of the nature of our thoughts, or the stress we incurred, the evening panorama always presented a phenomenal light extravaganza that was both distracting and palliative. Despite the perilous challenges of our profession, we were able to find not only serenity but the sense of calm we coveted, especially during missions.

I knew this part of the plan would be risky. A different breed of man was involved. But toying with men's minds was like playing poker. To win the game equated to identifying the opponent's weakness and possessing the skill to exploit it. I felt comfortable with the realization that I had gained expertise at this sport.

"May I join the party," Father billowed, lighting a cigar, fully conscious that if Shanna caught him he would be scolded like a small child surprised with his hand in the cookie jar. Benjamin and Françoise courteously excused themselves, understanding Dimetri wished some alone time with me and Ziva.

Not blessed with any female offspring, Father considered my beautiful love as a daughter, though I knew deep down he was thrilled the

Bastone name and company would continue for future generations, thanks to our efforts.

"Antonio, I have some news for you," Father began; exhaling a dense cloud of smoke. "I received a call from Frank Aiello. It seems a number of phone calls have been made by individuals seeking information about a man named Tony and a woman fluent in several languages who want to purchase huge amounts of cocaine. Nothing odd here, except there is the implication the couple is connected to Frank's group of friends in the United States."

Frank wondered if there was anything he needed to be told, and of course he offered full assistance. I took the liberty to assure him that at the proper time he would be well informed of all the events."

"Thanks Father, I believe that the less people know about us the safer we will be."

"Son, I never did ask how everything turned out; though I am sure you were successful as always."

"Yes—it went well. We were prepared. If I read Zarin correctly, once he receives information that Tony is an unknown in the business he will consider the Turks his biggest threat to the operation. Moreover, knowing Tito as well as I do, it is my opinion he will lie to save his own skin and not have any qualms about pointing fingers at his competitors, naming them the culprits behind the plan to get more money."

"Antonio I'm happy you're on top of it."

Pleasing my father was like a shot of caffeine upon rising. It empowered me to pursue our goals with even more drive and vigor. I felt secure with the knowledge I had of the players, and was certain Zarin was not enjoying tranquil days. He had to know something was brewing in the kettle.

Meanwhile across town in Turkey, Tito was surprised to receive a phone call from Hassan, Zarin's second in command, announcing he would be picked up in a half hour to attend another meeting. His questioning mind left him speculating what could have possibly changed in just a few short hours since their last reunion. The feeling in his gut was one of anxiety and ill omen. Something was wrong! Did Zarin discover he had been lied to about the events that had taken place at the deserted airstrip?

As the sole survivor, reason told him it was impossible. Furthermore, the mysterious man named Tony would not say anything, realizing Zarin would have him killed on the spot.

Tito gave strict orders to his men: "If I'm not back in one hour or if you fail to hear from me attack Zarin's compound and try to get him out."

Although a man of diminutive stature, he was a ruthless killer with the names of many victims listed in his curriculum vitae. Ultimately a man does not rise to top status of a powerful drug cartel without possessing a completely functioning brain, and spine of steel. However, Tito did admit in the secrecy of his own silent thoughts, that Tony left him soaking in his own sweat—and this was a first!

When the car pulled up, he climbed in noticing Hassan was seated in the rear behind the driver.

"Do you know what this unexpected convocation is about," Tito asked?

"You will know when we arrive," Hassan whispered, granting just a side glance in his direction. The little man could not help pondering if his time had come or if some unforeseen unknown was about to unravel.

"I have a problem, and I think you are the man who can help me resolve it," Zarin whispered making eye contact. Though his tone was soft to the ear, there was an icy hardness in his words.

"If I can I'd be more than willing. What is the problem?"

"I believe the man called Tony does not exist. I have contacted my sources in America as well as other regions and no one seems to know him or anything about him. Additionally, I'm told there are no new big players on the scene. There is only one explanation for what has happened, and I think you may have information that would be quite helpful in resolving my dilemma."

"Well I…"

Immediately Zarin pressed his index finger against his narrow shut lips, signaling Tito should hold his thoughts as he was not finished speaking.

"Have you heard any grumbling or words of discontent from the other growers? Has anyone made it know there was dissatisfaction about the price or conditions pertaining to our arrangement?"

A quick thinker, Tito grasped the situation at once, processing ways to take advantage of the question asked. Since Zarin was unaware of the truth, he assumed it was a set up by a group of growers to get more money for their product.

"Before I answer you question, I'd like to make a call that could prove very valuable in our discussion."

Without waiting for a response Tito stood and walked over to the opposite end of the room. He made certain Doust was not in earshot when he reassured his men all was proceeding according to plan, thus advising them to wait for his return.

"Zarin," he began rerunning to his seat, "although there is a great deal of discontent among some of the growers, only two have the smarts to come up with an idea such as you suggest—Nazaire and Rega."

What Zarin failed to realize was that these two individuals were Tito's largest competitors. In fact they had approached me from time to time, but I merely brushed them off as caterers of greed.

Zarin rose from his chair, and extended his hand toward Tito who instinctively grasped the outstretched limb. Both men shook hands firmly.

"Your help will be well rewarded, and never forgotten. Now I will ask Hassan to drive you back to your farm. I have a great deal of work to do and urgent matters to take care of."

When Tito was no longer present, Zarin busied himself summoning his suppliers to a meeting. The pretext was a discussion centered on adjusting the prices to a higher amount. Following the financial announcement, he planned to kill Nazaire and Rega, two sacrificial lambs chosen to teach the others a lesson.

Zarin contacted seven of his largest Turkish suppliers, inviting them to a dinner followed by a meeting to discuss his price increase agenda for the little flowers that not only built his patrimony but also strengthened his terrorist outlets across the Middle East. The *rendez-vous* was set for the day after tomorrow to allow everyone ample time to fly in.

Zarin phoned Tito to confirm the event, and invite him over before the official start of the meeting: Tito obliged, unaware of his motive. Quickly dressing, he hurried over. It was well known that Zarin was not one who enjoyed the waiting game.

When Tito entered his eyes focused on a grim faced individual. Something was not right—he felt it in his gut. The other invitees including Nazaire and Rega sat with stoic expressions, easy to read.

"Tito, do you think I am stupid?" Zarin shouted. From the tone and content of the opening words, the small man realized he was upset. "Did you believe for one moment I would not run a check on the mysterious Tony, a man no one has seen, a faceless individual who is merely a voice on the phone?"

Beads of sweat formed along Tito's brow. His pulse raced. Squirming in his chair, he struggled to keep his fear under wraps. Of course my existence was not a secret.

"You cost me nine of my best men," Zarin yelled, hardly pausing to catch his breath. From stoic the facial expressions of the others in the room turned to bewilderment. It was clear no one had an inkling why the boss was so enraged; no one except one individual. Whipping out his prized 1944 German Luger, Zarin fired two shots, immediately ending the lives of Nazaire and Rega while the others, flabbergasted from the harrowing scene, dove for cover.

"Hassan, remove these two traitors from my presence," he ordered, posing his weapon on the table. "Enough time lost—now let's get back to business."

The silence in the room was disturbed exclusively by Tito's sudden sneeze and muttered apology.

"Perhaps I have been a little harsh with the money arrangement,"

Hassan continued. Of course I realize costs have escalated; therefore effective immediately you will all receive a two percent increase for all future shipments."

Stiff up-right postures relaxed, as the men slid to the rear of their chairs, breathing sighs of relief.

"Tito, for the next few months, until things settle down, I would like you to run the farms of our recently departed friends. Any objections?"

"No Hassan, I accept the challenge," Tito replied.

"Good—does anyone have any questions or concerns?"

No one spoke up, giving him the response he wanted.

"OK let's finish our drinks and head back to work."

Eliminating Nazaire and Rega was a fatal mistake on Zarin's part. News not only of the assassination, but the brutal manner in which it was executed spread like a brush fire during a drought, reaching the ears of one of Turkey's fiercest group of bandits. Ruthless individuals they paid to protect the men who had been gunned down by the Iranian drug dealer, like rabid beasts. Two days following confirmation of the vile deed, a meeting was held in a perilous region of Turkey, few would dare visit.

A tall young man with a full dark beard, answering to the name Malik, sat on his horse gazing downward upon men he had engaged in battle with many times, leaving his enemies hopelessly defeated.

The group leader, he waved a weapon high above his head shouting; Nazaire and Rega must be vindicated or our word will mean nothing."

"We were well paid to protect and keep them alive; therefore the responsible assassins will pay with their own lives."

"İran köpekleri öldürmek—Kill the Iranian dogs," a voice screamed. A chorus of rahs shattered the quiet as throngs of men repeated in unison; "İran köpekleri öldürmek!"

"We must plan a course of action," Malik said. "I'll phone my close aids and begin strategizing a course of action. It is known that Zarin resides in a heavily guarded compound; for that reason a direct attack would result in unwanted casualties of innocent people. Bring Cari and Khan here at once," he said turning to the man seated at his right. "They are two of our most intelligent women. They will get us the information we need about Zarin."

All heads nodded in approval. Certainly women were far better suited for this kind of knowledge seeking, and would be beyond suspicion to Zarin's men. Malik's picks, Cari and Khan were far from novices though obviously neither elderly nor head-turning bombshells. Instead, they were bright, experienced, and fierce combatants. If anyone could excavate and find information, it was these two women.

Summoning the ladies, Malik waited, for their arrival, reviewing the plan of action in his mind. They arrived, ready for another challenging assignment.

"Go to the town were Zarin's compound is located," he instructed. "You must find a way for us to get to him without jeopardizing our safety. I will send two of our best men along as a safeguard, just in case."

"No" Khanh said; "that will be more of a hindrance than a safeguard. Cari and I can take care of ourselves. Having bodyguards would compromise our secrecy, draw unwanted attention and make the job more difficult.

"Alright it will be done according to your wishes," Malik agreed. "Take whatever you feel is necessary for the trip."

"It's the best way," Cari added as she and Khanh mounted their horses and left the forest, Malik's preferred meeting place as it provided his bandits the reassurance of safety and the concealment they desired.

The women headed toward Zarin's compound, a journey of at least three hours. Aided by the evening's darkness they planned to stop along the outskirts of the town to rest until day break. Zarin controlled this territory, monitoring arrivals and departures with a vigilant Big Brother eye.

Everything Zarin did was the result of planning, hence selecting a small inconspicuous Turkish village to locate his base was neither a haphazard decision nor left to chance. He knew the religious leader and most powerful man in Iran, {the Ayatollah} was a key voice in the destruction of Israel. He also knew the allies frowned upon the drug business as a way to finance the Holy War.

Zarin felt secure operating in Turkey, confident he would be protected from any possible reprisals orchestrated by the fanatics in his homeland. Precaution had led him to build a virtual fortress, including a prayer room for his twice daily implorations to Mohammad, the prophet and messenger of God.

Located one mile from his home was the small Mosque he had funded, a place of worship that enabled him to maintain a thriving association with Mohammad during his Friday evening visits. Thanks to his successful drug trade, he had the monetary possibility to isolate himself from other worshipers during prayer.

Although sentinels were paid to guard Zarin's compound, Cari and Khanh rode into the village unobserved. Such was their expertise.

Heading for a little cafe they were assured food and shelter since the proprietors, Turish and Zanish were Malik's relatives. The network was fully equipped to accommodate the information gathering process. Zarin did not have the exclusive in this camp.

Greeted warmly and treated to a nourishing repast followed by a warm bath, Turish and Zanish expressed their availability to be of assistance. However, discretion was respected as neither questions nor intrusive conversation took place.

"We are here to find all that we can, and as quickly as possible about the man I believe is called Zarin, who lives in the secluded house in the center of town," Cari said. "We already know he is well guarded 24/7 and when he leaves the fortress he travels in a helicopter, rarely taking the car."

"Give me a day or two and I will try to uncover some additional information. I want to speak with the domestic personnel who take care of his living quarters. Surely they will have something to add," Turish replied.

"Now tell me, how is my nephew? Is Malik well, and has that devil found a girl to bear him children yet?" Both women chuckled.

"Why should he settle for one, when he can have a multitude," Cari replied. "Let him live life and enjoy his youth. He is too young to be straddled with a wife and children."

"Thanks for the warm hospitality," Cari said, rising. "It is getting late and we should get to sleep. Tomorrow will be a busy day."

"And we must awaken early to catch the morning shopping crowd at the market," Khanah added.

Retiring to their room they planned a strategy for the information gathering process. For the next two days both women wandered around the market places and cafés, ears tuned to intercept any clue or echo of gossip that might be either of importance or interest to Malik. Unfortunately their efforts netted nothing of value; just the mention of his name followed by a few choice curse words. Apparently his reputation was truly not that of a beloved, well revered man.

Cari thought it best to up-date Malik concerning their unsuccessful attempts to discover any pertinent information about Zarin. Cell phones sure come in handy she thought swiping her finger over his name and number.

"Don't worry" Malik's voice rang loud. Eventually you and Uncle Turish will pick up on something. It's bound to happen."

In fact Malik was right. Luck has more than once played a major role in solving a problem. A couple of days thereafter, late on a Thursday evening two women walked into Turish's café. Immediately he recognized them as individuals he had been looking for. They seated themselves in a corner of the room, and waited to be approached.

"These two ladies come here almost religiously, every Thursday evening," Zanish remarked under breath as Turish walked over to their table.

"Iyi akşamlar, good evening; may I help you with your order," he asked smiling. "Is there anything special I can get for you lovely ladies?"

Waving their hands in a playful gesture they implied—we know you are a married man but we like your flirtatious teasing.

"We'll have the usual—potato leek soup, braised short ribs and a bottle of Pinot Noir." They eyed him coquettishly while ordering.

"Excellent choices, ladies: Would you like to have the wine as you pick on some bread and olives?"

Glancing at each other for mutual consent, they responded affirmatively.

"Enjoy your dinner; it will be here shortly," Turish said heading to the kitchen to place the order. Within minutes he had returned, with a basket of warm bread wrapped in a white and blue linen cloth, an olive oil mixture for dipping, and a perfectly chilled bottle of chardonnay.

"I notice you ladies like to come in on Thursdays," he said, uncorking the wine. Though curious to know why, he refrained from pursuing further for fear of disturbing with personal questions.

"We work for Mr. Doust, the Iranian importer-exporter, and for Iranians Friday is a day of rest—they don't work. I think it has something to do with their faith. We don't really care about his reasons. He is a strange man in many respects, but we do like having Fridays off."

The conversation was immediately referred to Malik as soon as Turish returned to the kitchen.

"*Amca*, Uncle, please ask them to keep their eyes on Doust and the compound all day and night tomorrow. Tell them to be super vigilant."

"Don't worry—Malik, I'll take care of it."

Turish hung up and summoned all who could be trusted, informing them their funding for time and effort would be provided upon request. However, not one of the volunteers requested reimbursement. They arrived, immediately to discuss his surveillance plan to scrutinize every square inch of Zarin Doust's fortress. There was neither room nor time for slip-ups.

Within hours of the call, all Turish's volunteers were stationed either on roof tops or the hills behind the rear of the compound. To insure security, it was enclosed within an eight foot barbwire topped wall constructed to prohibit unwanted intruders from trespassing.

The men carried high powered binoculars to enable them to clearly focus on all sides and angles of the property. No one and nothing could enter or leave the premises without their knowledge.

It was just minutes before sundown when a black armor plated stretch limousine with darkly tinted bullet proof windows exited the front gate and headed around the back. Like soldiers ready for a mission, six heavily armed men marched out from a well hidden door followed by Zarin Doust. All climbed into the limo.

The volunteer sentinels prepared to follow their subjects.

A small mud-incrusted car trailed behind the limo for about two miles until it arrived at an old building, which had been converted into a Mosque many years ago. Zarin emerged from the car, walked up to the front door and knocked. Seconds later, a man appeared, stepped across the threshold and planted two kisses, one on each of his cheeks. The body guards formed a circle around the Mosque, faithful to their Friday tradition.

Entering a narrow room which was separated from the main prayer area, Zarin unrolled his *seccade*, prayer rug, making certain the niche at the end was pointed toward Mecca as is required. Lowering himself down on his knees, he stretched out his arms and began the chant he had recited since his senior year in college, when he fully embraced Islam. Closed in his own conversation with Allah, his visual and auditory senses were tuned exclusively to his solitary presence and the sound of his voice in prayer.

About 20 minutes thereafter Zarin exited, imparted a kiss of gratitude to the man who had held the door open for him, handed him an envelope and headed toward the limo. Meanwhile to avoid any suspicion, his guards in the parked vehicle were instructed not to follow him back to the compound. All Zarin's activities were monitored. An up-date was promptly delivered to Malik who in turn referred the news to *Amca* Turish, awaiting further instruction.

In the interim his nephew selected Adem, Emire and Omer, three of his top men to accompany him to the village where Zarin lived.

"Each day, starting Monday one of you will go to my Uncle Turish's

Café and wait until all three of you are present. Be sure to wear simple clothing, nothing that signals you out from the norm. Indulgence in neither alcohol nor women is permitted, until the mission is completed. If any of you step out of line, even just once, it will be the last mistake you ever make. Have I made myself clear?"

"Clear," they uttered in unison, never doubting Malik meant every word.

"By our next meeting I will have finalized a plan to rid the world of this Iranian assassin who believes he can eliminate people under our protection without any accountability on his part. However, he will soon discover that his evil deeds carry a stiff bounty—his life.

"You may go now," Malik announced. Though not highly educated he was a natural leader whose mind already visualized how Zarin would take his final breath.

Recognizing the Iranian's affectation for privacy, he realized this very penchant for seclusion and confidentiality would be the *coup de grâce,* nipping him in the bud: his final blow.

As planned, one by one each of the three chosen men left their camp. By Thursday all were seated in a back room at the Turkish Café. When Malik pulled out his chair to join them, the group was complete.

"To my knowledge, which I believe fully reliable, Zarin heads to the Mosque every Friday to offer sunset prayers. He enters alone according to his specific wishes. No one is allowed in during his worship.

Our plan is to arrive at the Mosque an hour earlier making certain by whatever method you deem best, the elderly man who opens the door will not utter a word to tip him off regarding our presence.

You will keep an eye on him. But pay strict attention to anyone else who happens to be in the building. I will wait inside for Zarin. Uncle Turish has a concealed storage of weapons in the basement of the Café. *Teyze,* Aunt Zanish will take you down to choose a weapon of your choice."

After the final instructions, the men accompanied by Zanish walked down to the basement. The arsenal they discovered was sufficient to arm a small army. A long wooden table in the middle of the room was cluttered with weapons. Cari and Khanah stood cleaning each prized possession, one at a time. Suddenly from under his ankle-length robe, Malik extracted a long *kılıç*, a sharpened, single-edged slightly curved saber.

"This *Amca* Turish, will send our friend to paradise to meet Allah," he said, waving the sword high above his head. Now on to the Mosque!"

Hurriedly Malik made his way over to Zarin's place of worship. Focused and concentrated on his objective, he exited the car, walked over to the entry and with one knuckle slam against the door, made his arrival known. Immediately he was greeted by the elderly man who faithfully awaited Zarin every Friday at sundown.

"There is no need for concern," Malik said, stepping inside. Neither you nor your family will incur any harm if you do exactly as I say. My men will offer unfailing protection in your living quarters. You will let Zarin enter as in the past. There are to be no changes—not even a hint or you will die. This is a promise. Now take me to the room where Zarin prays."

Malik was escorted to a minute room, bare of any furnishings except the dark drapes in front of a large window facing east. He had found his perfect hiding place!

"What is your name?" Malik asked, signaling one of the men who stood directly opposite him.

"Bashire" he replied timidly. From his shaky voice and fidgety hands it was obvious the man questioned Malik's promise of safety for his family, assuming of course, he followed instructions carefully. He knew he had no choice but to follow his orders: a man must lookout for his family above all else.

"I will do as you have requested," Bashire replied, adjusting his head to establish direct eye contact. "But you must swear to me before Allah that you will keep your word regarding the safety of my loved ones."

"Fear not," Malik responded. "I want nothing from you or your family—this I swear before your Allah."

More than one person had misjudged Malik's integrity. Was he really a man of his world? The truth was not as transparent as he wished others to believe. If all went as planned Bashire and his family would live to spread the word: No one betrays, crosses or disagrees with him without suffering serious consequences.

According to habit, just as the sun prepared to set, Zarin's black limo pulled up in front of the Mosque. The six burly bodyguards jumped out, surveyed the area and waved an all clear signal, indicating it was safe for him to exit.

Zarin nodded, left the vehicle and as always strolled up to the entry door. He slammed his knuckles twice against the hard surface, announcing he had arrived. Promptly the keeper appeared, greeted him with the customary bi lateral kisses. Zarin entered and walked to the room where he felt completely at peace and distant from harm.

Unraveling his worn *seccade*, he dropped to his knees hands forward as he had done so many times before and started to chant, once again isolating his senses from any sight or sounds, but his own incantations.

Malik was ready to make his move, but decided to respect a man in prayer. Instead he waited until Zarin had finished, rolled up his *seccade* and exited into the foyer. From behind the drapes, he quietly extracted his *kılıç*. Taking a deep breath he stepped out and ran into the entry positioning himself directly behind his target. With one powerful stroke, he decapitated Zarin Doust. The last thought that entered the man's mind was the annoyance of a slight radiating pain located the rear of his neck.

Blood spurted, drenching the rolled prayer rug, spilling on the floor and oozing over toward the door. Careful not to soil his shoes with enemy body fluid, Malik stepped close to the wall. He cleaned his saber of all evidence rubbing it across the heavy brocade fabric, decorating the windows and entered the room where his men held Bashire and his family hostage.

Motioning to Bashire to join him outside, he whispered, "Now you must complete your task to assure your safety and that of your family."

"As you wish Malik," he stammered...."as you wish."

"Notify the bodyguards that Zarin suddenly felt ill. Summon them to come in to the Mosque immediately to assist him.

Shaking his head in agreement, Bashire opened the front door of the Mosque.

"Come quickly, Zarin is not feeling well. Hurry he needs immediate help."

Loyal to their boss, all six rushed past Bashire heading directly into the foyer. Greeted by the bloody mess, they stopped, paralyzed. Before they could regain their composure, three men appeared behind them, Uzis in action announcing their message of death.

In the blink of an eye, all six were pushed outside and left lifeless beside their headless leader who had been dragged out.

"*Afedin*—good job," Malik shouted, slapping Bashire on the back. "Not only have you saved your family, but you will now go forth and relate all that has taken place at the hand of Malik and his tribe of warriors."

He agreed though his complexion drained of all color. Malik and his men returned to *Amca* Turish's Café, boasted of their adventures, picked up Cari and Khanah and returned to the safety of the forest, completely unaware of the ramifications attached to their vile massacre.

# XXXIV

Zarin's death resulted in a fast-paced domino effect reaction, sending a rippling tidal wave halfway around the world. Outraged leaders of major terrorist groups were not resigned to forfeiting their main source of funding. Instead, taking root in their minds, were the seeds of reprisal to vindicate Doust's murder.

Meanwhile at the Bastone Villa I sat by the pool seeking a moment of relax eying Ziva's smooth movements as she completed endless laps in the glistening translucent water. Reflecting over the past several weeks, I realized how monotonous our lives had become. There had been neither scheming nor plotting: no discussions centered on specific plans. No orders from the Prime Minister to eliminate an inconvenient target were spoken. Now we sat eagerly awaiting the news announcing what we had set in motion had come to fruition.

Without removing my attention from Ziva's aquatic performance, I listened to the sound of my father's footsteps on the marble deck, signaling his arrival. He had a particular way to walk, especially when wearing his *ciabatte*, a leather flip flop style scandal he seemed to prefer.

"Frank just called me, Antonio," he said, immediately snatching my attention away from Ziva. "He had some gripping news. Apparently a big time drug dealer from the Middle East was decapitated by a crazed Turk after prayer in the entry of a local Mosque. In the process six of his body guards were also killed. Frank thought you might find this new turn of events interesting," he concluded with more than a hint of laughter in his voice.

"I just received word from the Prime Minister," Benjamin said before I could comment on Father's news. Walking across the patio he gave a quick glance at Ziva, still involved in her unremitting laps. "Her exact words were—'I don't know how you did it, however, it was undoubtedly well done. Now I would like to ask all of you to return to Israel. I have a very sensitive matter to discuss, but only face to face. Once again…well done.'"

"I guess it's time to go back to work," I said rising from my *chaise longue,* just as my beautiful girl climbed out of the pool. Her exit treated me to a luscious visual of curves and long limbs decorated with beads of gleaming silver drops. Reaching for the towel, she flung it around herself, ended my alluring vision, and strolled over.

"I saw your father arrive. Is there any news?" she asked.

"Yes—we are all meeting with Father, Benjamin and Françoise in 15 minutes."

"I was certain we would convene that's why I got out of the pool."

"And I thought perhaps you got tired," I teased laughing, though knowing better.

"No way—never happen," she replied taking off to shower and dress.

Precisely 18 minutes thereafter, we gathered together in the large dining room, each questioning the meaning behind the Prime Minister's message.

"I asked you here, to discuss our continuing strategy," I said, gazing around the table. When my eyes met, Françoise's I addressed her.

"You know how we all feel about you," I said smiling, and you also know you will always be well informed about our plans and the information and details we discover, however, I believe it would be best if you remained here at the villa while we meet with the Prime Minister for clarification of her requests."

Although I'm certain Françoise felt slighted, she tried her best to keep a stiff upper lip.

"I understand Antonio," she said, giving me a soft peck on the cheek. "I consider us family and decisions are made for the benefit and safety of all."

"You are phenomenal—thanks for understanding," I replied, winking.

"Get out your passports—we're leaving tomorrow for Israel. Father, will you please advise our pilot of the planned departure to make certain all is ready for a mid-morning take-off?"

"Consider it done, Son."

We parted company returning to our rooms to pack and prepare for the long journey ahead. Within minutes of hitting the pillow, I was out like a light, awakening the following morning to the enticing aroma of my freshly showered and perfumed Ziva, leaning over my bristly face.

"You're all ready to go," I shouted, sprinting towards the shower as Cuoco, tail wagging to the utmost, ran after me. "Just give me 15 minutes and I'll join you for breakfast."

"OK—Cuoco, come here, leave Antonio alone," Ziva said.

Surprisingly obedient, she turned and headed over to my love, who in appreciation gave her a pat on the head. Twenty minutes thereafter we united around the table for one of Françoise's delicious interpretations of *crostini di prociutto e uove strapazzate*, toasted Italian bread with thin slices of ham, topped with scrambled eggs. The bouquet of sautéed ham, melted butter and fresh brewed coffee, was intoxicating.

"Françoise," I said flashing a wide smile, this is fantastic as usual—you are absolutely a master in the kitchen."

"O Antonio, you like to exaggerate," she replied, her cheeks slowly flushing to pink.

"No No," Ziva, interrupted, "he speaks the truth. You are far too modest."

"I second that," Benjamin added.

Before parting company, we enjoyed a relaxing laugh while Françoise basked in the well-deserved praise we lavished on her. Breakfast concluded, we kissed grabbed our bags and climbed into the limo. En route to the airport we chatted and continued incessantly throughout the flight, until the sleek Bastone Jet landed on the runway reserved for dignitaries and leaders of foreign nations at the far corner of Natbag, Israel's Ben Gurion Airport.

Immediately I spotted the familiar black limo. Parked, it awaited our arrival. This time however, our customary driver was not behind the wheel. Regardless of the change, we climbed into the back seat and were whisked away to a diminutive building in the town of Ashdod on the Mediterranean coast, about twenty miles outside of Tel Aviv. Except for the heavily armed men and women stationed at strategic points around the simple structure, there was nothing odd, eye catching or questionable about the building.

Pulling to an abrupt stop, the driver leaped out, opened the rear passenger door and stood at attention as Benjamin, Ziva and I exited. Stoic and in silence he led the way into the building, and down a short, dimly lit corridor. Little did we know that behind the dark wood door in front of which he paused, sat a group of Israel's most powerful and influential people. Startled would be a mild classification of our reaction as we entered.

First to approach us with a smile and extended hand was Prime Minster Rachel Lagashie. Taking her cue, Ambassador Levy, stood to greet us.

"I would like to introduce you to David Barak," His Excellency said. The gentleman to his right rose to his feet followed by the remaining men in the room. "Mr. Barak heads the Mossad. To his left is Samuel Sharett, Director of Defense, beside him is Jacob Wiezman Israel's chief weapons developer, and last but not least we have General Abraham Cohen, Supreme Commander of our nation's fighting forces.

The presence of such high ranking military officials warranted our extreme composure and adherence to a protocol that required a stand at attention stance. Recognizing their names and rank I recalled having met General Cohen when I was commander of the company his tank unit was associated with.

"At ease," Ambassador Levy said allowing us to relax. "You are here today, because of the outstanding work you have done this past year.

This is a crucial moment for our country; therefore this meeting was called to discuss a problem that pertains to the survival of Israel."

"Thank you Ambassador," Prime Minister Lagashie said, rising from her seat. "The meeting will continue. First of all, I want to update everyone on the information we have received from Yazeed. Of course it has been verified by satellite photos produced by our highest ranking American friends."

"That's reassuring," Ziva whispered.

"Iran is much closer to obtaining nuclear power than we initially thought," General Cohen announced. While he spoke, the image of a building situated deep inside the bowels of Iran appeared on the monitor. "You will notice," he continued, pointing; "there are no windows, just tiny slits. Notice the dots—they indicate guards and helicopters flying above the building.

We have been told this is where the top scientists are working to complete the final pieces needed to arm the weapon that will be potent enough to reach Israel. Antonio—you, Benjamin and Ziva were summoned here at this time because your success in the first ever S.O.D. mission was commendable."

"What are you thinking General?" Ziva asked.

"At the present time we are exploring all our options, including bombing the building you are looking at."

"The fallout from such a direct action could result in almost as much damage as the bomb itself," the Prime Minister said. "Israel would become the global outcast and even our closest ally, the United States would not look favorably on such an action. Moreover, oil prices would sky rocket forcing many countries into financial chaos. Therefore, this must be our last resort."

I listened as the Prime Minister spoke, detailing how our planes would have to be refueled in midair. "It is important to note," she continued," that the countries they would have to fly over refuse to recognize Israel as a Sovereign Nation."

I formed a check list in my mind, and discounted many of the possibilities I was toying with for various failings and pitfalls which would compromise the mission. However, one idea that popped into my mind seemed obstinate and predominately unassailable. Feeling strongly about the risky aspects of a bombing strategy, I favored the accident simulation approach. If cleverly executed, this strategy would leave the Iranians believing they were at fault for the mishap. It was a foolproof plan.

"Forgive me Madame Prime Minister," I said interrupting her train of thought. "If I may, I'd like to discuss an idea."

"Of course Antonio—all ideas are welcome."

"If implemented, the accident simulation tactic would remove all reproach from Israel—in lieu of being a target for blame, Israel would be admired for restraint.

Your Excellency, can you give me a precise estimate regarding the time element? How urgent is this mission?"

"Mansur Raftab is scheduled to address the U.N. General Assembly five weeks from tomorrow. Consequently, it is our belief that he will announce to the world Iran's entry into the nuclear age," the Prime Minister responded.

"This does not give us much time," I replied, turning to David Barak. "Does Mossad have any high danger chemical weapons that could be used by one man, yet still have the potential to wreck serious havoc?"

"Nothing I can think of: Do you have anything in mind?" David asked.

"Is there a way to fill a 50 caliber sized bullet with some form of deadly gas and anything else that could cause panic and death?"

"Antonio, if we fill the nose of the bullet with cyanide pellets they would explode upon impact."

"Would high grade uranium result in the same reaction?" I asked.

"If you need that for your plan to work, it will be done," the Prime Minister, said. "What exactly do you have in mind?"

"I think the tiny dots in the satellite image are vents designed to supply fresh air to those working below. A sniper could fire six cyanide filled bullets from a great distance. The deadly compound would cause a silent death and the uranium would make the place uninhabitable for at least a century. But the best part is the haphazard catastrophe factor. It would seem as if the Iranians caused the tragedy accidentally," I said.

Listening intently, no one spoke. Excitement was building. Nevertheless, the simplicity of the plan left everyone stunned. But would it work? There were of course several wrinkles to iron out, though nothing major. I was confident we could pull it off.

"Who do you have in mind?" Lagashie asked, as if clueless. "Who will lead this potentially suicidal mission?"

"Who would be a better candidate than me?" I suggested smiling. "It's my idea. Besides who else can travel in the Arab world, welcomed as the son of a well respected man with whom they have business dealings?"

"You make a valid point Antonio," the Prime Minister replied.

"Now we have to focus on a way for me to get in and out safely, or you will all have to answer to my mother and grandmother."

"Getting you in is easy," Barak reassured. "As head of Mossad I have access to agents in both Saudi Arabia, and Kuwait City who can sail you across the Persian Gulf on their boat. Nonetheless, once on dry land, you'd be on you own."

"How far is the building from the Gulf," I inquired pointing to the satellite image on the wall.

"A ball park figure would be approximately 120 kilometers—75 miles from Abadan," Barak replied; "that is give or take a small margin in either direction."

"Once you get me into Iran, I can walk there. I've hiked more than that with an 80 pound knapsack straddled across my back."

"Since I will only travel in the dark to avoid any contact, it should take about two nights. I'm not the least bit concerned about this part of the plan."

"What worries you?" Barak asked.

"Well, the burning question is—how do I get out once the mission is completed?"

Benjamin stood up quietly: "I have the answer!"

All eyes darted in his direction, as curious, we awaited his suggestion.

"General Cohen, can you get a helicopter that is identical to the ones flying over for the target? And can you get your hands on their replacement schedule times?"

Following a brief silence, the General gave an affirmative nod.

"If the timing is precise, I see no reason for error. We can help Antonio get out, without incurring much risk," General Cohen said with conviction. His attitude gave the plan a simplistic nature, though everyone in the room fully recognized the importance of precision timing in such a potentially treacherous mission.

"Antonio, can you explain your plan in detail, and please no omissions," the Prime Minister requested, breaking her rather uncustomary silence. Standing she linked her gaze with mine. There was no doubting her wishes.

I obliged, though I had to admit this physically unassuming woman of petite stature had the power to wrestle with my nerves.

"My father can make arrangements for us to visit Saudi Arabia and Kuwait on business," I said, pausing to clear my throat. "Once there I will contact Barak's men and ask them to get me into the outskirts of Abadan. I will then proceed on foot, a distance of approximately two and a half kilometers—a mile and a half from the designated target. From that location I will be in prime position to execute my plan to fire six rounds into the air shafts. They will burst on impact, seeping lethal toxins through the ventilating system, causing the demise of most if not all the scientists working below.

"How will you get Antonio back safely?" The Prime Minister continued.

"I piloted helicopters before I moved to tanks," Benjamin replied. "I will fly the Iranian copter. At a certain point I will feign engine trouble, make an emergency landing near Antonio and then quickly fly off amid the post attack confusion and chaos."

"I understand there is a fourth member to your team," the Prime Minister said, "and I'm not referring to the dog."

"Yes that is correct," I replied. "Furthermore, Françoise is a person of trust and honor, invaluable to us. If for any reason we would loose her—we meaning in particular Benjamin, it would be a tragic loss. Therefore, she will not be participating in this mission."

Gazing into her attentive eyes, I had the confirmation Lagashie realized the significance behind my words.

"I hope Benjamin has found some happiness," she replied. He has given much to his country, to me and to all of you. I'd say he is duly entitled."

I could see the blood rush to Benjamin's face.

"She is..." he began...

"...a very valuable asset to our team," I said, finishing his sentence. She has proven to be intelligent, courageous and above all a loyal woman. Therefore, we asked Françoise to join us indefinitely during our stay in Monte-Carlo.

Personally I would feel lost, without Françoise," Ziva added. It was more than apparent the two women had a strong friendship.

"Did you really think we would not investigate a woman traveling the world with the three of you," the head of Mossad growled. The five individuals who ruled and protected Israel burst into laughter.

"We have information on Françoise, dating back more than a decade, Director of Defense Sharett said. I'm pleased to report we have discovered she is a good woman who lost her loyal husband. There is no need for concern—her dossier reports a spotless record.

We all breathed a sigh of relief, fully conscious these VIPs were well informed regarding Françoise's role in the death of her husband's assassin. However, I questioned as I'm certain Benjamin and Ziva did, just how much time would pass before the moment was opportune for them to reveal their knowledge.

Gesticulating with her raised left hand, the Prime Minister communicated it was time to put my plan into action.

"Mr. Wiezman," she said, "you have not voiced your thoughts. May I ask if high grade uranium can be infused in pellets that will burst open on impact?"

Eyes shut, brow furrowed, Wiezman sat motionless. Was he contemplating the riddle of the sphinx, I thought chuckling inside. Before I could pursue his reasoning, he was wide-eyed and alert.

"Madame Prime Minister," he said, "it would be tricky, but I do believe my staff could meet your requests."

"You do understand they must be transported in a lead lined container. And Antonio, you must wear special gloves when loading the weapon. Would that be a problem," she asked turning in my direction?"

"I don't think so," I replied. "I believe the noise from the helicopters overhead would drown out any sounds caused by my weapons."

"Good—I will need a few weeks to complete the preparations: a boat for crossing the gulf into Iran and Benjamin's helicopter."

"Be sure there is a smoke bomb aboard plus the radio frequency the Iranians will be using," Benjamin said. "Antonio and I will be able to use our satellite phones to communicate his precise location for the pick up and return."

"We have a lot of work ahead of us, and just a short time frame within which to finalize all plans," the Prime Minister replied, standing. "If there are no other questions or concerns, I suggest we meet again in three weeks for a progress report."

With her closing comments, the meeting was adjourned. We greeted each other with handshakes and Benjamin, Ziva and I departed for the airport to meet Calvin King.

A tall muscular man with short dark blonde curls and a ruddy surfer boy complexion, Calvin was the trusted pilot for the Bastone Corporation. His aviation skills were top of the line. Therefore calmly, we boarded the jet for the 2,082 kilometer, 1,294 mile flight from Tel Aviv to Naples, Italy. Within a few hours Mr. King steered the jet to a smooth stop in front of the family's private hanger at the Naples air strip.

Our faithful Domenico was standing like a sentinel, awaiting our arrival.

"Did you have a good trip" he asked, tipping his hat in Ziva's presence.

"Yes—thank you. It all went rather well," Benjamin responded.

We climbed into the car and were whisked off to the Bastone Estate where Mother, Father and Françoise eagerly waited for information about the meeting in Israel. Tired and hungry, we welcomed and reciprocated the hugs and double cheek kisses from Shanna, Demetri and, Benjamin's love, before re-uniting for a delicious meal.

Astute and experienced in the ways of the world, Father realized this was not the appropriate moment for excessive questioning. Curious yes, impatient perhaps, but certain he would eventually be up-dated, briefed and receive the much wanted answers to his questions. As always it was a matter of timing.

"I hope you will all sleep well," he said once we finished dessert. Tomorrow I'd like to hear about your trip to Israel."

"Thanks Father," I replied, flashing him a *you are a very wise man* look. Relieved for the postponement of the inevitable, I knew I had to find the right words to inform my parents of the imminent mission while trying my best to minimize if not conceal the high danger risk.

"And my thanks go to you Françoise" Ziva said, dabbing her lips with the white linen napkin. "I am filled to capacity, pleasingly satiated and now in need of a shower and at least eight hours of uninterrupted sleep." She rose from the table, grabbing my arm and then walked over to Shanna and Demetri.

"*Buona notte, dormite bene*—good night, sleep well" she whispered giving each the traditional two kisses before heading to her room, hand clasped in mine

Frustrated and anxious, Shanna remained in silence while Benjamin and Françoise trailed in their footsteps directly behind them.

It was so peaceful at the villa: a wonderful relaxing ambiance to enjoy before confronting another perilous mission. Less than ten minutes after my head hit the pillow, I was dead to the world.

Just as smoothly, I was fully awakened in time to catch the first burst of sun rays splash across the early morning sky. Walking toward the large bay window, I gazed through squinting eyes at the guest house across the court.

"What is wrong my love?" Ziva asked, yawning.

"You are so gorgeous, even first thing in the morning. I wonder what I ever did to deserve you. Why would God bless me so abundantly?" I questioned, turning to meet her glance.

"Truth conquers all—Antonio," she whispered circling her arms around my waist. " I too am disturbed by enormous worry this mission will cause your parents. It truly pains me."

"Generally speaking you are not a professional mind reader," I said, giving her a kiss, "however, when it comes to my mind you are phenomenal. It is almost eerie." I will try to be reassuring when I speak with Father."

"Do you hear the rustling from next door?"

"Yes Ziva—Benjamin and Françoise are up and getting ready for the meeting. Come on I'll race you to the shower."

Though the *douche a' deux* was more a rule than a luxury, somehow this shared shower seemed different. My love entwined her arms around me, pulling me magnetically, inviting me to feel as if she were an extension of both my body and soul. Hers was an embrace I prayed would be eternal.

"Ziva, we really must quicken our morning pace, dress and get to the meeting," I said reluctantly stepping back to rinse off. "I cannot postpone my conversation with Mother and Father any longer; we must speak to them now."

Unwillingly we separated. Within 15 minutes we were ready to meet Demetri and Shanna in the dining room.

"*Buongiorno*" Mother greeted as we walked in, and sat opposite my parents. The cappuccino aroma was penetrating as always.

"Françoise is a true gem," Father said sipping his steamy brew.

"I totally agree," Ziva responded, wetting her lips with the strong dark liquid.

"Now down to business," I began, interrupting the light chatter. I want to give you some highlights from yesterday's meeting in Israel.

I summarized the important points from our conversation, and mentioned the up-coming mission. Except for Shanna's taut jaw and a chilling look in Dimetri's eyes, there was an almost calm silence. They were certainly masters at self-control and the art of emotional camouflage.

"Is there anything I can do?" Father asked.

"Actually yes—you can contact our distributors in Saudi Arabia and Kuwait and inform them of my imminent business and pleasure trip with Ziva and our staff. We will provide the exact dates shortly, but we will take care of our own living accommodations.

Please emphasize our wishes for privacy, if they offer to host us. Additionally, it is important to convey our limited availability for social events. We will leave as soon as Mossad gives me the word everything is ready for the trip."

Much as it was not customary, I felt it best to cautiously omit a few details regarding the meeting in Israel, believing it was more opportune to avoid dwelling on the potential danger factor until a later date. However, I fooled no one. Dually wise and knowledgeable, Mother and Father were well aware of my concealing strategy, but agreed it was best not to pursue, certain they would have all the pertinent information in due time.

"I guess we are finished discussing," Dimetri said: "All has been said that was meant to be said. I will make all the arraignments to guarantee a profitable trip."

"Thanks Father, I appreciate your intervention. It is reassuring."

"I will do my best. Let me know if there is anything else you wish me to do."

We exchanged a final greeting before he departed to make good on his promises.

It was up to me to organize the rest of the trip. Time was an important element and we did not have a surplus to squander. There were incidentals that needed tending too.

"Ziva, I would like you to search on line for the appropriate garments for women in both countries. I want us to fit in and not be in anyone's eye. Meanwhile we will start settling the living accommodations as soon as I have more information regarding the locations of Father's distributors."

"Benjamin I'd like you to get me a full length camouflage suit. And please make certain it has a hood. I'll also need a flat two by four foot board, the night goggles we used during our battles in the desert, and of course sufficient rations to last two nights in Iran.

"I'll take care of it immediately," Benjamin reassured as he walked toward the door. "I'll phone Israel and the plan will be prepared, down to the last detail. Don't worry."

"I appreciate it," I replied and followed his departing footsteps, heading toward the guest house where I had my sniper's weapon and scope safely stored. They certainly had a track record of precision service.

"Well my friend," I said, patting him on the shoulder; "we must take extra precautions for this important mission—the mission with no option for failure because the very existence of our Country is at stake."

Within minutes I had my hands around the weapon. Carrying it to the kitchen, I began to clean it as I had done endless times before, only this time with eyes shut: such was my familiarity with the lethal arm.

"Antonio, you are going to Iran, "Demetri said gazing at the unassembled rifle, momentarily diverting my attention. Buried in my thoughts I had failed to hear his approaching footsteps. "You are the key player in the mission, just as your mother and I suspected."

"My plan—my job, Father," haven't I been training for the past years for something just like this?

"I will try to soften the explanation to your mother, although she has full awareness of what is coming to pass. Of course you do understand that it is her prerogative to worry about the safety of our only son, and rightly so considering the circumstances."

"I know, and I am sorry, but it is who I am, and what I have chosen to do."

"We do realize that, Son. Anyway I have contacted Zamal EL-Ralah our Saudi distributor as well as Hassen Mabbar from Kuwait. They have been informed you and your fiancée Ziva have requested a quiet, relaxing stay, after touring the facilities and visiting with the royal family. They assured me all social and business engagements would be kept at a minimum to honor your wishes."

Pulling a sheet of white unlined paper from his back pocket, Father thrust it into my hand.

"Here are the names of the men I just mentioned. Beside each are the addresses of both warehouses."

One glance was sufficient. A human Rolodex, I had already stored all the info in my mind.

"You are incredible, Antonio—you are really cut out for this," Father said, bidding me good night. And I tried my best to make it happen. Lying next to my beautiful love was a perfect catalyst. In her arms, I was soon fast asleep. I guess at times I did have nerves of steel—or was it the after-effect of our passionate love making?

The following days literally flew by. Having completed extensive wardrobe research, Ziva felt confident and well equipped to direct the seamstress. She listened and designed accordingly. Pleased with the integral coverage, lighter materials and more fashionable in an understated tone, outfits she presented, Ziva was ready to step into a mid-eastern culture where women dressed predominately in black. The girls would be fully concealed behind yards of heavy materials, without setting themselves apart from the majority of women.

Eventually, once all the details were organized, we were briefed, and ready for the departure. A villa and limo were available upon our arrival outside the City of Dhahran, approximately 16 kilometers, 10 miles from Hassen Mabbar's office and warehouse in Saudi Arabia. A major administrative hub for the oil industry, it was buzzing. According to Benjamin all was ready in Israel except a strategy for my safe return. This last part was still on the drawing board.

The Prime Minister's office phoned to announce a second meeting, scheduled for Tuesday at 1:00 PM, leaving us two days to prepare. Silence prevailed around the dining table, that evening, as the departure date for a journey with unknown outcome was imminent.

# XXXV

We busied ourselves getting ready for take-off. Organized and detail oriented, Benjamin and Ziva attended to the last minute particulars prior to boarding. Never falling short with preparations, we enjoyed a serene flight on the company jet, though each of us harbored unsettling feelings on behalf of the danger factor. Should the plan encounter a set-back, it had the potential to be a rather death-defying mission with serious consequences.

The skies were clear and the wind at minimum allowing the jet to land smoothly on a runway familiar to us from previous trips. As planned, a driver awaited, ready to speed us to our final meeting before the mission would be operative. Once again the ambiance in the limo was one of quiet and reflection. The probability of imminent danger begged for prayers, leaving each of us alone with our thoughts.

Within a half hour we were seated in the Prime Minister's office. Most of the individuals were familiar except for a tall, slender predominately bald gentleman. Thick, almost coke bottle black rimmed glasses were wrapped around his long angular face.

"Antonio, I want to introduce, Isaac Mandelbaum," Jacob Wiezman said as the stranger extended his hand toward me. The handshake was firm the eye contact direct.

Slipping his right index finger and thumb into his left jacket pocket, Isaac pulled out a small grey box. "I believe this is what you had in mind for your trip to Iran."

From his right pocket Isaac withdrew a pair of grey gloves, slid his hands in and lifted the cover of the box, exposing eight glistening 50 caliber bullets. Individually positioned in a slot they were held down by a strap slung across the casing attached to a snap on the opposite side.

"Each bullet is loaded with cyanide filled lead pellets and uranium, a hundred times more lethal than the gas used to kill our people during the Holocaust. They have the potential to disable the facility in which the Iranians' are working. Many decades would pass before it would be fit for human habitation.

Both the box and gloves had been sprayed with liquid lead to guarantee the quick and accurate loading of weapons," he concluded, placing the box on the conference table before seating himself.

"Well done Mandelbaum."

"Thank you Madame Prime Minister."

"You are welcome. Now on with business. Barak, what can you tell us about Antonio's safe return? Do you have a specific plan yet?"

"I am happy to report that we have met all Antonio's requests. Upon his arrival in Kuwait City, he will be given the lead case. Additionally, we have acquired a helicopter almost identical to the crafts flown in Iran," Barak replied. "There is just one little glitch to iron out. We have not yet located a building large enough to conceal the helicopter and the car which will take Antonio and Benjamin back to their living quarters. Another point to consider is the water factor. We must be in close proximity to the Sea. Also the craft must be stripped of all markings, until Benjamin is ready to fly it to Iran.

"I am more than certain you will devise a plan to assure Antonio a safe return—this is my primary focus at the moment. Now I'd like to hear from you, Sharett," the Prime Minister announced.

Obliging, the Defense Director rose to his feet delivering his report.

"We have broken the code used by Iranian helicopter pilots and have mastered the object-detection system. Currently we are aware of the wave length they use. This will keep us knowledgeable of their location, and any changes they may adopt in guarding the building.

"We now have confirmation that the slits visible in the satellite photo are indeed part of the ventilating system. I do want to mention an important factor. In ten days the moon will be almost at full eclipse. Therefore, if we can set Antonio ashore two nights prior, he will be traveling in almost complete darkness, yet return when the moon is in total eclipse. At that time he can communicate with Benjamin *via* satellite phone, and give him his exact location.

Antonio," he concluded, lowering his report folder, "I suggest you leave for Saudi Arabia as soon as you return home. I am confident you will resolve Barak's dilemma to locate a large building.

"Does anyone have any questions or concerns? Sharett asked. This is the time to speak up—after all our activities will jeopardize human lives as well as our relations with Iran. Remember—we don't want war.

This mission was designed quickly to take care of a pressing issue. I'll admit there was not much time for either lengthy preparations or a backup strategy that did not include the war option. Our people, however, are tired of intimidations, the foreshadowing of armed warfare and the anguish of living under the threat of total extinction at the hands of the Iranian terrorists."

"We must succeed," the Prime Minister responded, rising to her feet. "May God be with you. I will pray for you all."

With her good wishes and promise of prayers, the meeting was adjourned. Parting company, the participants shook hands with me, Benjamin and Ziva, expressing their well-wishes. Within minutes the room had emptied except for Barak.

"My men will respond to the password *Shalom,*" he whispered, leaning in toward my right ear.

We departed and returned to the guest residence now referred to as home.

"I hope the garments I ordered are ready," Ziva said.

"We will soon find out. We must pack for the trip. Once we arrive in Kuwait City, Barak and his men will take care of the rest." Benjamin added.

As soon as we returned I phoned my father both to up-date him and learn if he had any news.

"Antonio, I phoned Zamal El Ralah and notified him of your arrival later this evening. I mentioned that you and your team are heading directly to the rented villa near Bahrain approximately in the vicinity of his office. I also informed him you would make contact tomorrow."

"Thanks Father, I feel ready to undertake this mission."

Ready or otherwise, I was facing the determining moment. Thinking of loved ones waiting for news often with trepidation was standard procedure. And much as Mother and Father had grown accustomed to the protocol, somehow the mood was suddenly different. There was an air of uncertainty and danger that Demetri and Shanna could not shake, in spite of the repeated assurances.

Benjamin, Ziva, Françoise and I tried our best to calm both their expressed and silent concerns. Still, the parting words, "you have nothing to worry about," were about as credible as the guarantee of safety when swimming amid a school of famished sharks. They realized however, that this was my life—the life I had chosen.

Fully cognizant of the imminent danger, Ziva and Françoise tried their best to masquerade their own fears while horrendous probabilities crossed their minds at intermittent intervals. Both women realized everything had to proceed with unerring precision or they would never again see the two most important men in their lives.

"Ziva, if anything ever happened to Benjamin, my life would be worthless," Françoise confessed.

"I know—but let us not entertain such devastating thoughts." We must make an attempt to compose our fears.

In less than an hour we were baggage in hand and ready to board the flight to Bahrain. I chatted with my love to relax her, though I had to admit, my own nerves were all but still. She tried her best to be strong for my benefit. Her selfless consideration is just a fractional part of the extraordinary person she is. We kissed and I held her for a brief minute until it was time to board.

Thankfully the flight and landing were uneventful, and as expected the driver was waiting to accompany us to the villa. I hoped we would have some serene time to finish last minute business and of course relax.

With the exception of Frank Aiello who gave validity to my presence and served as a credible cover, I had never met any of the company's distributors. In a sense I was navigating in the dark.

This mission was risky on many fronts. Apart from the obvious hazards, what remained unsaid were the potential repercussions this could have on my father's business, if the plan failed, and I was caught. What better motivation to keep me vigilant and on my toes.

Once the landing gear was released, we all sat up-right. Moments later we rested on the runway and taxied to the assigned hanger. Waiting was a tall gentleman, with a thick dark beard, and gold framed sunglasses. His head was wrapped in a white and black cloth winding turban.

"Good evening," Abdul greeted in perfect English. "Did you have a pleasant flight?"

"Yes, thank you," I responded; "it was smooth."

"Kindly follow me. I will accompany you to the villa. Please know that I will be at your disposal any time day or night, compliments of Mr. Al Dalah."

"That's great—thank you again. We are looking forward to meeting Mr. Dalah in the near future," I said. "For the moment a nice meal and a good night's sleep would be our most pressing request."

"Your wish shall be granted. I prepared a light supper for you. I hope it is to your liking."

"I am certain it will be wonderful, Abdul."

I introduced Benjamin, Ziva and Françoise, as one by one, exhausted from the long day, we climbed into the car.

"We will be there in just about 20 minutes," our gracious driver announced. "There is no traffic at this late hour."

I noticed the ladies rode with closed eyes, while Benjamin and I sat alert and vigilant. They must really trust us, I thought, smiling. Not many women in this circumstance would rest easy in a foreign land under these circumstances.

"Here we are," Abdul said, coming to a smooth stop in front of a beautiful gated villa.

"It is as magnificent as it appeared in the photos," Ziva whispered. Our Realtor agent did a fine job. I will have to compliment him."

"Escort the ladies inside," Abdul said, opening his door. I will make certain all your luggage will be delivered to your rooms."

"Thank you." I said.

He kept his word in every respect. Our bags were brought in and deposited in the vestibule opposite the sleeping wing of the villa. The table was graciously set and before Françoise could find her way to the kitchen, Abdul was standing near the range, warming up the meal.

Literally famished, we consumed his menu selections in break-neck time, without even making an attempt to indulge in the art of conversation. Though different even from our pretty exotic inter-national diets, it was tasty and nourishing: The perfect pacifier to encourage a restful sleep.

"This is wonderful Abdul," Ziva said. I am certain my friends are as appreciative as I am." Three heads nodded in agreement. "Thank you for all your assistance."

"You are welcome Madame, may I help you sought your belongings?"

"No—don't worry," Françoise, exclaimed, realizing there were things packed, exclusively for their eyes. "Ziva and I can handle it."

"As you wish: I'll be back in the morning—have a restful evening," he said, placing a card with his contact info on the table before leaving the villa.

Françoise busied herself clearing the dishes, cutlery and glasses. She sent the others to their rooms to unpack, shower and crawl between the sheets.

Upon concluding her self-imposed task, she would join Benjamin. Although Abdul was a decent cook, like most men, he didn't concern himself with the pots and pans used to prepare the meal. Ziva offered assistance, but was promptly denied.

"Go take a shower," she suggested, "Antonio is waiting for you."

"OK—but don't work too hard."

Emanating a delicious post shower aroma after spraying Antonio's preferred perfume, 1000 de Jean Patou, Ziva climbed in next to her lover. Mysteriously all the pre-supper fatigue seemed to evaporate. Without even the slightest touch he was ready for her. Leaning over his rock solid manhood, she kissed it, grabbing as much as possible between her lips. Her mind raced with memories of her first gift of pleasure with Antonio. His blissful moans left her even greedier for him and somewhat surprised by the gratification she experienced until the point of climax.

It had been far too long since we last enjoyed such pleasure. I returned the favor leaving her gasping for air after she submitted to an orgasm so intense it bordered on painful. Reciprocally satisfied multiple times we drifted off to sleep, genuinely exhausted from the sheer delight of ecstatic, passionate love making.

Though Abdul arrived as promised shortly after the sunrise, he waited for a sign of life before entering the villa. Well aware of the VIPs in his charge, he was prepared to postpone his day's obligations until the opportune moment. Much as the beautiful women caught his eye, I noticed he seemed to have a curious fascination with me. Perhaps I intrigued him beyond the visual female delights.

Leaving the car to stretch his legs, and iron out the uncomfortable pressure he often felt in his lower back from sitting too long, Abdul heard a rustling from the slightly ajar kitchen window. He recalled that just a brief moment ago it had been tightly closed. Drawing a breath he walked around the villa listening for other signs of life. Once his ears confirmed everyone was awake, he tapped his knuckles against the entry door.

"Come in," Françoise called out, "I unlocked the door when Benjamin spotted your car."

Crossing the threshold, Abdul's gaze fell upon a striking petite woman honoring her Mid-Eastern visit by dressing in appropriate attire.

"May I offer you some breakfast," she asked, though it was more than 90 minutes past the noon hour.

"Thanks—but a cup of fresh brewed coffee will do."

"We will have a bit more than coffee to offer in a short span." She was grateful Benjamin took on the role of *sous chef,* though the extent of his culinary talents was not exactly worthy of either praise or discussion. Françoise however, gave merit to his intentions and loved having him around. Together they whipped up rations for an army of famished soldiers.

Meanwhile I made certain to phone Al Dalah to express my gratitude for the over-stocked cupboards and to offer my thoughts on Abdul, who I mentioned, was a perfect host. His was a strategy of unconditional availability, while respecting our need and wishes for privacy.

Two rings later I was greeted by a male voice.

"Mr. Dalah, I look forward to our meeting. Abdul will drive me to your warehouse as soon as we are finished breakfast."

"I share your enthusiasm Antonio. Please call me Al."

"I will see you shortly, Al."

As always the meal Françoise served was delicious and as always leftovers were non-existent. No wonder she loved to *don the toque,* and get in front of the oven. Moreover, we were such a satisfying audience for her delicacies.

"How long will it take you ladies to get ready for our visit with Al Dalah?" Benjamin asked, grinning. I knew better and kept a stoic expression.

"Give us 20 minutes," Françoise said. "Is that about right, Ziva?"

"Perfect."

When we arrived Al Dalah greeted me with the customary three kisses while bowing and flashing a genuine smile to welcome Benjamin, Françoise and Ziva into his company.

"*Salaam aleikum,* peace be with you Antonio. How are your father and your beautiful mother? I hope all is well. You know I have the deepest respect and feelings for them. They are wonderful people."

"They are very well, thank you, and send their warmest regards, to you, your wives, children and grandchildren. I do believe you have eleven little ones running around your home."

"Twelve, Antonio," he said chuckling. You're not up-dated. A new boy arrived last week, but I have not had the time to make an official announcement to my friends."

"May there be many more little ones to bring joy and immortality to your family especially in your later years," I said. "However, looking at you, I have to say old age is a long way off."

"Antonio you are a son worthy of your father and grandfather," Al replied, beaming: "so unlike the many affluent heirs for whom work is an unknown factor in the accumulation of their great wealth."

"Thank you—that is quite a compliment."

"More correctly stated—it's a well-merited consideration. By the way I don't know if you are aware, but I worked for your grandfather as his representative in my country. Actually it was your father, who provided me with the funding I needed to start my own distributorship of his as well as many other products. What touched me most was his reluctance to ask for any monetary recompense or interest. His sole objective was to assist me along my life journey. Individuals like Demetri Bastone are rare and must be honored for their beneficence to mankind. He is a true humanitarian."

Father had never told me about his involvement with Al Dalah, but listening to the man's words brought no surprises. This was who my father was, is and will always be.

"Come with me. I'd like to show you what your father's generosity helped build."

Eager to learn more about this charming gentleman, I jumped at the possibility to tour his facility.

"Lead the way," I said.

I followed Al Dalah into an approximately 100,000 square foot building housing endless tiers packed solid with merchandise from around the world. A quick glance of the area told me that about 30% of the cartons were labeled Bastone. No other olive oil company was represented.

"I would never do business with a competitor, therefore, you will never see another olive oil company's products in this warehouse or any other I might build in the future," he said, as if reading my thoughts.

"I never entertained the slightest doubt. My father speaks of you more as a friend than a business associate. You have done a wonderful job. I can see your employees work with a sense of pride, not because they fear you, but for the respect they have in your regard. Everything Father told me about you is true. He will be happy when I confirm his words upon my return."

"Antonio, I would like to invite you and your friends to my home for dinner this evening," he said smiling at Ziva, Françoise and Benjamin. Instinctively they reciprocated with broad grins. "My wives are eager to meet you. Abdul will arrive at 6:00 to accompany you. And I do promise all the little ones will be seen and not heard."

The ladies chuckled, realizing the prejudicial inclination of a doting grandfather may prove his comment to be merely the fruit of wishful thinking. Even an attentive and loving grandfather has a trite success rate in quieting energetic children.

After the friendly exchange of light dialogue, Abdul drove us back to the villa.

"I will pick you up at 6:00," he reminded smiling. Françoise and Ziva were grateful for the time to freshen up, and free themselves from their cumbersome *burqas*, the loosing fitting robe and head piece which is a unique veil/ hood combination, covering the entire body.

"How in the world do these women wear such heavy cloaks during this excruciating heat, day after day?" Françoise asked, pulling off the yards of material, drenched in her sweat.

"Like everything else in life, I believe one gets acclimated to it," Ziva replied, flinging her *burqa* on the bedside chair. "Plus you have to admit these robes cover a multitude of sins."

"Like you have physical sins to hide," Françoise blurted laughing.

"Well it is a positive aspect of the *burqa*. I'll see you later—I'm off to my room to get into another outfit for the evening. Here comes Antonio.

"See you at 6:00, Ziva."

Entering the room I noticed how flushed my love was as she stood practically naked, in an attempt to cool down.

"Thankfully you don't have to dress this way always," I chuckled.

"As I told Françoise, it may have some benefits. Tell me my love, how in the world do you know Al Dalah?"

"My father briefed me about him and Hassen Mabbar, although I have to admit I didn't know about their business. However, nothing he does surprises me. Now I am a bit concerned that Benjamin has not received word from Barak's men regarding the meeting place for my equipment as well as the plan for my helicopter departure.

At this point I feel it is best to leave tomorrow for Kuwait City. I'll come up with an excuse for Al Dalah to explain our brief stay. There is nothing more we can do here except perhaps try to offer assistance in locating a place that would be useful to Barak's men. Our chances are slim even if it is better than just sitting around doing nothing."

I was accustomed to living on the edge and risking my neck on more than one occasion, but this time I had to worry about Ziva and Françoise. Unlike Benjamin who could handle any situation, the ladies required a more cautious eye.

Decision made, I summoned Benjamin.

"Please notify Barak of a change in plans. Assure him we will be awaiting his information in Kuwait City rather than Saudi Arabia."

"I'll get on it immediately."

# XXXVI

Just as the clock chimed to announce it was 6:00, a double knuckle tap against the front door announced Abdul's arrival.

"He's prompt," I said, listening to Françoise's footsteps in the foyer.

"I'll get," she shouted.

"Good evening, Abdul," she greeted; "we're ready. They will be with you in a few minutes."

"No rush. I'll wait."

Before the hands on the clock pointed to 6:07 we were seated in Abdul's car en route to our dinner *rendezvous* at El Ralah's home.

"This is a rarity," our driver admitted. El Ralah hardly ever entertains guests in his residence with the exception of several members of the Royal Family. The truth is I have never seen him so excited and pleased to have you all meet his entire family. He must look upon you with great regard. You must be special people."

"We're honored," I replied as Abdul guided the car to a smooth halt in front of the villa's main entrance.

El Rahal greeted us at the entry door of his beautiful home. Standing behind him were his five wives, their ages, spanning two decades with the eldest pushing 50 and the youngest just tuning 30. Each was gorgeous and alluring. I didn't waste energy in commiseration. My father had informed me that although his first wife was the result of an arranged marriage, he adored her. Within minutes my keen eye and intuition confirmed it was this mature woman, the wife who ruled the house.

"Antonio, welcome: all this is due to the faith your father had in me," he said extending his right hand. I owe it all to Demetri Bastone! Now let me present the children," he said laughing.

Signaling each child and grandchild to step forward, the eldest first, he mentioned their name and age.

"My first born son is being groomed to run the family business, and two of my younger sons are studying in the United States."

Ziva overheard his three youngest girls giggling and whispering among themselves how wonderful it would be if their father would find them husbands like the tall handsome western man.

Once the formalities and introductions were completed, we were led through a corridor to a huge, ornate ballroom where much to my surprise colorfully attired dancers, and strains of exotic music waited. Undoubtedly we were honored guests at a thousand and one night feast. No table was ever more lavish. And our olfactory and visual senses shifted into high alert.

Françoise and Ziva were in western dress affording El Ralah the possibility to see both women full face.

"You have done quite well for yourself," Antonio, he said, poking me in the rib with his index finger. A wide grin subtracted years from his face.

"Yes—I'm very fortunate," I replied, winking at the gorgeous woman with whom I shared my life.

"Be my guest Antonio," he said, inviting me to enjoy the celebration.

The evening seemed to fly by. I savored the delicious delicacies on the table and on the dance floor while Ziva and Françoise danced with the other women as is customary. Some of the boys broke into patriotic songs of centuries past. When it was evident the festivities were winding down, I approached El Ralah.

"May I ask a favor?"

"Whatever you wish shall be yours, with the exception of my wives and children, of course."

"Of course," I reiterated laughing. "I would like to borrow one of your cars for about a week. I must visit Hassen Mabbar, one of Father's distributors in Kuwait City, and I promised Ziva a trip to the famous Water, Liberation and Dar Al Awadi Towers. I think she would be disappointed if I did not maintain my word.

"Well we cannot permit such a gorgeous woman to be disappointed. Come with me."

He took me by the arm escorting me toward a door off the entry foyer.

"Choose the car you wish," he said, pushing it open to reveal a garage populated with about 30 of the most prestigious, expensive and beautiful vehicles I had ever feasted my eyes on. "If you wish I will have Abdul drive you to your destinations."

"Thank you my friend, but I do not intend to take advantage of your kindness. Furthermore I have G. P. S. to keep me positioned and aligned should I falter. You have already extended yourself over and above for us. We would like to return as soon as possible to enjoy more of your country and of course your family as well."

"It would be my pleasure. Which car would you like?"

"I'll take that large Mercedes four door sedan," I said, pointing to a recently detailed black vehicle.

Walking over to a wood paneled cabinet, El Dalah pulled open the door to reveal a six by four foot safe. Pushing some sensors he entered in the combination. Once opened, he reached in and grabbed a set of keys.

"These will get you moving," he said, handing me the keys.

"Again my deepest thanks for everything. We are most appreciative of your extraordinary kindness. Don't worry about the car. It will be returned just as it is today."

"Never had a doubt otherwise, my friend. Have a good trip."

"Do not trust everyone. The man you are going to see is not as loyal to your father as I am."

We exchanged kisses and in a few minutes were heading back to the villa, to unwind, crawl into bed, and hopefully awaken refreshed and rested the follow morning. Joyfully it came to be.

After breakfast Françoise prepared and packed a basket lunch to keep us nourished and hydrated during the five hour drive to the office of the realtor from whom we had leased a villa in Kuwait City.

I was at ease knowing Father had completed successful business with this company in the past. Moreover, he had anticipated our arrival with a phone call to give strict instructions to satisfy our wishes and needs.

It was advisable to take King Fahad Bin Abdul Aziz Rd (40) to Kuwait City. As expected, the 480 horse powered Mercedes performed excellently, cutting the actual drive down to a bit more than four hours. Hardly any dialogue was exchanged, as all were in deep thought regarding the plan about to be executed. Although conscious of the danger, Benjamin and I would be risking, no one entertained any adverse *what if* scenarios. Instead, we used the time for private reflection and prayer.

I had received neither word regarding a meeting point for my crossing into Iran, nor any information pertaining to how and where Benjamin would acquire the helicopter needed for our safe return. However, I was optimistic everything would fall into place in due time.

Meanwhile the programmed G.P.S. guided us to the front door of Faran Realty where Mr. Faran eagerly awaited, keys in hand to accompany the son of Demetri Bastone and his friends to the villa.

"The house has been inspected and cleaned. The pool has been drained pressure washed, and treated as per your father's explicit instructions. Please follow my car. It is not a very distant ride," Mr. Faran said.

I slid behind the wheel and followed our realtor until he stopped in front of a rather charming residence.

"Wow—that looks like a home in New England—not Kuwait City," Ziva remarked, surprised.

"I hope this meets with your approval," Faran said smiling upon hearing her comment. "This once belonged to the daughter of the US Ambassador."

"Thank you Mr. Faran," I said outwardly pleased. "It seems perfect for us."

Smiling broadly he handed over the keys. "Please enjoy your stay, and if there is any way I can be of further assistance, do not hesitate to phone me."

"You are very gracious. Again thank you. I am certain we will be very comfortable here," I replied. Meanwhile, Françoise and Benjamin seized the moment to unload the luggage from the trunk.

"I'll leave the rest to you men," she said, grabbing Ziva under the arm. "Let's go for a tour of our new home."

Once inside I headed toward a huge royal blue club chair. Something about its soft, inviting look gave me a welcoming feeling.

"It is just lovely," Ziva said, giving a quick glance. "Come on Françoise let's explore the rest of the place."

Beside the chair, I noticed a tall narrow pine wood table, on top of which sat a black telephone.

"Not so fast Antonio," Benjamin said. Who knows if it is connected."

"There is only one way to find out," I replied lifting the receiver.

"OK—dial tone or no dial tone?"

"Dial tone, my friend. We're in business!"

I reached into my breast pocket, and pulled out the card my father handed me before leaving. Dialing the number scribbled I waited. After three rings, I was greeted by Hassen Mabbar's gruff voice.

"Mr. Mabbar," I began after presenting myself, I am here in Kuwait City and would like to meet with you."

My request was received neither with enthusiasm nor the gracious courtesy demonstrated by El Ralah.

Instead, Mabbar reacted with annoyance as if the scarcity and importance of his time made it a rare commodity, enabling him to dedicate it exclusively to matters generating financial revenue.

Hassen had bought out the previous owner about five years ago, and held no allegiance to any of his suppliers. In fact it was rumored he had made him an offer he could not refuse.

"Antonio, my only availability is tomorrow at 2:00 PM for one hour. I am a very busy man."

I felt the hairs on the nape of my neck stand at attention. Blood surging through my head, I gripped the phone so tightly my knuckles turned white.

"That would be fine. My plans include sightseeing in this beautiful city, fishing and a stint at the gaming tables. Business is really not my forte," I responded.

Hassen Mabbar smirked and chuckled, believing he was dealing with another rich play boy living off his father's wealth.

"I shall see you tomorrow. Be assured I will keep it brief to honor your busy schedule."

El Ralah was so right. Hassen was a man who should not be trusted. Undeniably he would sell his mother for the right price. Since he was totally irrelevant in my big picture, I gave neither his phone reaction nor involvement in my plan a second thought. Of course I never questioned the validity of my judgment. We ended the call and I focused on the tourist part of the journey.

We relaxed after a leisurely breakfast before satisfying our curiosity to see Kuwait City. I drove trying to please the different requests. Françoise expressed a desire to visit the House of Mirrors, Benjamin the Scientific Center and Ziva wanted to tour the Tareq Rajab Museum of Islamic Arts.

"What a beautiful city," I said; I'd certainly like to see it all. "We cannot miss the Grand Mosque."

"It's on my list," Ziva replied.

In unison my passengers agreed.

"I wish we had more time for sightseeing."

"I agree Antonio. But we are here on business," Benjamin whispered.

"Speaking of which, it is 1:30. We have just a half hour to drop Françoise off and get over to Hassen's office. Remember—I reassured him I would be prompt not to waste his precious time."

The chorus of chuckles lightened my mood as I proceeded to the *rendezvous*. When we arrived, a small heavy set man dressed in the traditional ivory *dishdasha* was waiting to escort us to Hassen. The floor length white robe with elongated side pockets seemed to exaggerate his short, portly stature.

Hassen's initial greeting was cold, diffident and unassuming, as I had anticipated. Obviously it was delivered from a seated position, until his eyes focused on Ziva. Instantly he was on his feet. It's amazing how powerful and alluring a woman's beauty and sex appeal can be in certain situations.

"Antonio, you did not inform me you were bringing such a beautiful woman with you," he gasped, never making eye contact with me.

"Forgive me, Hassen, this beautiful woman is my fiancée Ziva, and the gentleman is Benjamin, my driver."

"Fiancée—I am sorry to hear that. It is a troubling announcement. Too bad such a gorgeous woman is spoken for," Hassen replied. "Come with me, Ziva, and I will show you my warehouse." Walking over to my love, he lifted his arm, inviting her to take it. Together, arm in arm they exited the building. Benjamin and I trailed several steps behind.

When we entered the warehouse, I noticed the grim faces of the employees at work in a relatively restricted area. Stashed on the shelves were cartons of low-priced olive oil.

"This facility is too small for my expanding business. The new warehouse will be completed in about two months."

Ziva glanced at her escort, noticing his short stature. His grey *dishdasha* did nothing for his slight frame. She estimated his weight at about 140 pounds.

"Where is your new warehouse located?" Ziva asked flashing the same enticing smile that snatched my heart within minutes of meeting her.

"It's in an old hanger. Not only did I pick it up dirt cheap, but I discovered it has a boat dock. This will triple revenues for my export business."

It was evident a Napoleonic Complex plagued this tiny man, though his swelled ego often denied the obvious. However, what he failed or refused to admit was that we already had the info on his export business dealings with black market gangs. Shamefully they supplied the country's privileged class in the light of defaulting on the needy masses.

Ziva, bright, swift and cunning as she was, understood my glance.

"I would love to see your new location," she said, latching on to Hassen's arm. "Three tines the size of this one—I bet you're destined to become the biggest, most potent distributor in the Mid-East."

He was beaming and swelling as she flirtatiously pumped his ego.

'Be careful' I thought smiling behind my stoic facade, 'you might just explode.'

Puffed and enjoying my beautiful love hanging on to his arm, Hassen lost all concept of the time limitation he had imposed during our initial conversation.

When summoned, his secretary entered. "Reschedule my appointments," he shouted. "Tell the driver I need him right now."

Taking Ziva by the arm he led her out the door, while I trailed behind followed by Benjamin. It was as if we didn't even exist for Hassen. His focus was exclusively on my sexy woman.

Once in the car we were subjected to the endless bragging and boasting recital, typical of the little man trying to catch the gorgeous girl scenario. Exhausted from the braggadocio we arrived at the building, constructed of sand, clay and slit deposits from the river, cemented into solid rock. Directly to the left of the alluvium facility sprouted a long pier able to accommodate medium sized boats.

Factoring in time, direction and the speed at which we travelled from Hassen's office to the new warehouse, I was able to calculate the exact location with relative ease.

"Work will start in two weeks. I expect the place will be filled to capacity in approximately four months," he said as the vehicle came to a halt.

'Thank you Hassen,' I whispered soundlessly: 'Helpful info.' I filed the information in my mind, making a mental note to inform Barak and make a request for the building to be demolished once it was loaded to the rafters with merchandise.

Though he was putty in my hands, Hassen's brazen flirtation with Ziva started to fry my nerves, not out of jealousy, but for the blatant disrespect he was demonstrating in my presence. I had the information I needed. It was time to cut the smug man down to his true size.

"My compliments, Hassen, I said. "Thanks for taking time from your busy schedule to show us your new warehouse. But if you'll excuse us we have to take leave of your company. I don't want to keep the Emir waiting."

If the echo of heavy breathing could transmit a message, it would have confirmed Hassen's rage. Instead, his dark complexion flushed to red. I smiled inwardly, knowing my words had slapped him across his pompous face, wounding his pride.

As expected he did not utter a syllable during the return drive. Ziva playfully slapped the back of my head between bouts of blowing on my ear. I knew I would get even with her later this evening after she had her girl time telling Françoise about the day's adventure.

I think we were all happy to be in our car and heading back to the villa.

"Benjamin, phone Barak, and advise him we have the perfect location to hide the helicopter, and a plan to get me safely across the Gulf into Iran. Sometimes a little luck can play a major role in any mission, just as major as the most strategic and precise planning—kind of like poker."

"Good point, Antonio. I'll make that call now."

Barak was overjoyed with Benjamin's news and the information I provided regarding pinpointing the exact location.

"We can load the helicopter parts on a barge for transport, and assemble in the empty warehouse using the same barge to ship Antonio across the Gulf. It should take no more than one day to put together the copter, and with God's help Antonio will be safely on his way by tomorrow night."

# XXXVII

It was a well-thought out plan. We were scheduled to meet at sundown tomorrow, at the old hanger were the operation would be put in full gear. However, just because a plan is intricately and meticulously constructed, does not cancel out the unpredictability factor and the reality that nothing is flawless.

By the restless gyrations in bed, I understood Ziva was preoccupied and rightly so. My guess was that Françoise was not sleeping soundly either. Ours was a complex mission with very high risk. Consequently, the sunrise came all too soon for the ladies. In the backs of their minds they shared the terrifying thought of never seeing me and Benjamin again.

We had a wonderful leisurely breakfast before we left our ladies to review the plan, discuss any pitfalls or glitches, and to reassure ourselves we were on the same wave length. Later we met for lunch and kept the table dialogue light and up-beat.

"Benjamin, make certain everything is OK here in the villa before we leave."

"I already checked Antonio—no need for concern.

After my post-siesta shower, I phoned my parents. Denial took the lead in the conversation as we skirted the issue at hand in favor of light banter. Nevertheless, in our hearts we reciprocally felt the tension and fear attached to the mission. I had to admit my mother kept a stiff upper lip until the final goodbye when hard as she tried she could not control the tremble in her vocal chords.

"Everything will be fine, Mom," I said, crossing my fingers behind my back. "We'll be back at the villa soon, to see you."

Father, instead sought refuge in chuckling over Hassen's arrogance and how I had dismantled it in the end, a defense mechanism that seemed to work for him, at least outwardly.

"Son, he will be even more shocked when he finds out he's about to loose the Bastone brand."

"That's for sure. Now it's time to go. Father, Ziva and I love you and Mother very much.

"Be careful and safe Antonio."

"Thanks Father, I will."

"Antonio, I love you," my mother said, failing to muffle a sob.

"Don't worry I will be careful. I have too much to live for."

"We will be praying for you."

"Ziva and Françoise promised prayers too."

Turning to my beautiful love I kissed her goodbye deflecting from the motive for my departure, certain a similar scenario was occurring in Benjamin and Françoise's room.

"Go Antonio—call me as soon as you can," Ziva whispered, turning her head, though not quickly enough to hide the tear running down her cheek.

Just as the sun began its decent behind the horizon, Benjamin and I drove to the abandoned hangar to meet Barak's men. Except for the barge fastened to the pier there was no sign of life as we pulled up in front of the designated location.

"The door just opened," Benjamin whispered.

Immediately, two armed men emerged.

"*Shalom* Antonio," the huskier guy greeted, approaching the vehicle with long quick strides.

"*Shalom*," I reiterated.

"No need for introductions. Come inside, we have a lot of work to do."

He turned and hit a button on a remote nestled in his hand. The massive front of the facility opened. Five men were huddled together assembling the final parts of the copter which would secure my safe return.

"Just drive the car in," the robust man said. I obliged and guided the car into the designated spot in the hangar. "Park and walk across the room."

Again I followed his orders.

Opening a small crate he extracted a lead box.

"This contains eight, 50 caliber bullets filled with the material you specifically requested. Please handle with care," he said handing me a pair of special gloves to insure safe removal of the bullets from the box.

"Now come over here."

I trailed in his footsteps to a large tin container. Pulling it open he closed his hand on a long tan hooded garment and tugged it out.

"This is camouflage gear," he said thrusting it into my hands. "It protects you from the elements until you reach your destination. "I also have a folding shovel, and a searchlight visible only to those wearing night vision goggles. I have a pair for Benjamin too. There are rations which should suffice for three days and nights, plus a two inch thick slab of wood.

Reaching into the container he retrieved a manila envelope.

"In here is the latest satellite photo as well as a clear mapping of the suggested route you should be taking. One more thing—I also brought the newest 50 caliber sniper rifle in Israel's arsenal. It is yours if you wish to use it."

"Thanks, but I prefer to use mine. It has a proven reputation of reliability," I replied, handing it to the man packing the nap sack I'd be taking on the most important journey of my life.

I checked the Glock I had borrowed from Benjamin, Ziva's knife strapped to my leg and Françoise's folded razor. Everything was in place. They would all be with me, a thought bringing comfort and encouragement. Smiling I gazed down at the scuffed and well-worn combats boots with their battle scars, knowing they would surely eliminate annoying issues that could complicate my mission.

"I guess it's time to get moving," I said, lifting my nap sack. Strapping it on I glanced up at the moon, almost in total eclipse. "One more night and it will be a full eclipse—perfect," I whispered. Accepting only positive thoughts I went forward empowered.

"I am Abe," a man of medium build volunteered," walking toward me. "That's short for Abraham." Pointing to another man of similar stature, he continued; "this is Yosef. He will take you across. Reaching up to circle my shoulders with his arm, Abe chanted a prayer in Hebrew, asking God to bless me with a successful and safe mission.

"Please don't be late, Benjamin," I teased. "It can get hot as hell during the day time. Furthermore, I would like to be home by tomorrow night."

Taking the smoke canister from Abe, Benjamin nodded. Everything was in place. It was time.

"*Behatslacha*, Antonio, good luck."

"Thanks Ben—see you tomorrow."

Yosef and I climbed into the small boat, unfastened the knot that kept it anchored to the pier and glided across the Persian Gulf. Moments later, we landed on the Iranian shore. Hitting sand, I jumped out, waved goodbye to my captain and headed for the destined target.

Gazing at my watch I calculated I could count on eight additional hours of darkness. Quickening my pace I aimed to cover at least 40 miles before sunrise. Thank God I was in excellent condition having trained long and hard. Had I become lazy or lax, crossing the dessert with a 50 pound nap sack strapped to my back would have been an even more grueling task.

Mid way through the journey I paused, drank some water to keep hydrated and bit into an energy bar. Checking my mileage meter I was pleased to know my timing was flawless. I had covered 20 miles.

Encouraged by my excellent track record, I rose to my feet, strapped on my nap sack and completed the last part of the journey. The black sky faded to grey. When the radiant red circle peered out from behind the horizon I found a slightly wooded area populated with a few trees.

Certain they would offer a small amount of refuge from the torrid heat hitting as high as 130 degrees, I set down my sack.

Unzipping the top, I pulled out the long hooded tan robe, covered myself as much as possible, guzzled several gulps of water and chewed a few salt tablets. Realizing from my drenched garments that I was sweating profusely, I knew that if I failed to hydrate and replenish the lost sodium, I'd be flat on the ground.

Opening some of the rations, I consumed a bit of much need nourishment. It was a far cry from the meals our maser chef Françoise prepared, but it was life sustaining manna—the biblical miracle food. Stretching, I closed my eyes, and slept through the scorching day.

My parents, Ziva, Françoise, and Benjamin must have been praying hard. When I awakened, the last ray of the sun had vanished into the total eclipse of night. The moon was non-existent, flawlessly concealed behind the dense darkness.

"So far so good," I said aloud, just to hear the echo of a human voice. I stretched, stood and heeded the call of nature. Returning to my tree, I folded the robe, and washed down the remaining rations with several swigs of warm, but much treasured water. Fed and hydrated I began the last lap of a journey that seemed to have started a long time ago.

According to Mossad's information the copters next shift change would occur at 1:00 AM, allotting me approximately five hours to reach my destination, set up my weapon and wait for Benjamin's call.

To be on the safe side I quickened my pace and arrived at the location Abe gave me with 30 minutes to spare. Though distant a little less 1.5 kilometers, a mile, the top of the building housing the lethal weapons was already visible. It wouldn't be long now, God willing, I thought. Soon the weapons would be rendered useless and the responsible individuals halted. The announcement of powerful and destructive ammunition would never come to be. Israel's plan for peace and freedom would now have a chance to come to fruition. The world would breathe a sigh of relief.

I tried not to let my thoughts get ahead of me. I had to focus. Much was at stake here. Unpacking the nap sack, I withdrew the shovel. I dug a small trench, smoothed a strip of sand and placed the two by four slab of wood in front of the trench. Assembling my 50 caliber sniper's rifle in total darkness was not complicated since I had performed this operation a hundred times before.

My next task was the tripod. I pulled it out, opened the legs, stood it on the piece of wood and mounted the rifle.

After setting the scope dead on the first target, I inserted my hands into the special gloves, took out the lead box, slipped into my camouflage robe and waited. My drifting thoughts were interrupted by the buzz of my satellite phone.

"Antonio—can you hear me?" Benjamin's voice rang loud and clear. What a welcome sound!

"They're about to make the chopper change. No one will notice anything. There are seven coming instead of six. Are you ready?"

I took out one of the lead bullets and placed it into the chamber. I set my eye strategically over the scope locked in on the air vent.

"Ready when you are Benjamin."

Looking skyward, I glimpsed a puff of smoke; then heard Benjamin speaking in Arabic.

"I have a mechanical problem with the copter. I will have to land, find out what is faulty, and repair it!"

Immediately I flashed on the blue light beam, visible only to Benjamin thanks to his special goggles. This would allow him to pinpoint my precise location. Returning to my post at the tripod, I fired the first round into air shaft number one. Then in rapid succession I fired two, three, four, five and finally number six.

"My angels of death are on the way!" I shouted. "Soon the targets will be hit!"

Meandering through the building's ventilation system, the poison infiltrated the lower levels of the structure. The scene of people gasping, gagging and choking played in my mind. I imagined their panic stricken attempts to leave the building, falling unconscious as the toxic substance rushed into their lungs just as the millions of Jews gassed almost 70 years ago.

But I had to stay centered. Distractions in my world could be fatal. Drawing a deep breath, I saw the front door burst open. A worker probably exiting for a cigarette break staggered toward one of the guards. Two shells remained—maybe a gift from above. Immediately I fired them into the front passageway and dissembled my equipment, packing all my belongings including the eight spent shell casings.

When I head the buzz of whirling helicopter blades I emitted a sigh of relief, and waited for Benjamin to land. Thoughts of Ziva intensified my nostalgia for home and my loved ones.

As planned, Barak's men would dismantle and get rid of the chopper, thus eradicating any traces of our Iranian visit. Was it too soon to announce "mission accomplished?" I questioned. Perhaps it was best to wait. In the mean time I pondered what could possibly lay head for our team of four. Where would we go and what would we resolve in our quest for peace.

Impatiently puffing on his cigarette, pacing over his prestigious carpet, the little man waited, wondering why the phone call announcing all was completed did not arrive. Why this delay? Nervous he was eager to broadcast globally his imperial status now that he possessed weapons powerful enough to annihilate any nation that dared stand in his way. A knock on the door, halted his pacing.

"Come in."

"Did the call come?"

The phone rang. His pulse raced. It was happening.

"Listen the Ayatollah wants to speak with you immediately."

"Let me get the phone."

Raftab picked up the receiver. Two seconds later his breathing took on a labored rhythm. His dark complexion paled. His mouth moved without sounds. Dry heaves left him reeling on his feet.

"Billions lost," the voice shouted. "It will take at least half a century to get that building inhabitable! Hundreds of our best and most prize worthy scientists are all dead!

"Come home at once!" Total silence pursued, following the sound of a click—an echo that would sound into eternity.

*The End*

www.ingramcontent.com/pod-product-compliance
Lightning Source LLC
Chambersburg PA
CBHW062131170626
46813CB00002B/658